The Matter of the
DESERTED
AIRLINER

ALASKA DISAPPEARING CREW AND PASSENGERS CAPER

Steve Levi

Master Of The Impossible Crime

PUBLICATION
CONSULTANTS
PUBLISHING THE WORKS OF AUTHORS WORLDWIDE

PO Box 221974 Anchorage, Alaska 99522-1974
books@publicationconsultants.com—www.publicationconsultants.com

ISBN 978-1-59433-691-1
eISBN 978-1-59433-692-8
Library of Congress Catalog Card Number: 2016961629

Just because something is obvious does not make it true.
Detective Heinz Noonan

Chapter 1

Time with in-laws is not called *vacation*; it's called *obligation*. Every family is dysfunctional, some more than others. But those *others* are usually called *in-laws*. You refer to them as people with whom you would never associate unless you were linked by marriage. You can ignore the shortcomings of your own family. After all, you are related to them by blood.

Your in-laws are a different kettle of fish.

The best defense against in-laws is a good offense. Perhaps the best example of a successful campaign was Ferenc Molnar, the Hungarian dramatist and novelist. When he became famous his in-laws besieged him. When they came *en mass* to his hotel in Paris they were surprised to be treated so well by their now-famous-and-now-rich–relative. He even insisted they sit for a group portrait. After they left he gave the photograph to the hotel doorman and said, "Whenever you see any of the persons in this picture trying to get into the hotel, don't let them in."

Captain Noonan, the Bearded Holmes of the Sandersonville Police Department, was up to his ears in in-laws. He had been looking forward to a pleasant two weeks with those in-laws in Anchorage, Alaska. He was looking forward to it being pleasant but he was sure he wasn't going to get much pleasure out of it. After all, he had to put up with his four sisters-in-law and their families along with a gaggle of collaterals who wasted his time demanding he talk of old cases, new theories or prognostication of where criminal forensics was going in the next millennium.

However, there was a very big upside. The in-laws all lived in Anchorage which was a l-o-n-g way from Sandersonville, North Carolina. Alaska is a long way from anywhere. It is also a long way from anywhere so crowded you felt as though you were living on an anthill. It had just enough cabs you can always find one, few enough people you do not have to wait for a table in a restaurant and the largest, most delicious fish in the world which could be caught within city limits.

As long as Noonan visited the northland when it was the Land of the Midnight Sun the vacation was pleasurable. In July the sun came up at 1 a.m. and did not set until 4 a.m. He took this on faith because he made it a point not to be up and about at either 1 a.m. or 4 a.m. All he knew for sure was during the summer the sun did not rise in the east and set in the west. It circled the sky so you could never tell what time it was by looking at the position of the sun in the sky. Like Palm Springs, you were best served with sunglasses all day. Unlike Palm Springs, the temperature rarely got up to 80 degrees and the clouds came and went as the wind pleased, *clouds* and *wind* not being part of a Palm Springs summer.

Noonan had absolutely no desire whatsoever to visit Alaska when it was the land of ice and snow. It wasn't so much the cold bothered him; he'd grown up in Maine and spent three years with the Army in Butte, Montana. He had no problem with cold and snow.

But he did have a problem with darkness.

Even on the coldest days in Butte the sun did come up. In a lot places in Alaska, the sun did not rise or set during the winter. Because of the tipping of the earth on its axis, during the winter Alaska was the most distant swatch of land from the sun. This meant sunrises were later and sunset earlier the later in the year it was. In Barrow, the furthest north community, there were 67 days when the sun never came up at all. Even in Anchorage it was not unusual for the sun to rise at 10:30 a.m. and set at 2:30 p.m. If you worked in a building with no windows and did not take your lunch outside, it was possible to go through an entire week and not see the sun at all. You would go to work in the morning dark and return home in the evening dark. If you did this for too many weeks you would get what Alaskans call *cabin fever,* a type of claustrophobia brought about by being trapped in a cabin in a dark land for four or five months. Stephen King made cabin fever a well-known phenomenon with THE SHINING and the basic theme repeats in movies of people lost on desert islands or during long voyages on space ships.

What will make cabin fever worse is being stuck with your in-laws in the same cabin. Then it doesn't have to be just in a cabin during the winter. It could happen on a crowded cruise liner anchored off Acapulco.

That being said, Noonan was not in Acapulco.

He was in Anchorage.

So were his in-laws.

This was a prescription for disaster if one did not temper his vocabulary.

This particular morning had not started well. The Bearded Holmes was slowly working his way through the morning copy of the *Anchorage Tribune*, the local newspaper with the thickness of a napkin, as he sat on the white wood bench in his mother-in-law's gazebo. The gazebo was the only place he was safe from children, in-laws and the gaggle of neighbors because it was so small. Small enough to give someone cabin fever if they spent the winter there—or an afternoon listening to in-laws and neighbors.

Looking up from the newspaper Noonan was displeased to see his son Fritz coming toward him with a cell phone. Cell phones were a blessing when you were at work but the spawn of the Devil between 5 p.m. and 9 a.m. The only people who used them between those hours were wives and salespeople. Of all the years he had owned a cell phone he had yet to receive one cheery message after 5 and before 9. When he did get a call between those hours it was either his wife demanding he pick something up at the grocery store on his way home or a late assignment from the office, something the Commissioner wanted done **Right Now** which always could have waited until the next day.

Or the Second of Never.

Fritz, the oldest of his twins – by three minutes – handed him a cellular telephone. *Handed*, however, was a polite of way describing how the possession of the phone was transferred. *Thrown* would have been a better verb. One moment the lord of the North Carolina manor was pleasantly reading what business page there was in a newspaper the thickness of tissue paper and the next he was clawing for a telephone the size of a pack of cards as it somersaulted toward him through the air.

Today he was in luck. The phone was actually headed in his direction. The day before he had been forced to root around in the rhubarb to find the phone by tracing the outraged voice coming from the other end of the electronic beam. Had Fritz been younger, he would have tossed the phone like a sack of sand. Now, at 13, the phone-to-dad transfer was a casual lob, not quite a lateral but, considering his growing size, the transfer would be honed in high school in the fall.

Noonan dropped the newspaper and bobbled the instrument one-handedly because the other was full of a coffee cup. He finally secured the phone between the heel of his left hand and collarbone. He shouted an exclamation at which his wife would have frowned as Fritz made a mad dash for the garden gate, fishing pole in one hand and king salmon net in the other.

Ever since Fritz and his brother Otto had discovered Alaska was famous for its salmon –king, red and silver – they were spending every moment of their vacation with their grandfather on the Chulitna River. Each morning they would pile into the old man's pickup and head north. Every evening they would arrive home dog-tired and covered with mosquito bites and more stories than fish.

Clearly the only thing stalling the trio this morning was this phone call. Dad now had his phone so they were like the Hittites: history. In fact, Fritz had crashed out of the back yard so fast the phone was still mid-air when the good captain heard the back gate slam and the instantaneous roar of Grandpa's pickup as it backed out of the driveway.

Actually, it was perfectly acceptable for Noonan for his kids to go fishing with their grandfather. This kept three of the family out from underfoot all day. His wife, Lorelei, was usually off with her childhood friends, Alaskans all, and this was fine as well because it got her out of his way. All day. The litter of in-laws were working, or pretending to work, and their kids were in summer school or art camp. All of these circumstances kept them from being at bay until suppertime. It was what made a vacation *a vacation:* being with the family without having to be around them.

There was, however, one **significant** drawback to being in Alaska and it was a dilly. With everyone else gone, it left the Captain alone with his mother-in-law. While it was true she could not be described as a stunning conversationalist, she could not be called a wallflower either. In fact and unfortunately, she was like a shark in a feeding frenzy when she got her chance to talk. Now, with husband, daughter and grandchildren gone from her home, she would lurk in the bushes waiting for someone to engage in a lengthy, inane conversation, the bulk of which was one-sided. While the Chief of Detectives desired nothing more for his vacation than the silence of the Alaska wilderness, what he got was an ongoing verbal onslaught of kindness, advice, concern and suggestions from the time his family left in

the morning for their various adventures until they returned in the evening at which time his mother-in-law would have exhausted her store of
advice and slipped into the blessed lethargy of 40 years of connubial bliss.
Noonan suspected his father-in-law looked at him sympathetically in the
evenings but as the old man was the perfect grandfather – other than the
moments when he would delight the kids by flopping onto his back on
a picnic table and proceed to arf like a seal, his arms and legs flailing like
flippers – Noonan had no complaints of the old man.

Thus it was with great enthusiasm Captain Heinz Noonan, Chief of
Detectives of the Sandersonville Police Department and one of America's
top crime fighters, hiding behind the white lattice of his mother-in-law's
gazebo was pleased to get a phone call. Any phone call. At the very least
it meant he would not have to converse with the walking catalog of trivia
of his mother-in-law. Speaking of which – at this very instant – he could
see her cutting her way toward him through the clover. It would only be a
moment before she lumbered into the gazebo full of enough advice, concern and suggestions for a year of newspaper columns.

"Hello."

"Captain Noonan?"

"I hope so. Otherwise I've got someone else's ID."

"I hate to break into your vacation, Captain."

Noonan looked through the trellis at his approaching mother-in-law
and said with gusto and volume, "Not a problem. What can I do for you?
Or rather, who are you?"

"This is Ayanna Driscoll. I'm the head of Airport Security here at the
Anchorage International Airport. I've got kind of an odd story but I can
assure you . . ."

As soon as he was assured he could stretch this phone call long
enough to dissuade his mother-in-law for a least another 15 minutes,
Noonan stepped out from behind the white bracing of the gazebo and
gave a planned, surprised look and pointed at the cellular phone with
his coffee cup-filled hand. He gave a helpless "sorry but I can't talk now"
look and gesture. His mother-in-law got the message and broke off her
approach to the gazebo. With great satisfaction, Noonan smiled as she
turned her back to him and began walking back toward the house lost in
a grove of evergreens.

"Ms. Driscoll,"

"Call me Ayanna."

"OK, Ayanna, every story I get is odd. Give me what you've got."

"Your name was given to me by the Anchorage Police Commissioner, Charles Dabenshire. I know him casually and professionally. He suggested I give you a call. He knows you're on vacation at your in-laws here in town but . . ."

"Crime doesn't take a vacation. Yeah, sounds like Charlie, work first." He paused for a moment, looking at his retreating mother-in-law. "As it happens," he continued, "I've got nothing but time today."

"This might not take long. Actually, at this point it's more of a 'what's going on here?' problem."

"That's the way the big problems always start. Tell me what's happened."

"OK. At about 10:15 this morning Unicorn Flight 739 from SEATAC landed in Anchorage after routine instructions."

"Meaning?"

"Oh, I'm sorry. I'm talking jargon. Before a plane lands there is a flurry of communication, mostly about local weather conditions, wind speed and direction, if there is any ice on the runway, which runway to use, at which gate to dock and other routine information."

"Go on."

"Unicorn 739 landed without incident. It rolled into Gate A-17, shut down its engines and then just sat there."

"Just sat there?"

"Right. As in nothing happened. The ground crew cranked the walkway out to the fuselage door and waited for it to open. It didn't. The ground crew assumed it was jammed on the inside so they tried to raise the pilot by radio and intercom but got no answer. Then they tried waving to the pilot through the terminal window but there was no pilot in the cockpit."

"Is this unusual?"

"Not really. We do have doors stick every once in a while – events we do not mention to the FAA – but it does happen. Not being able to reach the pilot by radio or intercom is a bit unusual too but not surprising. The pilot and copilot could have left their seats, say to go to the restroom. If she didn't have her headphones on – the pilot was a woman, by the way – it is also possible."

"It's always good to see women in the workplace," Noonan said. "Go on."

"We tried to wave through a terminal window to the pilot but the cockpit was empty. It's a bit out of the ordinary since there's a lot of shutting down before the pilot and crew can leave the plane. When we finally got into the plane we found it empty. That, I must say, was unusual."

"Empty?"

"Yes, sir. Empty. As in no one on board."

"I thought you said . . ."

"I did. It was a routine landing. The pilot and the control tower had a standard conversation. The aircraft followed all the rules right down to the docking procedure. There was no one on board when the ground crew finally made it into the plane."

"No one?"

"Not a soul."

"Can someone get out of an airplane without being seen, like through an emergency exit?"

"There weren't any emergency exits open but there are a few ways to get out of an airplane without using an emergency exit. We assume the pilot exited through the wheel well. We didn't see anyone on the control tower security camera tape so we have to assume whomever was flying the plane just kept under the aircraft until she got to the terminal overhang and just walked through the baggage holding area like she belonged there. The security cameras are there to keep people from heading the other way – in from the street, not out from the aircraft. If the pilot dressed like the ground crew, no one would have been the wiser. After all, we didn't know there was a problem until we couldn't get the main hatch open. It was long enough to give our girl about three or four minutes to make a clean getaway."

"Now you want to know where the pilot is?"

"Not really. We want to know where the 89 passengers and crew of 6 are."

Chapter 2

Ayanna was easy to spot. First, she was the only woman on the A Concourse of the Anchorage International Airport. Second, she was only one of the three at the end of the concourse at all. It made spotting her even easier.

Approaching the police tape was a lot more difficult than spotting Ayanna. It was summer time and the Anchorage International Airport was packed with tourists. While Anchorage is a small city by American standards – it has all of about 300,000 people depending on whether you count the two military bases and the bedroom communities – it will see one million tourists in the three summer months. There are not a lot of tourists in the other months. Lots of ice and snow but very few tourists. There is an old saying in Alaska; every year has nine months of snow and three months of relatives.

True to human nature, the moment the police tape went up there was a crowd of lookie-loos. Everyone wanted to know what was going on. But nothing was going on. All anyone could see were three figures at the far end of concourse just standing around. There was no body, no hustle of men-and-women in blue with their guns drawn to hint of a hijacking. Hijacking a plane in Alaska?! Where would you demand to go? There were already scheduled flights to Russia and Cuba was a l-o-n-g way from the land of ice and snow.

Noonan fought his way through the crowd like a defensive lineman until he came to the tape. He was stopped momentarily by a very tired Anchorage Airport security guard who looked about as old as Noonan's son Otto. He was old enough to be carrying a revolver, which, Noonan was pleased to see, was buttoned down in a nylon holster. Noonan liked guns in holsters. He liked them even more when the holster was buttoned down.

There was a moment of confusion before the guard let Noonan under the tape. Noonan showed him a badge from the Sandersonville Police Department and the guard grunted something sounding like "OK." His facial expression read he didn't know why he was on duty anyway. He had been told it was crowd control except for some guy with a badge who would be coming. Then some old guy with a badge showed up so what's a minimum wage security guard to do? So he let the old man through.

Noonan ducked under the police tape, to the titter of the crowd. They couldn't go to the crime scene but he could. (What a shame, Martha!) But then again, the crowd was only going to stand around for a moment or two. No body, no blood, no reason to waste any time at the airport when they could be spending their afternoon fishing for salmon or sucking up suds at any one of half-hundred places in town which catered to the three-months-and-then-gone crush of humanity.

Noonan proceeded down the empty carpet toward the far end of Concourse A. The only other individuals at the far end of the terminal were a pair of Alaska State Troopers who appeared more as bookends than officers of the law. Both stood well over six feet tall, carried a good 250 pounds apiece, and looked like weight lifters. Both also had small tooth-brush mustaches making them look a bit like Adolf Hitler on steroids. Why anyone would *want* to look like Adolf Hitler was beyond Noonan but clearly here were two men who did. The uniforms enhanced the image. They fit as if they were tailor-made, odd because police uniforms were supposed to be loose enough to chase felons. These two were obviously for show not sweat. Noonan could tell because both men had shoes so shiny they reflected the overhead lights like strobes on the runway.

Noonan could smell politics in a hurricane. Even before closing the two dozen yards between himself and the trio the stench of bureaucracy and incompetence was overpowering. Just what he needed on vacation, more of what he was escaping in North Carolina.

In the real world there are two pillars in the chain of command. One is of sweat and the other for show. Those of the sweat did the work; those of show took the credit. They were like oil and water, always together but never combining. Show people are like spiders: they come in pairs. Whenever you found show people in the singular they are looking for a telephone. They were members of the penultimate mutual admiration society, party animals in the sense they needed a litter of their own to feel comfortable. They passed around the blessings of the credit they did not earn to make sure every one of the good old boys – and, this day and age, good old girls – received the blessings of playing politics the right way.

You will always find people of sweat alone. They did not work alone because they so prefer. They work alone because it is the only way to get anything done. People of sweat do not come in gaggles; they work best when not hindered by the people of show. People of show leave people of sweat alone because, without them, there would be no credit. So the people of show let people of sweat work alone. People of show are never far away. They circle like vultures waiting for the right instant to snatch the victory they could never earn by themselves. The two Alaska State Troopers reeked of the stench of people of show.

The troopers dwarfed Noonan, not a tall man by any definition. He still stood a good head above Ayanna. She was slight and weighed in the range of 110 pounds, small enough to make her attaché appear to be a suit-case. She wore a rumpled uniform looking as though she had slept in it, which she clearly had, and her boots were a cross between hiking gear and combat footwear. Un-shined they showed the scuffmarks and scratches of years in the field. The toes were solid, probably steel-toed, which was par for the course for a person of sweat. You never knew when you were going to have to crawl over luggage or around machinery.

Ayanna's jet black hair hung straight and limp, the conditioner sheen it probably had possessed the previous day had been replaced with a dull greasy look. A fleck of white, possibly a strand of the cottonwood which filled the late summer sky, clung to a strand at the nape of her neck. If either of the troopers noticed it, they had clearly not mentioned it. The only thing on Ayanna which shined, was a yellow gold necklace chain with a small medallion. Noonan could see it was not religious but appeared more of an antique, something a woman of class would have worn proudly a century earlier.

Ayanna may have been exhausted but there was no way to tell from her posture or body language. The troopers were like all people of show, always on stage. Noonan introduced himself and there was a round of per-functory hand-shaking. Ayanna indicated they should move toward the walkway to the plane and one of the troopers raised a section of police tape stretching across the end of the concourse. Why this tape was at the end of the concourse where they were no people was beyond Noonan.

The crowd was already being contained behind the first tape he had ducked under. He smelled bureaucratic incompetence, again a stench he was well used to avoiding in North Carolina.

From the terminal window at the Anchorage International Airport, Unicorn 739 looked just like every other airliner waiting for passengers. The cigar-shaped 737 filled Gate 17 at the far end of the A Concourse and other than the fact Gates 14 through 17 were closed it looked just like any other plane about to receive passengers. Noonan did not know much about aviation but he did know a 737 when he saw one. It was not hard to spot a 737 since it was the workhorse of the aviation passenger business.

The most visual product of the Boeing assembly line, it had been around since the 1960s. Over the years it had morphed into variants, from the 737-100 to the 737-800 with a 737-900 probably on the design boards. And why not? It was the most commercially successful civilian aircraft since the Second World War. At any one moment there could be as many as 1,000 of them in the air. They didn't crash. They needed little maintenance and, most important of all, passengers had complete faith in them. If you were on a 737 the only problem you were going to have would be a broken coffee machine. There was not a single design flaw of common knowledge. The 737 was such a dependable aircraft that after American airline companies flew the planes into obsolescence they were sold to Third World countries who flew them into oblivion. A century from now, Noonan mused, there would probably be some pilot somewhere flying a 737 over a remote landscape and the plane would be just as dependable then as it was the day it came off the assembly line.

Looking out of the terminal window–and considering the two police tapes–Noonan expected to see a flurry of activity around the plane.

He was in error.

The only visual indication something was amiss was a squad of airport security people sitting in parked cars strategically scattered around the plane. The cars were just there in the sense they were not moving. The personnel inside those cars were not moving either. It did not look like a crime scene with people scurrying hither and yon. It looked like a used car lot around an airplane at the end of the concourse. The plane wasn't going anywhere and neither were the security people. Everyone was just sitting, waiting for the curtain to rise in the next act of this drama.

One of the vehicles, a heavy van, was parked directly behind one of the massive back wheels of the 737, clearly to block the plane if it tried to back-out of the gate. Noonan gave a soft snicker and said to himself, "a bit late, eh?"

"Sorry?" said Ayanna as she scanned the scene below to see what Noonan was referring to.

Noonan indicated the van with a tilt of his head. "The security van behind the back wheel of the plane. It's a bit late, don't you think?"

Ayanna smiled and now she looked tired. "Well, yes, I guess so. You have to understand we have procedures here at the airport we have to follow even if they seem stupid. We do everything by the book. When there is a problem involving a plane, we block the plane. It's in our rule book."

Noonan gave a slight grunt. "True. But as we get into this case keep in mind the bad boys and girls know your procedures and there are going to use them against you. I'm not saying to stop doing what you are supposed to do. What I am suggesting is you force yourself to start thinking outside of the box. We are up against some very clever people."

"Well," replied Ayanna tiredly, "at this point we don't know what is going on so we are not going to take any chances." Then she backtracked a bit and said, "If you have any suggestions . . ."

"Oh, no. All I was saying was we are a long from over on this case and every detail has been planned in advance. We, rather, you, are only going to get through this successfully if you become just as clever as your adversaries. Yes, if I have a suggestion I will let you know. For the moment, follow your procedures. Just do not let them get in your way of making a quick, creative decision."

"I'm not sure what you mean but I'll keep it in mind."

"That's the first step to being a creative thinker."

Noonan turned from the terminal window and looked back down the concourse. Other than it was old and clearly in desperate need of repair, upgrade or, probably, total demolition, it looked pretty much like any other terminal in any other small city in America. The carpet wasn't threadbare yet but it has hardly new. It was a facsimile of the galaxy with a brightened constellation of stars making up the Alaska Flag every dozen or so feet. The carpet must have been stunning when it was new – and during the decade it had been installed. Now it was old. Visibly old. Threadbare with a footpath right down its center where millions of passenger shoes and boots had trod their way to waiting aircraft.

There were alcoves of seating on both sides of the terminal carpet, which extended three deep all the way to the windows except where the gate entrances were located. The front wall was glass to capture whatever sunshine there was during the summer. There was an ocean of surface of industrial ceiling squares stretching down the concourse, all of them old and loaded with asbestos. A lot of Alaskans were going to be very happy when the concourse was upgraded because, from experience, Noonan knew every one of those ceiling tiles was going to end up as insulation in cabins and hunting lodges from Katmai to Talkeetna. Waste not want not was the Alaska way of life.

"This is a pretty old terminal for an international airport."

Ayanna smiled. "Alaska's a bit different than the rest of country. Before there was oil we didn't have much of a tourist industry other than along the coastline. Now we get about a million tourists coming through this terminal during the three months of the summer. We are so packed during the summer we can't do any repair or upgrade work. We have to do all the upgrade in the off-season."

"Doesn't look like a lot of work has been done on this concourse." Noonan pointed to some loose ceiling tiles and the buckling of some of the wainscot panels along the wall below the windows.

"This is the last concourse to be upgraded. We started the renovation three years ago on Concourse C," she pointed down the hallway, "at the other end of the airport. Where the dignitaries land. We're been progressing this way year-by-year."

"So this is the last concourse to be worked on?"

"Yes. It should be finished before next summer." She stalled for a moment. "Is it important?"

Noonan smiled.

Ayanna was learning.

"Until we know what is going on, *everything* is important. Was this the actual gate where the plane arrived?"

"Yes. Why?"

"Because it's at the end of the concourse – and the oldest concourse. Odd."

"It was where Unicorn 739 was scheduled to arrive. Being at the end of the concourse was just the luck of the draw. Gates are assigned weeks ahead of the arrival but lots of things happen which move planes around. Planes are late, it takes longer than expected to off-load cargo or emergencies come up, the usual. So planes get moved around. Gate 17 was where Unicorn 739 was supposed to dock."

"You might check just to be sure."

"The luck of the draw?"

"I'm guessing there was a reason the bad boys and girls wanted the plane to be here. Why don't you check to make sure it *was* the luck of draw and not something which was somehow engineered into the system? It might also give you a clue as to who might be in the inside person."

"You think there was an inside person?"

"Had to be. Even if there was no inside person it's the place to start. Planes do not land without pilots, passengers do not vanish into thin air and crimes like this usually have a cash motive. Cash means an inside job."

"What cash are we talking about?"

Noonan gave Ayanna a fatherly tap on the shoulders. "This case is very young. Believe me, before it is over there will be a cash motive. No one goes to this kind of trouble for a prank."

Noonan scuffed the carpet while Ayanna dug around in her attaché for a pad. The carpet here was even more discolored than the concourse walkway. The traffic was clearly more concentrated where people boarded the planes.

Noonan turned back from looking out the window at the 737. "OK," he said to Ayanna almost excitedly, "Let's take a look inside the plane." This was clearly better than spending the day listening to his mother-in-law prattle on and on and on.

One of troopers raised the crime scene tape while Ayanna and Noonan went under. Three steps later one of the trooper bookends posted himself beside the check-in carrel like an oak and immediately picked up a phone to report his location. The other escorted Noonan and Ayanna as far as the entrance to the ramp. There he stationed himself and started scanning the empty concourse cul-de-sac as if there was a crowd and he, a Secret Service agent, was looking for assassins.

Noonan and Ayanna proceeded down the elevated ramp as if they were going to enter the plane from the walkway. At the bend in the walkway, Ayanna stopped and opened a door in a side wall. From there they descended to the ground on a rolling walkway and walked to a ramp at the rear of the plane.

"Why are we entering the plane from the rear?" Noonan asked as he blinked in the bright Alaska summer sunshine.

"Sorry for all the Security, Captain, but . . ."

"Call me Heinz. I'm on vacation, remember."

"Uh, OK," she paused, clearly at a loss to call a captain by his first name, "Heinz."

Noonan smiled. "Relax, you'll get used to it."

Ayanna smiled nervously for a moment and then relaxed. "There's a bulkhead at the front of the airplane dividing the cockpit from the passenger compartment. Are you familiar with cargo hauling in Alaska?"

"Not really."

"A lot of flights from the Lower 48, or within Alaska, carry cargo as well as passengers, often together. Because the cargo is heavier, it is put to the front of the wings. It's loaded first. When all of the cargo to be taken is loaded onboard, a bulkhead is slid into place. The bulkhead separates the cargo from the passengers. The more cargo there is, the less room for the passengers."

"What you are saying is the area in the plane between the pilot and the passengers is chock full of boxes and crates and bags and whatever else is being transported as cargo?"

"We say *carried*. *Carried* as cargo. Yeah but it's more complicated than how you expressed it. You are thinking of cargo as boxes and crates like you were filling a U-Haul. Air cargo can be sheets of plywood, pianos, hospital beds, thousands of feet of steel pipe, whatever. I've seen elephants."

"Elephants?"

"Two, actually. They were small but they were elephants and they were alive."

"For the zoo?"

"No. They were part of an educational project funded by a federal grant. Someone came up with the idea of flying elephants around in the bush so Natives children could see there really were such things as elephants."

Noonan chuckled, "If you can't go to the zoo then the zoo comes to you."

"A nice way of putting it. Carrying live animals is not unusual. Large animals are carried in the cargo area while cats and small dogs go onboard with the passengers as carry-ons. I've seen a lot of chickens going into the villages and a number of years ago a Japanese Airlines jumbo jet broke open on the runway. It was loaded with cattle and when the plane finally came to rest the cattle still alive were running all over the runway. We didn't have a fence between us and the park," Ayanna said as she pointed the south across the runway, "to Kincaid Park. I'm sure there are a few cattle still out there, roaming around and wondering how they ended up in the land of ice and snow."

"There's a fence there now?"

"To keep the moose off the runway."

"Does it work?"

"Must. No plane has hit a moose since I've been here."

"So the cargo between the pilot and the passengers could be anything of any size of any configuration?"

"Welcome to Alaska. You can see for yourself when we get onboard."

Noonan thought for a moment, "Can the pilot get from the cockpit to the passengers?"

"Sure. It's dark because the cargo has covered the windows and not all of the cargo stacks perfectly so you might catch a knee or a shin if you're not careful. So passengers load from the back of the plane. Insurance reasons. Only here in Anchorage. It's a whole different matter in the bush. The further you are from the FAA the less you do things by the book. I've taken flights in the Aleutians where I was sitting on cargo. Didn't even have a seat. Cargo pays more than passengers and there's an old Alaska aviation expression 'cargo doesn't talk back.'"

Noonan chuckled. "The Alaskan expression I like is 'there old pilots and bold pilots but no old bold pilots.'"

"You've got that right. In the aviation business you can't make too many mistakes and live. Which is a very good reason to do things by the book."

The runway apron was dry as a bone. There was not a speck of dust on the pavement. Noonan stopped Ayanna for a moment and went over to look at the airplane's tires. Ayanna waited while Noonan did some poking.

"Looking for anything in particular," she asked when he got back.

"Not really. Planes have to land. Tires are old, not new. If the tires had been new it might have been a lead."

"What would new tires have meant?"

"I don't know if they would have meant anything at all. Clues are where you find them. If something is out of the ordinary, it's worth investigating."

Ayanna said something which sounded like "hu" or "um."

"Was it usual for this kind of a plane to be taking cargo? I mean, this is a 737. It's a passenger plane. It has windows. Cargo 737s don't have windows."

"Yes and no," Ayanna said stopping at the foot of the stairway to the back of the plane. "There is more money in passengers than cargo so the larger companies want to take as many passengers as possible. After the summer, the tourist traffic drops to zero. So the larger companies cut their service to Alaska and consolidate their flights. They are in the business for the passengers. Companies like this one, Unicorn," she pointing at the plane, "are here year-round. To keep good will with the cargo companies they carry cargo year round even if they could make more money with passengers. They don't *lose* money with cargo; they just don't make as much as they could. They are low in cargo in June, July and August. Unicorn then makes up for the loss by hauling cargo the rest of the year."

Noonan nodded his head as they climbed the tail staircase. The staircase bounced gently as he ascended. He asked Ayanna if this was unusual.

"There is another yes and no answer when it comes to boarding from the rear. In most cases planes do not use the tail staircase. It's too cumbersome and most of the time passengers deplane from the front only. Now if passengers have to enter from the rear they go up a mobile staircase we drive out to the plane. It's more efficient and more stable."

"When I went to Bethel last year we entered the plane through the back. It was up a staircase with a truck attached but we didn't go through the tail. We went in what was basically the side of the aircraft."

Ayanna pointed to the outer side of the 737. "You were basically going in through an emergency exit. It's unusual these days in large airports. Even in the bush the tail staircase is rarely used. We had to force this staircase open because the front door was locked from the inside. For this trip all of the passengers in Seattle had to enter from the rear because of the bulk head. They entered through a mobile staircase, not these stairs. We had to break the front hatch door open from the inside. Now it's a crime scene so the hatch is closed off until the forensic people get here."

The pair went up the tail staircase and into the aisle of the airliner, empty seats disappearing toward the bulkhead at the front. The plane had a flown-in look, as if it had just been cleared of passengers. There were blankets tossed about willy-nilly on the seats, magazines were half in/half out of seat pockets, and the floor was littered with plastic wrapping, paper prayers from the meal trays, as well as some salt and pepper containers along with bits and pieces of paper. Noonan popped one of the overhead compartments and discovered it was full of carry-on luggage.

"It's almost as if everybody was sucked out of the plane leaving only their luggage and carry-ons," noted Ayanna as she popped open another overhead compartment to reveal it was full as well.

"Well, wherever they were sucked off to, they went with the clothes they were wearing," said Noonan slyly, "and they didn't take their carry-on luggage."

"Or their make-up," said Ayanna as she opened a cosmetic case on one of the seats and examined its contents.

Noonan walked down the aisle, stopping occasionally and probing a seat pocket here and an overhead bin there. He pulled the curtain back from the kitchen and looked at the counter. Then he popped open what passed for a refrigerator onboard.

"Nothing looks as though it has been touched," he said. Then he gingerly pulled the trash can box out from underneath the counter. It was partially full. "Here," he said as he handed the plastic container to Ayanna. "Have your lab take a look at this."

"The garbage? Why?"

"To see if you can match any fingerprints. If you can match the flight attendants fingerprints to the trash, you will know they were on board. If you get a strange fingerprint, or even only one set on everything, we'll know this was a set-up."

"The matching is going to take some time."

"Naw, maybe forty minutes. You know the flight attendants' names and they had to have flight passes to get into secure areas. All those passes required fingerprints. Just get the names of the flight attendants, email their names to SEATAC and you'll have their prints on line within an hour. By then a good print man will have the prints off those bottles," Noonan indicated the contents of the garbage container. "All you have to do is confirm a match. If you get one, bingo, it confirms the flight attendants who were supposed to be on board were. If not, you've got another problem on your hands."

"Like terrorists?"

"You won't be *that lucky.*" Noonan smiled sadly.

"You mean this is some kind of a scam? Are we back to a ransom you were talking about?"

"It has to be. Unless you believe in space aliens, little green men transubstantiate into airliners and they suck everyone out . . ."

". . . with their clothes on. Right, Heinz, I'm afraid to say I'm not a believer."

Noonan leaned back against one of the chairs. "Bring me up to speed on everything you know at this time."

Ayanna shook her head slowly, her hair slopping about more than bouncing. The very motion gave every indication that in spite of her high spirits, it had been a l-o-n-g night. Noonan knew the feeling.

He had been there before.

Many, many nights.

He called them *Naugahyde Nights,* the hours spent kind-of/sort-of nap-ping on the Naugahyde furniture in his office waiting.

Waiting for lab results.

Waiting for a fingerprint match out of Washington D. C.

Waiting for a judge's signature.

Waiting for an interrogation to come to a close.

Waiting for a hunch to play out.

It was waiting for whatever was supposed to happen and hoping it would happen soon. So he didn't have to go home, get two hours of sleep only to be dragged back to the office.

Just as bad, every Naugahyde Night inevitable came with *caveat.* No matter how long the wait or how important the matter, there were always *a few items to work out.* Things that did not fit. Loose ends and holes in the sequence of logic. The Devil was certainly in the details.

Noonan could tell Ayanna was tired. Well, in this business you had to get used to it. If she thought she had problems now, she was in for a real surprise. Things were not going to be getting any better any time soon. Noonan gave Ayanna time to collect her thoughts. She was young; she'd learn how to go days without deep sleep and still be professional, compe-tent and composed.

Ayanna settled back against an arm rest. "Well, there's not much to tell. The plane took off from SEATAC a bit late, about half an hour. Everything was routine until it approached the Juneau area when the plane requested permission to land for a medical emergency. According to the pilot, a woman, one of the passengers was having what she said was described by the flight attendants as 'mild convulsions.' Unicorn 739 descended to an altitude below the radar's horizon as if it were going to land in Juneau and then came back on radar about five minutes later. The pilot stated the pas-senger had recovered to the extent the trip could continue uninterrupted."

"I know this is a foolish question," Noonan said as he rubbed his fore-head with the tips of the fingers of his left hand, "but are you sure there wasn't a plane switch there, as in one plane rising above the radar horizon as another falls beneath it?"

"Again, another yes and no answer." Ayanna shifted on the airplane seat. "Yes, we looked into the possibility but we discounted it. The plane, which landed in Anchorage, was the same plane, which took off from Seattle. The serial numbers of the aircraft matched. The luggage onboard was loaded in Seattle and the passengers were listed as having boarded in Seattle. The passengers were on the plane when it pulled out of the gate in SEATAC. Considering the time involved, it would not have been possible for the plane to have landed, dropped off the passengers, and taken off again."

"Improbable but not impossible."

"Correct. Not impossible. However, there are a number of other problems. First, the plane never landed at the Juneau airport and it could not have landed anywhere nearby. Have you been to Juneau?"

"Actually, no."

"Well, there are only three things in whole area: steep mountains dropping right to the water's edge, very small cities and lots of rough water. We're checking every landing strip within a 30-minute flying radius of Juneau, regardless of its condition. We're still only talking about three places a plane this size could land – maybe."

"No help from the Air Force?"

"We don't know yet. We've asked Elmendorf Air Force Base to check with their AWACS . . ."

"AWACS?"

"Airborne Warning and Control System. Those are the big planes you see with the large saucers on top. The saucers are actually downward-looking radars. They can spot and track all aircraft and anything on the ground composed of metal."

"If they are downward looking then they could tell you if the plane actually landed."

"Right. If they want to tell us. If their command structure will tell us. See, we civilians are not even supposed to know AWACS exist. So when we called and asked for the AWACS to check its tapes we were asked what AWACS was."

"Nice."

"Military intelligence in action. So we just asked if they would 'look around' to see if there was anything like downward looking radar and if there was any information we could have. Then we asked the FAA to ask the Air Force. I'm afraid the Air Force won't tell us diddly. They'll tell the Pentagon who might tell the FAA who might tell us. Do you know how stupid you feel when you call the FAA and say 'Hey, we've just lost 95 people and can't find them?'" Ayanna rested the plastic garbage can down on the leading edge of the seat.

Noonan thought for a moment. "What did the FAA say, I mean about the AWACS tape?"

"They said they'd check with the Pentagon but the FAA said it was unlikely AWACS would have any record of the flight. In Southeast Alaska there are so many steep mountains if a plane drops below the mountain level, the downward looking radar can't track it."

"You mean if the plane went below the tops of the mountains, the AWACS can't track it?"

"Probably. I don't know the specifics on AWACS but I'll bet they can't follow a car on the road in the mountains. Too much ground clutter. The mountains probably scramble the image. For a plane, if is moving fast and flying low it will, quite literally, disappear into the ground clutter. It doesn't mean it crashed; it just disappeared off the scope. So we're stuck with the time difference. We'd have to calculate how long the plane was off the scope to determine if it could have landed, dropped off passengers and then taken off again."

"What do you think?" Noonan asked almost uninterestedly as he looked back toward the bulkhead which blocked off the back of the airplane.

"I think anything's possible."

"I agree with you." Noonan began walking down the aisle toward the front the plane. Ayanna watched him for a moment and then followed, the garbage can in tow.

When Noonan got to the front of the seat section he took a close look at the bulkhead. The bulkhead itself was nothing more than a sheet of particle board covered with carpet identical to carpet on the floor of the plane. It had two massive unicorns, one on either side of a doorway, which now stood open. Noonan stuck his head inside the doorway and looked at the back of the bulkhead particle board. It was sturdier on the inside. There were a handful of metal bars forming a webbing pattern on either side of the doorway which ran to the side of the fuselage where the beams were bolted to the aircraft chassis.

As Noonan leaned inside the bulk head area and extended his right hand to test the stability of the metal arms, he heard Ayanna say "Those metal bars are to keep the cargo from coming through the bulk head if the plane hits rough weather."

"Seem solid enough," said Noonan as he pulled his hand away. He stepped into the bulkhead area and gave the particle board plug a push. It was solid from plane ceiling to floor making the first bank of seats in the airplane Row 15. "Kind of cuts down First Class seating doesn't it?"

"There *is* no First Class seating on Unicorn, Heinz. It's the economy airline."

"Good point."

When Ayanna had said the bulkhead was crammed with cargo, she had not been kidding. The carpeted floor of the passenger section of the aircraft had been removed leaving the brackets and beams of the aircraft fuselage bracing exposed so ropes and wires could be attached to hooks to secure the cargo. The area was dark because all of the window shades had been pulled down. The only light came from behind him and the faint glow of the cockpit windows somewhere, 15 rows ahead of him.

There were a half dozen igloos stacked strategically on both sides of the plane for balance and a pile of plywood sheets was wedged on one side of the craft. Boxes, canvas bags, cartons, and every other description of cargo was neatly and efficiently stacked and roped securely around the cargo containers. Noonan picked his way around the cargo until he found where the door to the walkway was located. While the pilot and cockpit crew could easily get out of the main hatch, the rest of the forward section was filled with cargo, primarily boxes stacked as high as Noonan could reach. There was also a hospital bed strapped to one side of the bulkhead and a motorcycle, complete with full-face helmet padlocked to the crossbar running parallel to the handlebars.

"There's an odd collection of cargo here. Is it always like this?"

"Not always," replied Ayanna, her voice muted behind him. After she entered the bulkhead area and came toward him, her voice got clearer. "Every plane coming from Seattle takes a certain amount of cargo. During the winter when the tourist traffic goes way down Unicorn runs almost exclusively cargo. Sometimes the bulkhead is pushed all the way back to the center of the plane. Unicorn is a small airline so it can't afford to run exclusively on passengers. It runs just enough cargo during the summer to keep its winter customers happy."

Noonan pointed to the hospital bed. "This doesn't look like something an industrial client would want transported by airplane. Wouldn't a barge be cheaper? Or a truck?"

Ayanna tapped the bed. "Sure, if you didn't need it tomorrow. Any airline which has cargo space is not too picky about what it carries as long as the customer pays. In the case of the bed," she reached over and grasped the cargo tag with her left hand, "it's going to Lime Village. It's out on the Stony River. If whoever wanted the bed in Lime Village didn't make arrangements for it to be on the barge this spring, it had to come in by air. There's no other way in. Except dog sled and I don't see dogs pulling this puppy," she tapped the bed, "across the frozen tundra – even if it were taken apart."

"Wouldn't it have been cheaper to buy a hospital bed in Anchorage?"

"Maybe. If you could wait a year. Even then the cost would not be a lot less. Lime Village would still be paying the same transportation costs from Seattle to Anchorage–plus the overhead and storage and profit charged locally. It can be expensive. Once they get the bed to Anchorage it goes postal rates, not cargo rates. It saves the village money."

"Postage?"

"Right. In Alaska you can send anything to anywhere in Alaska through the Post Office, bricks, beds, motorcycles."

"You mean just like mail?"

"Right. It is mail. It's got a special name: bypass mail. This bed is coming north from Seattle as cargo. Once it gets to Anchorage someone picks it up in a truck, drives it over to the Post Office where it's mailed."

"Then the Post Office flies it out to Lime Village?"

"No, then the Post Office puts it on a truck and drives it right back to the airport where it's put on a plane flying out to Lime Village as mail. Sometimes it's the same plane."

"Why not just send it as cargo? It seems as though there is a lot of shuffling around here."

Ayanna gave a smile indicating **Welcome to Alaska, the land where we do things differently.** "Air cargo rates are twice postage rates. It's cheaper to put the bed on a truck and drive it to the Post Office than to pay cargo rates."

"Wait a minute," Noonan scratched his head in amazement. "Hum, if the bed only costs the hospital in Lime Village $300 if it's sent through the Postal Service, so I am guessing the air cargo company is not carrying the bed for $300? They would be losing money at $300."

"Believe me, Captain, er, Heinz. No air carrier loses a dime in Alaska on mail. No, the air cargo carrier charges the Postal Service $600, its usual rate."

"If the hospital only pays $300 and the air cargo company charges $600, who makes up the difference?"

Ayanna looked at Noonan with the same amused expression. "Do you want my answer or the Post Office's?"

"I know *your* answer: the taxpayer. What's the Post Office say?"

"It says on the average it all works out. While it costs $600 to send the bed out, in essence the rest of the mail is so light it flies for free."

"Yeah," said Noonan. "I can see some Postal public affairs person making that statement. It sounds logical but is not. The epitome of the bureaucracy for you." He swept his index finger side-to-side. "Is all of these stuff going to remote villages?"

"Could be." Ayanna started looking a number of cargo tags. "This motorcycle is going to be picked up here at the airport; these skis are going to Talkeetna so they are cargo transfers." She tapped some of the smaller boxes in one of the cargo nets. "Some of these are going to be delivered here in Anchorage and others are on their way to the Mat-Su Valley for distribution."

"Mat-Su as in Matanuska-Susitna Valley?"

"You know your Alaska geography well."

"No. I know the Mat-Su has some of the largest king salmon runs in the world. That's where my kids are today."

"Then they are going to have fishing stories for the rest of their lives. Do you have salmon in North Carolina?"

"Only in the supermarket."

Ayanna laughed. "Where my father does his fishing. Comes home with a fish every time he goes out."

"Smart man."

"And successful."

They both chuckled and Noonan gestured with his left hand to indicate the stacks of cargo. "I see, so you've got a big collection of a lot of little deliveries."

"Except for those large crates." Ayanna pointed to a mountain of crates, all the same size. They were strapped together and all had the same logo printed on all sides of the cartons. "They go to the Alyeska Pipeline. Probably tools or technical equipment too delicate to travel by barge. Or too important. I don't think any of the cargo has anything to do with the passengers. It was loaded long before the passengers were brought on board. And it's here. They're not."

Noonan gave a *hum* indicating he had heard what she said. Then he stepped back through the particle board bulkhead and surveyed the interior of the airplane. Ayanna followed him and shut the panel door behind her.

Noonan wandered down the corridor not sure what he was looking for. About halfway to the tail staircase he turned around. "Can one person fly an airplane this big?"

"Sure. It's not safe and quite complicated. One person could do it. Flying itself is not difficult; it's the takeoff and landing. Landing and takeoffs are where all the busy work happens."

"Would Seattle have known there was only one person in the cockpit?"

"Probably not. The Control Tower doesn't talk to everyone in the cockpit, just the pilot. There would be no reason to talk with anyone else. And the Control Tower can't see inside the cockpit so there would have been no way to visually confirm there was only one person in the cockpit."

Noonan looked down the aisle and nudged a pillow with the toe of his right shoe. "Once the plane got aloft," he paused for a moment. "Aloft, the right term?"

"It'll do. We just say 'up.'"

"OK, when the plane got up could the pilot have put the plane on automatic long enough to come back here and spread out this trash? I mean the blankets, magazines and napkins?"

"Modern automatic pilots don't really work so easily. It's not like you hit a switch and the plane flies with no one in charge for hours. It has to be updated and re-entered every ten or fifteen minutes – just to make sure some external force like a storm or wind isn't affecting the route of the plane. But, the answer to your question is yes; someone could have come back here and messed up the cabin. They'd just have to be back in the pilot's chair before the automatic pilot shut off."

"What happens when the automatic pilot shuts off?"

"Don't know. Never heard of it happening. I'm assuming some kind of an alarm goes off in the cockpit. Maybe some lights flash. I don't think the plane goes into a power dive or anything so severe. I'll bet some kind of alarm flashes in some control tower somewhere."

"You might want to check and see if something similar happened for this plane," Noonan said as he poked around inside of one of the overhead lockers. "I don't see any laptops up here and I didn't see any on the seats. Some of the passengers probably had laptops. If they are on the ground you might be able to get an email through. There have got to be relatives waiting in the terminal," he angled his head toward the terminal. "You might also ask for cell phone numbers. Some of the passengers probably had cell phones."

"We've got a passel of relatives in the terminal and they are not happy campers."

"I imagine not," Noonan took another long look up the aisle. "When you finally got into the plane it was empty. Just like this?"

"Yup. We haven't touched anything. It's a crime scene right now."

"Well, I guess I've seen all I want to see here. Will you make sure you get your print people to work on the trash can?"

"Not a problem."

"OK. Let's go to your office and quack. I still need some information."

"Quack?"

"When you live in duck country, you quack."

Ayanna was silent for a moment. "I knew there was a reason I didn't want to live in North Carolina."

"If I lived in Alaska," Noonan said quickly, "I wouldn't want to live in North Carolina either."

Ayanna found it funny and laughed. It was a light laugh, at first kind of nervous and then with a bit of relief. "I needed a laugh," she said. "It's been so tense lately, the passengers missing and all."

"Well, don't relax yet," Noonan said darkly. "Those passengers aren't the only mystery here."

"You still think they're being held hostage? Why? How?"

"*Why?* For lots of money. How? Another matter altogether." Noonan extended his arm out toward the rear door of the airplane indicating she should lead the two of them out of the plane.

Ayanna preceded him down the back stairway. As they crossed the tarmac she nodded to the security teams who were on alert around the aircraft. Well, they were supposed to on alert but to Noonan they looked to be snoozing. No one was actually asleep, as in sawing logs, but it was clear to Noonan no one was expecting anything to happen soon. Most of the men were bleary eyed as if they had just been rudely shaken awake, not as if they had been up all night. They had probably been on the clock all night but, as Noonan knew from sad experience, it was not the same as being wide awake for the same period of time.

Noonan stood for a moment in the bright sunshine and took in the entire operations area, from the terminal building across the apron and then across the runway to where the trees to the far south indicated vacant land or a park. He saw absolutely nothing out of place. He didn't know what kind of activity an airport was supposed to have on the apron side of the terminal but there wasn't a lot of activity here. Anchorage was certainly not SEATAC or LAX but he would have expected more movement. There was none. Maybe it got busy when a plane came in? Actually, he knew this probably wasn't true. Whenever he had landed in Anchorage all he saw through the window was the usual crew of six or seven taking luggage off the plane and maybe two or three more inside the plane cleaning it out for the next load of passengers. There were 17 gates and even though he could see the tails of six or seven Alaska Airlines jets, the face of the Eskimo proudly on each one, he saw no flurry of trucks and people on the apron. Odd, he thought.

Then again, this was Alaska.

Noonan followed Ayanna across the tarmac to the edge of the apron. Ayanna used a pass key to open an outer door and they mounted the same stairway they had used to get onto the tarmac earlier. When the door slammed shut behind them, it was pitch dark. No reason to have windows here.

At the top of the stairs Ayanna handed the trash can to one of the gorilla-like Alaska State Troopers watching the docking bay. "Please have this taken over to the crime lab," she said to him. "Have them check for any fingerprints on anything. Then get a copy of the fingerprints of the flight attendants and crew from SEATAC. See if we can make a match."

The trooper gave her a look of annoyance, the way people of show do when they have to deal with the people of sweat. Annoyance because *work* is what people of sweat do. *Work* is not what people of show do. Then again, Noonan was standing next to Ayanna and one of the unspoken rules of being a person of show is to never upset someone you don't know. They could be important, you know.

The state trooper grunted rather than said anything. He wrapped his fingers around the lip of the garbage can and held it away from his body as if it had some odious smell emanating from within. Noonan had seen the look too many time to mistake it. It was the don't-let-anything-stain-my-uniform-because-I-look-so-good-in-it expression. With the trash can at arm's length he was off, striding down the concourse with seven league boots.

The other trooper still stood oak-like overlooking the check-in desk. He had a phone in one hand and was waving Ayanna toward him with the other. "For you," he said as he passed her the phone.

"Driscoll." She listened for a moment and then her face went pale. When she put the phone down, her face had the pallor of a corpse.

Noonan looked at her with a sad smile as if to silently say he knew what was coming next.

"They want $25 million in diamonds and other precious stones." She took a deep breath. "They want it within 48 hours."

Chapter 3

In Alaska, fishing is neither a sport nor a passion; it is a religion. It is a polytheistic creed with the king salmon as the most holy divine and the lesser gods descending from sockeye and coho to halibut and sheefish, grayling and cutthroat and thence to pike, chum, dog, hooligan and finally Irish lords. An Alaskans who does not fish is as rare as a Californian without a car.

Alaska is, quite literally, the land of fish. Fish made the land. In the days before canned salmon the fish of profit was hooligan. These smelt were so rich in fish oil if they were held upright they would burn like a candle. The market for this oil was so great what became known as the Inside Passage, the waterway connecting Juneau with the Seattle, was *Grease Alley*. Long before the hooligan fishery died the canned salmon industry rose. Beginning in the early years of the 1900s salmon became the cash crop. It supplanted the other two other great industries in Alaska history: fur and gold. Even with the rise of the oil industry, fishing is still the second largest employer in the state.

The solitary fisherman is the symbol of the summer in Alaska. The man, or woman, with the pole and fish net is the royalty of the north. From late May to early September Alaskans plan their weekends based on which fish run is open. King salmon are so plentiful they can be caught in Ship Creek, the stream on which the original town of Anchorage was established. Within the boundaries of the Municipality of Anchorage, depending on the date, the wily fisherman can catch silver and pink salmon, hooligan, Dolly Varden, rainbow trout, grayling or Arctic char.

There are so many fisherman on the open rivers Alaskans refer to the sport as *combat fishing*. Anglers stand shoulder-to-shoulder-shoulder along the shoreline casting their lures into the water or dip netting the in- and out-going tide for their limits. The runs are so strong everyone has a chance of getting at least one fish. With limits being as high as 25 fish per person, a family can stock a winter's worth of fish in a dedicated weekend of fishing. In the Upper Cook Inlet, a leisurely drive from Anchorage, the total yearly harvest is 25 salmon and 10 flounder for the permit holder and 10 salmon for each additional household member.

Salmon runs are so popular most television and radio stations have several minutes during the news hour to report where the fishing is hottest. Newspapers have colored maps of fishing areas and the most popular publication in Alaska during the summer is the State of Alaska Department of Fish and Game tide chart.

For the angler who wants to increase his chance of getting a king salmon, he fishes from a boat rather than along the shoreline. Though boats there are plenty, the ocean is a huge expanse and one can always find a secluded area to drop in a little tiny hook to catch a very big fish. Since the salmon migrate, there are no fishing holes as they are known in the lower states. In Alaska you fish the migration streams. If you time it right, you can catch a king salmon which can weigh upwards of one hundred pounds–and every ounce not skin, guts or bone is very good eating. After you have hooked your monster, all you have to do is get him into the boat. For the smaller fish, an ice chest will do; but you fill ice chest with beer **just in case** the salmon aren't biting.

The sun was still high in the sky, which meant nothing in July in Anchorage, as the Fisherman lugged the ice chest onto his boat. He had to make sure it would fit. Perfect planning was the key to success. He didn't need any last minute surprises. It wasn't hard to load the ice chest because it was empty. It was supposed to be empty. You didn't go fishing with a full ice chest. You came *back* with a full ice chest. He didn't need any ice now. He was just setting the stage. He'd get the ice tomorrow. Six or seven pounds would be enough. Not a lot of ice. He was not after big fish. He didn't need much ice.

He would need beer. No Alaskan fisherman would set off after king salmon without a six-pack or two of beer. It would be uncivilized, un-Alaskan. More beer made more friends. Make it three or four six-packs. Fit in with the crowd.

Chapter 4

It took less than 23 minutes for the Anchorage International Airport to go from a contained crisis to Pandemonium. It was bad enough the President of Unicorn Airlines in Seattle was notified of the ransom demand by an anonymous phone call within minutes of Ayanna – on his private line. Worse, both Anchorage newspapers and every radio and television station in town were tipped by the end of the hour – and Ayanna only got the call with 23 minutes left in that hour.

Before she had hung up the phone, every one of the relatives of the passengers knew the ransom call had been made. Those who had not picked it up from the radio saw it blasted across the Internet.

Welcome to the age of electronic communication

They were not happy.

In fact, they were extremely upset.

This was the good news.

The bad news was they were telling everyone about the ransom.

And anyone.

Radio stations as far west as Denver were running live interviews with relatives within the hour and 60 minutes later Los Angeles television stations had live feeds from the airport using Anchorage affiliate commentators. File footage of the 737 and construction experts clogged the airwaves and there was talk of the *return of D. B. Cooper*, a name so unfamiliar to the average television watcher the entire historical saga of the lone hijacker had to be brought back to life.

It was as if the center of the entire news universe had shifted, west from New York and north from Washington D. C. The President of the

United States canceled a news conference because she didn't think any of the stations would preempt the Anchorage drama and Congress went on an extended vacation because no news of the floor was making the cable channels.

For better or worse, the Alaskans were loving it. Local broadcast feeds were going worldwide and freelance reporters were inundating the airport as if it were a red carpet event. There were so many people descending on the airport there was gridlock in the parking lot, singular, and both the Approach and Departure lanes. Inside the terminal a dozen state troopers were assigned to keep the crowd away from the end Concourse C and back from the windows overlooking the plane. Another dozen were assigned in-terminal duty with two dozen more handling the traffic – foot and vehicular – outside on both sides of the terminal.

Then things really got out of hand. A freelance cameraman was discovered in the chassis of a food van supplying planes on the runway apron. This lead to a search of all vehicles on the landing apron and three more *paparazzi* were discovered. Two small surveillance cameras were discovered bolted to the backside of the terminal facing the plane and tents began appearing on the far side of the runway from where a bank of telephoto lenses could be seen glinting in the sunshine.

The calls from the extortionists, quite literally, shut the city down. Anchorage, Alaska was not a large city to begin with. During the winter it had a population of about 300,000 making it, at best, a modest but small American city. During the summer, the city was packed. Every hotel was filled to capacity and it was easier to find a walrus with a gold tooth than an open restaurant table. When the *paparazzi* arrived, the bed-and-breakfasts filled. More rooms were needed so citizens were asked to open their homes to the visiting news teams – at $250 a night breakfast not included.

What made Anchorage unique was its isolation. There was no 'next town.' In Los Angeles someone could drive from the Pacific Ocean to the desert, about 50 miles, and pass through a dozen cities the size of Anchorage. But Anchorage had no neighbors of similar size. The nearest large city was Seattle, 2000 miles to the south. The next smallest city was Fairbanks, 300 miles to the north. Other than a limited selection of bedroom communities, Anchorage was as geographically isolated as it had been before the Second World War. The miles between it and the lower 48 states had not changed, only the time it takes to get there.

Because the population was so concentrated, Anchorage had the feel of a small town. Everyone knew everyone else's business. The best stories never made it into the newspaper but everything else did. Whether it is a cotillion at the high school, a murder on the military base or what's being served for lunch at each elementary school, the Anchorage newspapers covered it all. Unicorn 739 moved everything out of the papers, thin as they were, until they were running nothing but passenger relative profiles and the comics.

The extortion of Unicorn Airlines wasn't just big news for a city like Anchorage. It was big news worldwide and it stopped the city cold. One concourse of the airport was completely shut down and the other three were staggering flights around the clock. There were quarter-hour updates on radio stations across the country and minute-by-minute in Anchorage. Freelance journalists and every lookie-loo within 50 miles were at the airport or on their way. Both military bases were on alert and Kulis National Guard Base, just off the runway of the Anchorage Airport was set up as a command post for the Anchorage Police.

For the moment there was not much Noonan could do. He had no trouble dodging the press because they – individually and collectively – did not know who he was – or knew he didn't know anything more than was being given out at the makeshift press conference. Or they didn't care. Maneuvering himself away from the end of Concourse A he meandered down to the Mezzanine Plaza where the four concourse wings of the airport merged.

The upgraded airport was actually not very large. Compared to a Denver, Atlanta or Miami it was positively small. It was large enough for Anchorage which saw the bulk of its passengers from May 15th to September 15th and spent the rest of the year as a regional cargo hub. This was clear from the large cargo area, which was conveniently situated at the western end of the airport.

The airport itself was cleverly designed for the tourist traffic. The massive windows stretching the length of the structure faced due south to gather every ray of sunlight possible: during the summer to remind the tourists this was the Land of the Midnight Sun and during the winter to remind Alaskans there *was* a sun. Concourse A and B stretched in a straight line, from the cargo holding area to the frontage road with offices of the air carriers on the east. Concourse C, dedicated to bush travel and cargo operations, ran at an oblique angle to the north northwest. It had a western exposure, looking across a runway toward the sewage treatment plant barely visible through the trees and set against the stunning landscape of Mt. Susitna just across Cook Inlet. The last concourse was the international wing, which was isolated from the rest of the airport by a quarter mile of roadway and parking lot asphalt. Noonan knew the international wing was by far the largest of the concourses because Anchorage was an international hub for FedEx, among others cargo transport services. Anchorage landed more cargo daily than LAX and Kennedy combined. He knew because his wife kept telling him whenever he said Anchorage had a "small town feel."

With the exception of the international wing, the concourses were on the second floor. The ground floor was dedicated to baggage handling and operations. This made sense as it put the tourists a good dozen feet off the level of the runway and gave them a better view of the Chugach Mountains to the east of the airport. Once again, the design of the airport was to impress travelers that Alaska was a beautiful land – at least during the summer – and well worthy of another trip north sometime soon.

Tourism was one of the largest industries in the state. Alaskans, however, were schizophrenic when it came to tourists. On one hand they appreciated the dollars which cycled through their community from the incoming hordes. On the other hand, they were appalled at the absolute ignorance of the travelers. Some tourists actually believed Alaska had six months of unbroken sunshine followed instantaneously by another six months of pitch darkness. It was not unusual for people from the Lower 48 to ask where they could see a penguin, why Alaskans did not live in igloos and if Eskimos really did buy refrigerators. Alaskans generally and Anchorage-ites in particular usually welcomed the tourists in the early weeks of the summer with open arms. By September the attitude was "Welcome to Alaska; now go home."

Noonan had nothing better to do than wander the airport, which was a better option than returning to the conversational desert of his mother-in-law. So he wandered. Even though there was a strong contingent of Alaska State Troopers in the terminals, no one bothered him. At least not until he headed downstairs to the cargo area. There he was stopped.

"Sorry, this is a restricted area," a squat trooper said. "You'll have to go back upstairs." Noonan handed the guard the pass Ayanna had given him. The trooper kind of scoffed at it. "This isn't any good today. You'll have to go back upstairs."

Back upstairs Noonan got clearance and then it was back downstairs. "Can I get in now?"

The trooper kind of grunted but insisted he have an escort. So there went about ten minutes of his life. Then the trooper checked his credentials again. Then he called upstairs for confirmation. When Noonan showed him his Sandersonville Chief of Detectives' badge the trooper just smiled. "My ex-wife is back in North Carolina. One very big reason I'm in Alaska. Best way to have it."

After another good half-an-hour of waiting, a young man in a poorly fitting uniform showed up. It was an Anchorage International Airport uniform, one used by service personnel, not law enforcement. He was young enough to be Noonan's son and sauntered more than walked. He had the look of a man who was saying to himself *what am I doing here and why*? He checked in with the trooper who checked his credentials as well.

"This is your escort," said the trooper curtly to Noonan. "Don't touch anything."

Noonan wasn't sure what it was he was going to touch. The cargo floor of an airport is not like a china shop where you could pick up and examine merchandise. The irony of the remark did not seem to bother the trooper. He didn't smile; he just turned away.

"Noonan," said Heinz as he extended his hand toward the young man in the ill-fitting uniform. "Heinz Noonan. Call me Heinz."

The young man took his hand. "Dabney the Dogman.

"Dabney the Dogman? Not your real name, right?"

"Nope. I'm the dog man around here. So I'm Dabney the Dog Man. Doesn't bother me. I'm employed."

"Good for you," Noonan chuckled. "Not a lot of call for a drug sniffing dog today, eh?"

Dabney kind of shook his head. "You got it right. Half the airport's closed down. No incoming flights to this concourse and I don't scan outgoing. So I'm your escort." He smiled. "What would you like to see, Mr. Noonan?" Dabney took a close look at Noonan's pass. Noonan hated the term "Mr. Noonan." "Mr. Noonan" was his father; he was Heinz.

"Well, why don't we take a walk around the area, son." The "son" was said with a jab. If he was going to be "Mr. Noonan" even after he told this whippersnapper to call him Heinz, Dabney might as well be "Son."

"Whatever you want, sir." The "sir" grated too.

"Why don't you just call me, Heinz? OK?"

"Sure thing, sir."

Noonan shook his head sadly. "Do you work for the Anchorage International Airport, the Anchorage Police or are you a private contractor?"

"I work for everyone – including the federal government and the State of Alaska. Just depends what I'm doing at the moment. I'm assigned to the airport to work with its security force. Since I have to go into the international wing a lot, I need clearance there. So I'd guess you'd say I work for everyone. I don't handle the paperwork; just the dogs."

"Good for you," Noonan said. "As long as everyone pays you. I'd like to see the underside of Unicorn 739."

"It's a quite a walk from here. Are you up to it, sir?" Noonan glared at the young man who instantly got the message. "I see your point," he said quickly as he pointed to the east. "Right this way, sir."

Far from being a labyrinth of belts, storage bins and luggage channels, the ground floor was more of a long garage. Baggage wagons were driven into the building and up to any one of the six belt systems. The luggage was then lifted out of the wagons by hand and placed onto the moving belts. When the wagons were empty, they were parked in a holding area to the rear of the belt system. If the gate was not in use, the sliding doors were closed. There wasn't a lot of activity on this day but Noonan was sure when the concourse was open for business it was like a beehive.

"How soon before a plane lands do you open the gateway doors," Noonan asked.

"Depends," Dabney said. "During the winter when it's cold the gate is only opened at the last possible moment. This time of year the gates stay open pretty much around the clock. No real reason to keep the doors closed."

"Doesn't that make it headache for security?"

"Not so far. In addition to the people on the ground we also have security cameras inside the building, on the outer wall and overlooking the entrances," he said as he pointed up onto the wall. "No one's slipped through our system yet."

"As far as you know."

"The only person who *may* have eluded the cameras," the young man said as he emphasized the word *may*, "was the pilot of Unicorn 739." He gave a pause and then said "if he came through the baggage area."

"You think he didn't?"

Dabney looked at Noonan with a look of skepticism. He was silent for a moment and then said, "I don't know. Everyone in security has looked over all of the camera footage and we didn't see anything out of the ordinary in those critical five or six minutes. I mean nothing. No one. Nothing. We accounted for everybody, and I mean every *body* . . ."

"What do you mean by *every body*?"

"There were two corpses in coffins and we even checked those out too. Popped the coffins open to make sure the bodies inside were dead and the paperwork matched."

"Did it?"

"Absolutely. Just because we're Alaskans doesn't mean we do slipshod work. Everyone here went over those tapes. And over them again. No one saw anything unusual. No cargo or luggage came off the plane so there was no way to smuggle anyone into the building with the offload."

"Maybe the pilot didn't get off."

"Then he's really well hidden. I went through with a dog twice and didn't find diddly. No bodies, not drugs."

"Does the dog know to look for live bodies? I mean, I thought dogs were only sniffing for drugs. Cadaver dogs only look for cadavers. How do you get a dog to look for real people," Noonan asked. "I mean live people."

Dabney smiled. "Dogs aren't like machines, sir." (There was *sir* again.) "They are attuned to everything. Yes, drugs are the Number One item of interest. If the dogs find something suspicious, like a human hiding in a box, they will sit next to the box to indicate something is not right. They'd sit and wait for me to say it's OK to go on." Dabney shook his finger at Noonan in friendly admonition. "Dogs did not find anything suspicious so I'm willing to say no one was onboard, living or dead."

"Well, if the pilot's not on the plane and you didn't see her get off, where is she?"

"Didn't know it was a *she*. You sure?"

"Yeah, why?"

"No reason. Just most of the pilots are men."

"This one wasn't. If the pilot's not on the plane and you didn't see her get off, where is she?"

"That's not what you originally implied, sir. You originally implied our security arrangements are less than standard and somehow the pilot slipped through our security net unobserved."

"Well, I didn't mean . . ."

"It's OK. Everyone's taking heat on this one so I can understand how you feel. Cop to cop, there's not a single shred of evidence a woman came through the baggage area. She's not on the plane either."

"Then where do you think she is?"

There was a moment of silence. Then Dabney said "Well, there are a lot of theories."

"Give me one or two."

Dabney looked in the direction of the 737, as if he could see it through the wall of the cargo bay. "Getting *out of* the plane would not have been hard. There are a whole bunch of ways depending on how small you are and how much squeezing you want to do. Once on the ground there's the question of avoiding the cameras. Now there's where the pilot's got a problem. The instant she steps out from under the plane in any direction, the cameras are going to spot her – and we didn't see so much as a shadow under the plane."

"So she didn't go out from under the plane."

"It's one of the theories. The best bet we have is she just waited until the hubbub started and then walked out dressed as airport security. There were enough people running in and out of the plane she could have easily slipped into the crowd. It's easy to keep track of people on the cameras in the baggage loading areas but out there when the plane was being mobbed by our people, well, there were just too many people. At best she would only have been on the camera for two or three seconds. If she had on a uniform, we'd never have spotted her."

"Two or three seconds? That's not very long."

"Right. The entrance to the security area is right across from the gateway. There were security people scrambling back and forth the whole time. If the pilot kept her head down and walked from the plane to the security door, she'd of been in and out of the camera's eye in a half dozen steps. Then, *poof,* she's gone."

"Did you actually look over the footage?"

"Yup. We all did. And we saw nothing out of the ordinary. Sure there were a lot of people and security people running around but we didn't see anyone we couldn't identify. Then again, the pictures on those security cameras are not very good."

"Where do you think the pilot is?"

"If I knew, I'd be the Chief of Detectives. That's your title, isn't it?"

"Yeah, but I don't know where the pilot is either so I guess neither of us should have the job."

They both laughed.

Noonan and Dabney spent a few more minutes poking around the cargo bay. To Noonan it looked just like a storage area except all of the material to be stored was out in the open. There was not any luggage because all of it had been dispensed to the passengers. What was left was cargo stacked for flights yet to leave. It was orderly but still out in the open.

Noonan wandered about the piles of crates occasionally looking at a label or packing slip. When he was finished looking around he indicated with a point of his index finger he wanted to go outside of the cargo bay. Dabney, who had been leaning against a pile of crates, nodded his assent and the two of them stepped out of the cargo bay into the sunshine. Then they proceeded down the apron to the 737. Dabney waved the security men aside before they got out of their cars.

Arriving at the parked aircraft, Noonan walked under the plane where he did an intensive examination of the belly of Unicorn 739. He knew next to nothing about airplanes and didn't really know what he was supposed to see–or if what he saw was suspicious. What he saw was pretty much the same thing anyone else would see whether they were an aviation specialist or a bagel maker. It just like the belly of any other plane of similar size and even after the three possible exit routes were pointed out, Noonan couldn't see how the pilot could have used any of them. To have stayed out of the camera's view the woman had to have been a magician.

Maybe she was, Noonan mused aloud.

"Nope," replied the guide. "She landed the plane and she got off the plane. She was just a little cleverer than we are. All she needed were a few seconds and she got 'em. It may take us a day or two but we'll figure it out."

"I like your attitude," Noonan said as he pointed at the sliding doors of the gateway entrance to the cargo garage and then down the length of the building. "When Unicorn 739 landed, were all of these gateway doors were open?"

"Probably. I can check if you want."

"Please. I notice the airliner is situated immediately underneath the camera." Noonan pointed up to the security camera. "Actually there are two cameras, both pointed in opposite directions. Is there a blind spot immediately beneath the camera? Maybe our pilot didn't exit the plane from beneath it but went over the top."

"Good guess." Dabney scratched his head. "I don't recall there being a blind spot there but I'll check with security. Even if there was a blind spot immediately under the camera, where could our pilot go? If she tried to scale the building she'd of been picked up by one of the other cameras. She couldn't stay there or we would have spotted him. Her."

Noonan nodded his head. Then he walked out from beneath the airliner and onto the landing apron.

"Don't go too far out there," the guide warned. "Got lots of activity and I'd hate to see you get run over."

"Oh, I'm as far out as I'm going to be," Noonan responded as he looked down the length of the building. "It looks like there's a lot of repair work going on." He pointed to several of the window frames covered with plastic sheeting rather than glass. There were ramps beneath the frames with the logo and name of the Anchorage Glass Replacement Company boldly emblazoned on the side. Further up the building, strategically placed so it would not block any tourists view of the Chugach Range was a construction chute which ended in a dumpster at ground level.

"There's always repair work going on," said Dabney. "We have to do the outside repair work during the summer because, well, winters get real cold up here."

"Really," Noonan said in mock surprise. "I hear a lot of people say so (a slight pause) up here." He turned around and then looked across the runway, south. "What's over there?" He pointed to the far side of the runway where trees could be seen edging up against the cyclone fence dividing the airport from the forest. A line of tents was going up.

Dabney shaded his eyes as he looked south. "Other than those reporters setting up, not much. The airport shares the end of a peninsula with a large park, Kincaid Park. There's a cyclone fence dividing the two but once you get to the other side there's nothing between you and Cook Inlet but about two miles of wilderness."

"Don't you get moose on the runway every once in a while?"

"Every blue moon or so, yeah, but the fence was constructed to keep them in the park. We do have a number of moose gates along the fence so just in case one somehow wanders onto the runway we can scare them back to the park. You know how those moose gates work, don't you."

"A moose can go through but can't get back."

"Yup."

"So the fence does have breaks in it."

"Yes. However, the fence is half a mile away. I know what you're thinking but no. Our pilot could not have gone out through the fence. Even if she tried to head out there she'd of been picked up on the security cameras."

Noonan slowly did a 360 degree turn drinking in the details of the airport from the apron. After a dozen seconds he indicated to Dabney he was ready to go back inside.

"Find what you were looking for?"

"Haven't a clue," said Noonan. "I don't know what I'm looking for."

"Well," said Dabney. "Welcome to the club."

Back inside the terminal Noonan threaded his way through the throngs of tourists onto the main floor. The news of what had happened to Unicorn 739 had sobered the crowd, as much as such was possible for tourists on holiday who didn't have to drive. Knots of passengers were talking about the apparent hijacking, one of the few times in Noonan's life he had actually heard the word *hijack* spoken in an airport with no one getting arrested. Even more surprising, there were so many uniformed security personnel meandering around Noonan wondered who was watching the security cameras. It was also the first time he had actually seen uniformed police officers in an airport. In most cases the only uniforms were TSA personnel who were, frankly, not law enforcement personnel. They were bureaucrats. Men and women with ball point pens and metal detectors, not nervous law enforcement agents with pistols on their hips.

When he arrived back at Gate A-17 there was a note from Ayanna asking him to join her in the Command Center which had been set up in the Staff Conference Room. It wasn't hard to find the Staff Conference Room. All Noonan had to do was go to the police tape across the administrative exit. There he was told he could not go to the Staff Conference Room, which was, according to the TSA person at the door, "somewhere else." Noonan gave his name and suddenly the TSA person knew where the Staff Conference Room was. Ah, the joy of political connections.

Noonan started down the hallway and was joined by two other guards, these Alaska State Troopers, who just appeared out of an empty rooms on either side of the hall. There was a moment of checking his name and then he was taken to a security elevator at the end of a hallway which seemed to converge at a point of oblivion. Noonan stepped onboard and the magic box whisked him up a floor and then disgorged him into another long hallway which also visually pinched to a point in both directions. He walked to his left first and progressed halfway down the hall before he stumbled on what had to be called a Command Center. He stepped into the room and was stopped by one of the statuesque state troopers he had seen at the gateway earlier in the day.

"He's OK," Ayanna's voice came from across the room. "He's cleared to be here." The trooper stood aside and after Noonan stepped past him, replanted himself with precision in front of the door.

"We're going to need all the help we can get, unfortunately," Ayanna told Noonan quietly when he reached her side. She waved him toward the group of men gathered around a table the size of a record halibut and was the same color. "Let me introduce you around."

Ayanna introduced Noonan to those assembled and there was an orgy of handshaking. Noonan knew he wouldn't remember even one of the names. So their names didn't matter. It was a good bet they'd never remember his name either. Probably could have cared less who he was. After all, he wasn't in uniform, was not in their chain of command and clearly too old to be of political use to a single one of them. Noonan could read it in their eyes. He wasn't even a *guru*; just someone who had the juice to be there.

There were about 20 people in the room. With the exception of Ayanna and Noonan, every one of them was in uniform and not a single of them with stripes. The Anchorage Police and Alaska State Trooper uniforms were self-evident but there were some other uniforms Noonan did not recognize and assumed them to be airport security. A cadaverous man dressed in a mismatched outfit in the back of the crowd was talking on a cell phone. He had to be FBI. The FBI was always on the phone. It was part of the job: look important by being on a phone.

"Let me guess," Noonan said quietly to Ayanna as she ushered him into an office alongside the table. "The FBI says they're in charge and haven't done anything, right?"

"You've been here before?" It was a snide remark, meant to be and interpreted as such.

Noonan shook his head sadly. He had the been-there-done-that look on his face. To Ayanna he mumbled, "Just every time they show up. What's going on and what can I do to help?"

"You can help me by holding my hand and giving me advice. We're barely an hour into this and everything has broken loose. We've got the family members under control. We gave them the news as we have it and then took them to the Intercontinental Hotel just down the road. They've got an open bar and all the food they want to eat. They're still talking to the press. We can't stop them from talking but at least we can keep them from nosing around the airport getting in our way. Then we've got the press and every freelance journalist is the state walking the terminal. We can't keep them out but we can keep them away from the concourse."

"Good move."

"What's going on?" Ayanna shook her head, tossing her hair from out of her eyes. "Well, a lot of little things. We're working with the Anchorage Police to get the precious stones those guys want. We've fast-tracked a $25 million loan from First Seattle National Savings and Loan and are using collateral to get precious stones from the jewelers here in Anchorage. So far the jewelers have been cooperating."

"Of course they are," chortled Noonan. "They're getting top retail dollar for their wholesale stones. Here's a deal that doesn't come down the pike every day."

"Whatever." Ayanna did not give the impression she was aware of the dollars-and-cents reference Noonan had made. Probably didn't care. It wasn't her money. "We don't have time to dicker. The first drop is to be tomorrow at 10 a.m. We're going to receive instructions as to when and where."

"How nice."

"Isn't it though? I'd like you to go along with the drop."

This took Noonan by surprise. "Do you think that's such a good idea?"

"No. But the extortionists asked for you by name."

Here was another eye-opener. For Noonan. "They asked for me?" He was incredulous. "Really? I find it hard to believe. Are you sure they said me. By name?"

"They asked for you by name." Ayanna raised her hands in a help-less gesture. "We had them repeat the request twice just to be sure. Not only did they ask for you by name but they gave your rank with the Sandersonville Police Department. Then they asked if they would have to call Sandersonville to get an official Okey Dokey."

"Okey Dokey?"

"The very words used. It's what they said and we said fine. At least the FBI said they would check into to it. The clearance came back within a few minutes."

"They called?"

"Both the FBI and our friends who want the stones. Both of them. A Commissioner Lizzard," she said and pronounced the name as if it were an animal.

"Lizzard," corrected Noonan, "accent on the *double z*. I'd say we have some very well-prepared customers."

"I'd say." Ayanna fiddled with a cell phone but before she started to talk she told Noonan, "The fingerprints on the trash can from the interior of the airplane came back."

"Anything unusual?"

"Nope. The fingerprints match one of the crew who was on the flight."

"Not much help there."

Chapter 5

The only thing which interested Geraldine "Gerry" McComber more than a bottle of fine wine with the man of her choice – and she was choosey with both wine and men – was a good news story. There was good reason she was so choosy. Wine and men came and went. News stories did not. They appeared when they did and were ephemeral. Yesterday's news was like three-day old fish; it did not get better with age. Some wine got better with age but most men did not. They were best when fresh and grew stale quickly.

A freelance reporter on prowl, she was so good at generating her own leads the Anchorage *Tribune* and one of the local television affiliates gave her a budget and a free hand to develop her own stories. She was a rarity, a freelancer who was paid by both print and electronic media for the same stories. They both had her on payroll as staff and paid her New York style: what she asked. She was worth every dollar they spent. She had a desk in both newsrooms she rarely used and a cell phone with 1,000 minutes per month; and she used every one of them.

"News is where you find it," she said anytime someone higher up the food chain demanded she spend more time in either of the newsrooms and make at least one editorial meeting a month. "You get it where you find it. If you don't like what I'm producing, fire me." No one ever fired Gerry McComber.

She wasn't demanding in the sense she was a *prima donna*. She got what she wanted because she wasn't just good at her job. She was great. And she knew it. But it didn't go to her head. She kept turning in the quality stories because she had a reputation for fairness, intelligence and never divulging where she got her information. And her sources were highly placed. In her special on medical billing fraud she brought the largest hospital in town to its knees. It had been charging questionable fees for a decade – the reason it *was* the largest hospital in town – and after the IRS followed her footprints into the books, there was an exodus of administrative personnel south, most of them to federal prison. Her investigative work on walrus poaching prompted a sting operation by the United States Department of Fish and Wildlife and led to a dozen arrests.

The story of Unicorn 739 was going to be her best. Not just because it was a great story.

It was. The story of a lifetime in Anchorage, Alaska, in the proverbial middle of no place. No, it was the story of the century for McComber. It was the story of the century and a Pulitzer Prize for sure because she had the best inside source there was. It was the ultimate inside source. You could not get better than a hot line to the extortionists on an open case with the whole world watching. Well, she couldn't actually call them. They had called her.

Gerry's cell phone erupted into a *fugue* as she was sitting in the back of Crown Bagel, the in-spot for artists and the out-spot for anyone who wore a tie. The music touched off a flurry of patrons pawing for their cell phones. A glance at the incoming number told Gerry it was from a pay phone. Her heart began to beat with anticipation.

"And what do you have for me now?" She was smooth and she knew it.

"Gerry, dahling," the smooth male voice purred through the ether, "You didn't think I'd forget you?"

"Of course not. Are we ever going to meet?"

"We're meeting now, my love."

"No, I mean in person."

"Maybe you already have met me. Ever considered the possibility?"

"Yes. But when are we going to meet when you've identified yourself?"

"Who knows? Stranger things have happened." The voice gave a merry chortle. "But I do have a tip for you."

"So far you've been a very good boy."

"I **am** a very good boy. I just have this larcenous streak I can't control. It is so expensive to keep it satisfied. Do you want the lead?"

"Is the Pope Catholic?"

"Actually he's an Argentinian Italian but his heritage is neither here nor there. Here's your lead. Ayanna Driscoll, the Head of Security for the

Anchorage International Airport, and Heinz Noonan, Chief of Detectives for the Sandersonville Police Department. . ."

"Heinz who?"

"Noonan. N-o-o-n-a-n." The voice spelled it out.

"Where is Sandersonville?"

"North Carolina. He's up here on vacation."

"What does North Carolina have to do with all of this?"

"This is my story, love. You can ask him when you meet him."

"When am I going to meet him?"

"You'll be able to see him tomorrow at 10 a.m. He and Ayanna are going to be delivering the first of four payments to our little enterprise. They're going to have a little bag with about $5 million in precious stones with them so bring your camera to get all kinds of nice pictures, eh?."

"Where are the stones going to be delivered?"

"Uh, uh, uh," the voice chided. "If I told you it would spoil the surprise! You just be at the Wickersham Hotel lobby phone bank by 10 a.m. Not a moment late, now. The lobby is where the pair will get their first call of the day. Then they will be off like hounds after the hare. Don't be seen though."

"So you're going to run them around town, phone to phone, before you let them make the drop?"

"It's what they expect me to do so I don't want to disappoint."

"Them."

There was a moment of silence. "Right. 'Them.' I don't want to disappoint *them*. You are as bad as my English teacher."

"I used to be an English teacher."

"I know, Gerry, dahling. In a little town outside of Boise."

"Your information is very good."

"*And* why I haven't been caught." With the comment hanging the phone went dead.

Gerry did a quick redial but there was no answer. Whoever he was, he was long gone. She snapped her phone shut and slid it into its carrying case on her belt. A woman with a cell phone on her belt, she thought. How unfeminine but how necessary on days like this.

Gerry slowly sipped her coffee and looked over her notes.

"Noonan," she muttered to herself as she pulled her phone out again. She snapped it on and called the *Tribune* library. "If we don't have a file on this Noonan character at the *Tribune*, he surely must have one in North

Carolina. What's the biggest city in North Carolina? Raleigh? Durham? Who do I know in Raleigh?" She drummed her pen on the table.

Then she called the best cameraman at the television station.

Between bites of her bagel she pulled him off covering the Anchorage Chamber of Commerce prayer breakfast and told him to meet her at the Wickersham at 9:30 the next morning – and to wear tennis shoes. When he asked why the tennis shoes, she replied, "because we're going to be doing quite a bit of running around, both literally and figuratively."

He said he didn't believe her and she snickered as she hung up.

"And now we shall see what we shall see," she muttered as dipped her bagel in a cup of black coffee.

Chapter 6

"So this is what $5 million in diamonds looks like," muttered Ayanna as she took a small leather bag from a rotund man in the uniform of State Security and Fidelity. He looked like Porky Pig. His uniform fit as though he was Porky Pig. He even had a high squeaky voice like Porky Pig. Ayanna wondered if his wife told him he looked like Porky Pig when they came to verbal blows.

"Do you want to check them?" The voice fit the man but lacked warmth. He might as well have been a banker. Probably had been. Or an accountant.

"How would I know if I was being cheated?"

"Ms. Driscoll," the voice had an edge. "State Security and Fidelity is insuring these stones. We know they're authentic. We have the papers of authenticity. Even if they are not, what do you care? You're not the final recipient, if you know what I mean. Let *them* take us to court."

Porky Pig thought the statement was funny.

Ayanna didn't.

"You'd better be right because there are 95 people whose lives depend on these stones. Any phonies get mixed in and there could be real problems. So, once again, I'm asking if all of these stones are legitimate."

Porky didn't bat an eye. "Yeah. They are all legitimate. Every one of them which is why your thieves are asking for them in portions. They want to make sure all the stones are real. Four drops means they have three times to check the stones. As long as they hold the hostages, the last load has got to be legit too. We know our business, Ms. Driscoll."

"A lot is riding on these stones. We can always get more stones, we can't get back a hostage if he gets killed."

Porky was unimpressed. There was no reason he had to be. His ham hocks weren't on the line. Or the griddle. "Just sign here, Ms. Driscoll," he said as he indicated a spot on piece of paper on a clipboard, "and everything will be peachy keen."

From the look Ayanna's face it was clear she didn't think everything was going to be just peachy keen.

Noonan was standing in the only quiet space left in the Command Center: behind the coffee machine. Noonan stood with his back to the soft drink machine and stared out of the southern windows at the trees on the far side of the runway. He noticed Ayanna had cleaned up in the last few hours. She had clearly managed to snatch a few hours of sleep and her energy level was significantly higher. Now she was dressed for speed, jeans and a short sleeved blouse, tennis shoes and a fanny pack.

Noonan was dressed for the runaround as well. Been there, done that. He was wearing his only pair of jeans, a grey pullover and his favorite cross trainers, comfortable on the inside and scarred from his aerobics class on the outside. His socks were the thick white athletic kind and there was a GIS strapped around one ankle. He was not carrying a pistol. "I don't believe in them on a case like this," he had told the Anchorage Police Lieutenant who tried to give him a Glock. "These guys don't want trouble; they just want the gems and we are going to have to make more than one drop. We've got time. Let's play their game for the moment."

"Yeah," snapped the Lieutenant. "I don't like dealing with bad guys even for the best of reasons."

"Nice quote," replied Noonan. "You can use it for the Chamber of Commerce next week. Right now I'm worried about 95 people sitting in a dark room hoping we're going to make the right decision."

Ayanna was having problems with paying the thieves too.

She didn't like it.

She didn't like it at all and it was clear from her voice as she talked to Porky. Porky clearly didn't care. Then again, why should he? His company only insured the stones if they were stolen on the way to the drop. When the thieves got the stones, his company was off the hook. The Anchorage Airport had bought the stones and they couldn't sue.

"Relax, Ms. Driscoll," said Porky with the enthusiasm of an undertaker. "All is well. The stones are authentic, we've insured them." Then he made the only human motion Noonan had seen him make in his 15 minutes in the Command Center. He put his left hand to the center of his chest, over his heart, and gave it a little press. "Cross my heart." There was no telltale lift to the outer corners of his lips indicating he knew he was making a humorous statement.

"I didn't know insurance people had hearts," snapped Ayanna.

"An occupational liability," said Porky with as much emotion as if he were counting pennies.

Ayanna opened the leather pouch and looked inside. All she could see were a bunch of loose stones.

"Isn't it bad to have all these stones together in the bag? Won't they chip?"

"Maybe but not likely," said Porky. "Besides. We weren't asked for the papers of authenticity, only the gems. As soon as the thieves get the stones they are going to cut them up anyway."

"Why do you think that?" Noonan broke in.

"Simple," replied Porky, craning his neck as he spoke with a look on his face which said we-*professionals*-have-been-through-this-before, "with the papers of authenticity, there's a paper trail. Without the papers of authenticity, they have to re-create those papers. That's a whale of a lot of paperwork and if any one stone is recognized, then the FBI has a clue to follow. If they cut the stones, there are new signatures and the chances of any one stone being recognized is very, very low."

"We're talking about a lot stones here," said Noonan as he reached over Ayanna's shoulder and fingered the bag. This is just one-fifth of what they've asked for. There's going to be a lot of paperwork. Why not just sell the stones overseas and take the cash?"

"Good point. A better question is why not just sell the stones in New York or Los Angeles? $25 million may be a lot to you but on the world precious stone market it's not even a drop in the bucket. The answer is simple: traceability. Once again, the thieves have the problem of recognizability. Even a reputable dealer can't show up with a million dollars' worth of gems with no paperwork. Sure, he could dribble them into the market over time but there are lots of people watching for stray gems to show up. These are not the good old days where you could drop a few million on the market and no one cared."

"A few million!" said Ayanna in surprise. "A *few* million?"

Porky looked at her with all of the enthusiasm of a lode stone. "Twenty-five million is not even close to small in the precious stone market. But, like I keep saying, what is important here is the stones have no papers.

Which means the stones are going to be cut up before they ever make it onto the market."

"Are they going to make more with the cut stones than the whole ones?" Noonan cut in. "I would have thought big stones, if *big stones* is the correct term, were more valuable than small ones."

Porky seemed pleased to show his expertise. "Precious stone thieves are an odd bunch of felons. In many cases the jewels are simply stolen for the insurance money. It's cheaper for the insurance company to buy the gems back from the thieves at, say, 15% of their value than pay out the total loss."

"Insurance companies do that?" Ayanna was surprised. "Is it ethical?"

"Maybe not," said Porky clearly carefully about how he was phrasing his response. "But it's legal." Porky was emphatic about it. "That's the way it's done. If a thief wants more than 15% he has to handle the stones himself. Then things get dicey. No one in the United States or Europe is going to buy a stone without a letter of authenticity. This means they have to take the jewels to Asia or South America to sell."

He took a breath.

"More than likely these guys are jewelers or have a connection to a jeweler. They'll get the gems, cut them, and place them in jewelry. Once they are in settings the individual stones do not need any letters of authenticity. The entire piece of jewelry has its own fingerprint, so to speak. We may never find one of the stones as a stone but a lot of people will have jewelry with stolen gems inlaid."

"What you are saying is these guys could get away with it?" Ayanna was not happy.

"They could," replied Porky, "but I doubt it. This is a big heist of computer-identified stones. It's unlikely all the stones will slide into the market unrecognized. The thieves will have to be careful every time they sell a stone; we only have to be lucky once."

But Porky gave a tell. He may have said the cops only had to be lucky once but his facial expression indicated he didn't believe what he was saying. Noonan, who was hardly an expert on precious stones, figured the truth without an explanation: these guys were going to get away with it.

Ayanna shook her head as she stood up and tucked the bag in her fanny pack. "I don't like this at all."

"Not part of your job description, was it?" Noonan smiled wryly. He tightened his belt unconsciously.

"Not *even* on the radar scope of skills I thought I would need to do this job." Ayanna raised her hands to indicate the building. "I'm supposed to be saving the airport from bad boys and girls, not paying them ransom."

"All part of the job," said Noonan spryly. "You will make up for it when the hostages get free and the bad boys and girls are caught."

"You sound so confident." Ayanna pulled on a light jacket and zipped it shut. Then put her hand on the .38 on the table.

"Oh, I am," replied Noonan as he put his hand on her. "We are a long way from finished here." When she tried to pick up the revolver Noonan nixed it, "Not yet. There is no danger with this drop."

Ayanna pulled her hand back, looked longingly at the pistol and then nodded.

Chapter 7

The water was always calm along the shoreline.

This was good. The bank was steep. At high tide the water lapped the roots of the overhanging brush. At low tide – 30 feet down and 6 hours away – the shoreline wasn't much of a line of shore. It was a sheer cliff. And the cliff line didn't stop where it joined with the surface of Knik Arm. It kept dropping. Thirty feet from shore at low tide the water was 50 feet deep. On the bottom was mud. Deep mud. With the exception of this part of the shoreline, the Knik Arm reached the shore across deep mud flats. As the tide rose, the mud was swirled about. When the tide receded the mud was so loose a man could be sucked down to his waist. He would not be swallowed alive, but he would find himself stuck in the muck. If he could not get out he would drown with the advent of the next tide. The mud flats always got one or two tourists every year. More than the bears. Alaska was a dangerous land if you were from Iowa or Missouri and didn't listen to the locals.

A lot of people did not know Anchorage had some of the highest tides in North America. This was probably because of the city's unique landscape. From the air Anchorage was like a giant triangle. The rugged Chugach Mountains formed the hypotenuse while Knik Arm to the north and Turnagain Arm to the south formed the other two sides. The Knik Arm and Turnagain Arm joined just beyond the end of the runway at Anchorage International Airport. When the salt water was plowing up from the Pacific Ocean it enters Cook Inlet, the wide mouth spreads and flattens the incoming tide. Then, like honey being poured on a table, it layers as it moves.

As the tide moves south into Turnagain Arm, it often arrives in steps. Known as the bore tide, it arrives in four-foot high sections. From horizon-to-horizon, a four-foot wall of water advances down the arm. Behind the aqueous wall is another with another behind it as well. On good days – good if you are a windsurfer – you can ride two sometimes three bore tides in a single day. On bad days, the water just rises 30 feet in 6 hours and there is no bore tide to ride or jump.

Captain James Cook named Turnagain Arm in May of 1778. He had sailed into the arm hopeful it would lead him to the fabled Northwest Passage. He didn't get very far because the arm is only about 40 miles long and not very deep at low tide. He ran with the tide coming in and when the tide turned, he found himself stranded on the mud flats in the center of the mud-filled fjord. A dozen hours later he had to *turn again* and come out leaving nothing but the name of the arm on his nautical charts.

Knik Arm, on the northern flank of Anchorage, does not get bore tides. It does get good, deep water for ships, the reason the *anchorage* at Ship Creek gave the city its name. It still gets tides. They can be vicious during the winter, particularly because the Knik and Matanuska rivers feed into Knik Arm.

It isn't the water making Knik Arm so hazardous; it's the ice. The river which feeds into the Knik Arm, freezes from shore-to-shore during the winter. Then snow falls on the river ice and freezes in place. Layer by layer the ice builds.

Until Spring.

Late Spring.

Then the ice sheet on the river breaks and several hundred miles of river ice bergs gouge their way downriver. When they tumble into Knik Arm they come as a flotilla many the size of small houses and some the size of skyscrapers. Ships choose their passage carefully into and out of Anchorage during the days when the ice is running. The oil rigs fur-ther down Cook Inlet cannot dodge the big ones. Built to withstand the impact of massive boulders of ice, the workers on the rigs are always wary of the "the big one," a berg so large it will snap the legs of the strongest rig man could build. It hasn't arrive yet but every spring the chances of "the big one" arriving gets better.

Chapter 8

"Who?"

"Noonan. Chief of Detectives from Sandersonville, North Carolina, I think. Some hick town on the Atlantic coast. I'm really not sure where. Just in North Carolina somewhere." Gerry was looking at her palm pilot as she spoke. "He's in his 60s, about six feet tall, thick but not fat, athletic and looks like someone you'd miss in a crowd."

The cameraman was built like an athlete, young enough to be training for the Olympics and dressed for speed. He was wearing a track suit and had on running shoes. His long hair was tied back in a ponytail and a tattoo was half-visible at the back of his neck. He and Gerry were wedged in a corner of the lobby of the Wickersham Hotel behind an artificial fern. They had moved the table and four chairs behind them so they get the camera in the right position. Now the two were pressed so close together than Gerry could feel Sam's muscular buttocks on her thighs. She couldn't see his face. It was glued to the eyepiece of the camera focused on the bank of telephones.

"Geraldine, . . ." Sam was whispering.

"Gerry, Sam. Gerry. We've worked together long enough for you to call me 'Gerry.'"

"Gerry," Sam said. "Every time I work with you I get in trouble."

"Correction," said Gerry. "Every time you work with me you have an adventure."

Sam smiled, half of it hidden by the camera. "I'm dressed to run but this camera is heavy. Why don't we get a backup car to follow us around?"

"Because we're not going to have much of a runaround. With a 60-year old guy doing the drop, I don't think they are going to have him run around too much."

"Who are 'they?'"

"They are the kidnappers."

"We're on a kidnapping drop? Hey, exciting! Is this part of the story about those folks who got snatched out of thin air?"

"Same folk. They disappeared on a flight to Anchorage from Seattle."

Sam pulled back from the camera view scope and looked at Gerry carefully. "These guys aren't aliens or anything are they?"

"Nope. Flesh and blood types, just like you and me. You know how I know?"

"No. How?"

Gerry gave Sam a look which said 'you are so easy.' "They're asking for $25 million in precious stones. Asking for money doesn't sound like aliens to me."

"Sounds like someone who wants to get rich quick," replied Sam. "How'd you get the lead?"

Gerry made a mock expression of surprise. "Why a little bird told me."

"Speaking of birds, is that our pigeon?" Sam gave a brief forward jerk using his camera. He wasn't being careful and one of the ferns slipped across the camera lens and slapped back striking him in the face. Another fern covered the camera lens for a moment before he shook it off.

"Be careful there," snapped Gerry. "We need every second of footage we can get."

Gerry stared through the veneer of fronds. "Looks to be. He's old enough and I recognize the woman from the Chamber of Commerce. Has to be Ayanna Driscoll in the flesh."

The camera began to grind as Sam shot a few seconds of the pair leaning against the jade telephone counter.

"Make sure you get them on the phone," whispered Gerry hoarsely as she leaned into Sam. "Then get ready to run. The second they put the phone down, they are going to be off and away."

Sam pushed back against Gerry. "I'm ready when you are!"

Chapter 9

The Wickersham Hotel in Anchorage was legendary for its silence. This is not to say the hotel was a quiet place to stay. Actually, the opposite was true. In terms of the audible range, it was notorious for being the worst possible place to hold a meeting. It had floors of Travertine tile and oaken walls, which, together, allowed sound to bounce from floor to ceiling to wall to floor as though it were an echo chamber. The food was bad, the liquor expensive and the décor abysmal. But if one were looking for an establishment where the staff was as blind as the clientele, the Wickersham Hotel was the place to be.

The hotel had originally been built with fish money. Rather, it had been constructed with funding from the large salmon canning companies wanting a luxurious home-away-from-home for their executives when they came north. These executives, almost exclusively male, were most often accompanied with secretarial help, almost exclusively female, and every effort was made to make sure these executives were not saddled with pedestrian difficulties. Those difficulties included such indignities as liquor raids during Prohibition or the unexpected arrival of wives of the executives on the Alaska Marine Highway ferries. Until the advent of the oil industry, the Wickersham did not bill its guests. The company for which they worked checked them in and the Anchorage office of those companies then handled all charges with no questions asked. It was said the only thing higher than a liquor bill at the Wickersham Hotel was an incoming cold front.

No one had ever been arrested in the Wickersham. Certain people had been arrested on the sidewalk thereof but not within the hotel itself. It was like a city unto itself. It had a doctors, barbers, lawyers and other professionals available at all hours of the day and night who, for a fee, could resolve any problem. Judges, mayors, governors, movie stars, police chiefs and illustrious foreign officials frequented the establishment and not a single one of them had ever been subject to even a passing legal or ethical glance. No one was ever asked why they were in the establishment when they lived in Anchorage or, if they lived out of town, what they were doing within the confines of the oaken walls of the hotel. It was a proverbial city of silence. One went to the Wickersham Hotel for silence and to associate with others who were as blind, deaf and dumb as you wanted them to be.

It was thus the perfect place to begin a fruitless enterprise and exactly why Heinz Noonan and Ayanna Driscoll were there in the morning, leaning against the solid jade telephone counter of the Wickersham Hotel, their backs to the bank of telephones.

"How do you know?" asked Ayanna as she scanned the lobby for the press. Clearly the last thing she wanted was for the press to be there. Being new to law enforcement, she did not know how to spot the press. Her point of view was simple. If she did not see anyone who looked like the press there was no press there. There were no light flashes, cameras being lugged or men and women with pen and pad. It was actually a relief to be away from the airport where every other person had a press pass and very one of them had a question she could not answer.

"Believe me," said Noonan casually. "They're here. Just because you can't see them means nothing. The bad guys we are dealing with are going to make our lives as difficult as possible – which means tipping off the press. The press is here. We just can't see them yet."

"What good will it do?" Harried asked. "I mean, won't tipping the press make the drop more difficult?"

Noonan shook his head. "Keep in mind the bad people are very clever boys and girls. They are calling the shots and they want the press on top of every aspect of this story as fast as possible. Using the press will clog the information system. While the police are trying to satisfy the press, the bad guys are screwing up the time schedule, anything to throw us off of being prepared. Every second we spend spinning our wheels or dealing with the press is one second the bad boys and girls will use to their advantage. It means they are pretty sure their drops are going to be safe."

"I don't like that kind of confidence," snapped Ayanna.

"Get used to it," advised Noonan. "These guys are pros. They've planned this right down to the second they make the call." Noonan looked in the direction of the artificial ferns in the corner where he saw a camera lens peeking out from the shrubbery. "I see our reporters are here right on cue."

"Where?" Ayanna, to her credit, did not begin searching the lobby with her gaze. She just looked casually at Noonan.

"Far end of the lobby, behind the artificial ferns. At least a camera. Every camera has a commentator so I'd say there were at least two people there."

"Just two?"

"Just two. Means our friends have selected a single ally. They want to clog the airport with the press so they called everyone. But they want us to have an almost free hand in delivering the gems so they only called one press person. Very clever, I must say. They get the gems and we look bad for delivering the stones."

"What do we do?"

"Nothing. If the kidnappers want them to follow us, so be it. But," there was a twinkle in Noonan's eye, "we shouldn't make it too easy for them. When we get the phone call, you go out the front door and get in the car. I'll head out the back and catch a cab. Maybe I can shake them. At least it's worth a try. We'll meet wherever we're told."

"Who do you think they'll follow?"

"Me. They figure they can always catch up to you later. I'm the unknown here and that, my dear Ayanna, is where the story is."

"You've done this before, haven't you?"

"No," replied Noonan sadly. "I know human nature."

The two relaxed against the counter when the suddenly one of the phones in the bank of instruments behind them began to ring. Ayanna tensed and answered the phone.

"Ah, Ms. Driscoll. It's such a pleasure to talk with you at last," came a soothing male voice over the line. "I applaud your choice of clothing. I assume the valuables are in the fanny pack?"

Ayanna looked around.

"You can't see me, Ms. Ayanna," the voice continued without missing a beat. "Take my word for it. Now, I assume you have the precious stones in your possession? A total of at least five millions of dollars? Correct?" The voice was smooth and professional, not a hint of excitement.

Ayanna nodded though she clearly had no idea who was going to see the gesture. Then she said, "I have what I was given and I have been assured there are at least $5 million in the bundle. We're holding up our end of the bargain. How about letting some of the hostages go?"

There was a chuckle on the line. "With twenty millions of dollars still on the table? I think not. It was a good try, Ms. Driscoll. I applaud audacity. Just not now. We'll talk about all matters later." The phone suddenly went silent.

Ayanna waited for a moment, looked at the phone in a panic. Then she looked at Noonan. Noonan had no expression on his face. Ayanna spoke into the phone again. "Are you still there?"

"Of course. You don't think I'd leave without telling you where to drop off my gems?"

"Let's play as few games as possible," Ayanna said cautiously. "There's a lot at stake here."

"Jolly fine for you to say! You don't have the police looking for you!"

"That's not exactly my fault," Ayanna snapped. "The gems?"

"I like a woman who comes right to the point. You do have on your running shoes so let's get a running start on this," the voice chortled at his own pun. "There is a pay phone outside the Alaska Railroad terminal on Front Street, on the east side, the mountain side of the passenger terminal. In reality there are three phones but only one of them has an 'Out of Service' sign. I will call you there in exactly five minutes. Five minutes as in one, two, three, four, and five. Should give you time to dump the reporters and make it to the phone on time."

"What reporters?"

"Ms. Driscoll!" The voice was humorously testy. "I know they are there because I told them where to go. My gift to the press of the city. We mustn't, cannot, make it too easy for them. Don't you agree?"

"Well, I don't know what to say."

"Don't say anything. Just make it to the pay phone in five minutes because I will not call twice." Then the phone went dead.

Ayanna kept the phone to her ear and, looking straight ahead, mouthed a message to Noonan. "Our first stop is the pay phone at the Alaska Railroad passenger terminal. The pay phones on the east side of the buildings, toward the mountains."

Noonan didn't say a word. He just stepped away from the counter and started walking toward the back entrance. Ayanna put down the phone and headed in the opposite direction, fast but not at a run.

Chapter 10

"Which one?" snapped Sam as he dropped the camera to his knee and looked at Gerry. "Or do we split up?"

"Not a chance. We'll follow Noonan. The old guy. We can always catch up with Ayanna later. She's local. He's not."

Almost tumbling over each other they pushed past the ferns. The pot holding the artificial plants fell forward as the two trampled them in their haste to get out of the building. The pot continued rolling as they rushed into the main lobby and made a beeline for the back entrance to the Wickersham lobby. Not a single person in the Wickersham gave them a glance, least of all the bellman who righted the plant and called janitorial to clean up the mess. Sixty years after it had been established the Wickersham was still living up to its reputation as the quietest hotel in Alaska.

Gerry and Sam made it out the hotel onto the sidewalk just as Noonan got into a cab at the carriage entrance, the only one where a line of cabs were usually waiting. They watched helplessly as Noonan's cab made a right on Fourth Avenue and headed east.

"What do we do now?" Sam was out of breath.

"We're not out of the ball game yet," snapped Gerry. "He got an Orange cab. We should be able to track him. Let's go." In the next instant she was dashing across the carriage entrance and out onto the sidewalk.

As luck would have it, another Orange cab was just passing but going in the opposite direction. Gerry dashed out into the street, directly in front of the cab. It slammed on its brakes to avoid hitting her.

"What are you doing?" The driver stuck his head out of the open window and cursed at her.

"We need a ride and we need it now!" Gerry and Sam piled into the cab, Gerry in the front seat and Sam in the back, surprising the elderly couple already in the back seat.

"Emergency," Sam said to the couple. "We're on a hot story."

"Go! Go! Go!" yelled Gerry as the astonished cabbie looked from Gerry to Sam to the elderly couple in the back. "Go!" she yelled again. "This is an emergency."

With gusto the cabbie was off.

It was wild ride. First, and most probably only, because the cabbie assumed his new passengers were police officers working under cover. The camera was a bit hard to fit into the scenario but the cabbie was clearly not going to take the chance he was wrong. No one, and particularly a cabbie in a small town, wanted to be on the wrong side of the Anchorage Police Department.

The elderly couple clearly thought the two were with the police. There was a gold glow in the cab with both the cabbie and his initial passengers believing they were assisting the police in apprehending some miscreant who had purloined valuable property from person or person unknown. The cabbie even went so far as to get the destination of the other Orange cab: the Alaska Railroad terminal. The glow ended when the octogenarian asked Sam if the police "always filmed their pursuits?"

"We're not the police," said Sam. "We're reporters trying to capture the kidnappers of those people on Unicorn 739."

With those words the cabbie slammed on his brakes and tossed Gerry and Sam out of his cab. He drove off, leaving Gerry and Sam standing on the corner of Fourth and F watching helplessly as the cab drove away, the elderly couple waving at them out of the rear window.

"What now?" asked Sam.

"We get another cab," Gerry said simply. "Now we know where we're going!"

A minute later they were in a Cheechako Cab on their way to the Alaska Railroad terminal.

Chapter 11

Two fishing poles went into the row boat. So did the trash can liner. Everything had to be perfect. A lot of people were depending on perfect. P-E-R-F-E-C-T. The empty beer cans clattered in the trash bag. The Fisherman dragged the bag back and forth across the bottom of the boat before tossing it forward. The bag had to look used.

It wasn't a large boat but it was a good one. Good enough for a two-person fishing excursion. Got the bug juice for the mosquitoes. Sun screen. Ripped shirt and worn jeans, old socks, Sitka slippers. Couple pair of sunglasses, old and twisted. Lots of fishing gear. Gotta be authentic.

Chapter 12

Ayanna was already at the pay phone when Noonan arrived. She had stripped the Out Of Order sign off the phone in the center and was leaning against the telephone shelf, her left hand on the phone. She had a pen and a pad of paper in her right, pen poised for action.

"I see you lost our friends with the press." Ayanna searched the parking lot for the reporters and verbally expressed her pleasure at seeing none of them. She knew better than to assume she had lost them – particularly since they had been tipped where to start looking for herself and Noonan.

"Hardly," said Noonan. "I slowed them down. Maybe. I doubt I lost them. The press has a tendency to be quite tenacious."

Noonan was correct in his assessment. Just as soon as the phone started ringing, a Cheechako Cab pulled up. Gerry and Sam tumbled out as Ayanna answered the phone. The cameraman was setting up for a shot even before the cab stopped moving. Gerry could be seen throwing money at the cabbie. The cabbie didn't seem to mind. He just took the money and sat. He knew a paying customer when he saw one.

"Ah, I see our intrepid reporters are still on scent." The voice on the phone was still cool and confident.

"Very funny," said Ayanna. "If you wanted them to follow us, why didn't we all go together like a big happy family?"

"It would take all the fun out of it! Now, your next stop is the Federal Building. You shouldn't have any trouble getting in with both of you carrying badges. It should slow the reporters down. Go in the east entrance, next to the hideous modern art monstrosity hanging on the north wall. Do you know where I mean?"

"Oh, yeah," replied Ayanna. "The pink walrus with the hanging bird nest."

"Yes, yes. The very one. Hideous artwork such as it is. It's amazing what the Federal government will do with its money. Talk about a poor excuse for art."

"... and when we get there," prompted Ayanna.

"Proceed toward the library in the main lobby. There you will find another bank of pay phones. Then go ..."

"Let me guess," broke in Ayanna. "Go the pay phone listed as 'Out of Order.'"

"You are getting very good at this, aren't you?" There was humor in the voice. "Very, very good. Correct. Go to the phone listed as 'Out of Order' and I'll call you. Once again. Three minutes. No longer."

"We'll be talking to you." Ayanna hung up the phone. To Noonan she said, "I don't think we can outrun the press but the next stop will slow them down. We're going into the Federal building."

"The big square one with the ugly art?"

"Ah," said Ayanna in mock surprise. "I see you've been there before."

"Worst art I have ever seen." Noonan shook his head sadly, "What the public pays for what some people call art!"

"But," said Ayanna cautiously raising an index finger. "We have a bit of an edge this time. We can get in easily because we've got badges. Our friends with the press," she inclined her head toward Gerry and Sam trying to look inconspicuous in a parking lot where they were the only ones with no luggage "are going to have a hard time getting through security. It'll give us a minute or so to plan our next move."

"Let's go. Let's not make it too easy for the press."

The actual drive between the Alaska Railroad terminal and the Federal Building in Anchorage was five blocks so the three minute limit was adequate for the drive. But it was not adequate to find parking. Parking in downtown Anchorage, particularly during the summer, was another matter altogether. Ayanna's car didn't have police plates so she was just as likely to be impounded as anyone else. In reality more likely because the Anchorage Police knew the State of Alaska would pay for every ticket issued–promptly. Besides the ticket, she could not afford to be impounded because she was going to need the car for the next destination.

Ayanna did have two distinct advantages. First, she was driving a car with State of Alaska license plates. While such was bad news when it came to parking on the street, it was good news when it came to parking lots.

There were a lot of state-funded parking lots in downtown Anchorage. All she had to do was pull into one of the state parking lots and leave her car anywhere. No one was going to impound a state vehicle in a state parking lot.

The second advantage was she had been a probation officer before she was hired to run security for the Anchorage International Airport. The Probation Office was right across the street from the Federal Building. So she pulled into a space marked "Director, Adult Probation" just off 8th Street and turned off the engine. Her old job. Her old space.

"How many more of these stops are we going to have to make?" asked Ayanna as she hit the flasher button on her car. Instantly all of the lights on the dashboard started pulsing.

"No way of knowing," replied Noonan as he opened the passenger door and stepped out. Out of the corner of his eye he could see a nondescript car pull into a handicapped parking space on A Street alongside a mail box across the street from the Federal Building. Noonan pointed out the car to Ayanna. "These guys are pros. They know the FBI are following us – somewhere out there," Noonan pointed obliquely toward the sidewalk choked with professional dressed men and women hurrying along. "They know the FBI is going to be moving as fast as we are but they don't appear to care. I think they just want to make sure the press is close enough to get a story."

"They clearly want the publicity."

"Yes, I agree with you," said Noonan. "I haven't figured out why yet. Usually the bad boys and girls want to keep things like this as quiet as possible."

"Kidnapping 95 people kind of makes it public."

Noonan gave a humorous grunt.

Ayanna and Noonan carefully crossed the street and headed for the back entrance to the Federal Building as Gerry and Sam snarled traffic on the adjacent street as they jetted from a taxi cab and dashed across the street. Traffic swerved, honked and cursed.

"Our friends had better watch what they are doing or they won't be alive to make tonight's broadcast," said Ayanna snidely without looking at Noonan or in the direction of Sam and Gerry.

In the next instant Ayanna and Noonan were inside. Waving badges they were given a cursory check and stepped through the metal detectors – preceded by apologies from the security personnel.

"Sorry, Sir, Ma'am. Everyone has to go through the detectors."

"Not a problem," Noonan said, casually looking over his shoulder at Sam and Gerry rushing up the steps. "Just do your job."

Free of the security checkpoint, Ayanna and Noonan headed for the phone bank. The phones were not hard to find. The phone with the 'Out of Order' sign was exactly where the voice had said it would be. It was on the last phone next to a hallway disappearing into the bowels of the building. Noonan took a quick look down the hallway and noticed a dozen office doors, all of them open. No one seemed to be lurking in any of them.

The Federal Building lobby was surprisingly empty as well. There were three people sitting on the benches next to the pool of water and sculpture dominating the back wall of the massive mezzanine. A handful of people could be seen at the cafeteria entrance next to the security checkpoint at the back of the building and the checkpoint at the front door was devoid of anyone except three security personnel lounging with cups of coffee waiting for their next victim.

Sam and Gerry had made it through the checkpoint and were trying to make themselves appear as paint on a sidewall. They might have been inconspicuous had it not been for Sam's lens staring at Noonan like the unblinking eye of a Cyclops.

Then the phone rang.

"It is us," said Ayanna into the receiver.

"Of course it is," replied the voice. "I never had any doubt you would arrive on time and with the press still in tow."

"OK. We're here. The press is here. What's next?"

"Nothing. This is you last stop. Without looking down, slide your hand underneath the writing desk of this phone, where the telephone book is supposed to be."

Ayanna slid her hand down and felt for the phone book.

It wasn't there.

It was nothing but an empty ledge.

"OK. There's nothing here."

"Pre-cisely," the voice said. "Now, still without looking down, put the little bag of gems on the empty shelf."

Ayanna reached around behind her back to the fanny pack and extracted the leather bag. She gave it a little shake and slipped it onto the shelf.

"Now what."

"Now, you leave. Go back the way you came in. Do not look back, just keep walking." The phone went dead.

Ayanna hung up the receiver. "He wants us to go now."

Noonan nodded and they headed toward the back entrance avoiding looking at the lens following their every move.

Nothing happened until they passed the bank of elevators when there was suddenly the distinct, acrid smell of smoke. Then the smell became overpowering. In the next instant, every fire alarm in the Federal Building erupted into a screech at the same moment. A heartbeat later the lobby was jammed with a wave of humanity moving in one direction: out. Ayanna and Noonan only had time to look back once before they were picked up by the frightened human wave and swept outward. Noonan lost sight of Gerry and Sam in the melee.

Chapter 13

"What the ...?" was all Sam had time to say before he was capsized by the wave of oncoming humanity. In one instant he was peering through the camera lens at what could only be called an abandoned mezzanine of the Federal Building. In the next instant he was being pummeled by frantic pedestrians, *pedestrians* being the operative word, as they were running over him. There was no building of a panicked mob; it was the abrupt appearance of the same. Had he and Gerry not been near a recess for a door entrance, they might have been trampled to death. The unexpected fire alarm combined with the smell of smoke was enough to turn reasonable men and women into a mob. One second the lobby of the Federal Building was empty and the next it was packed with hysterical people trying to get out. Nothing was going to stand in their way of safety, least of all two reporters. As the human wave went, so did the reporters. By the time the stampede thinned, Noonan and Ayanna were long gone and the two reporters had no choice but to return to the station.

At least they had a tape to look at.

"What do you think we have?" Sam asked.

"That," Gerry replied thoughtfully, "remains to be seen. I don't expect much, though."

Back at the television station, Gerry pulled out the tape they had been shooting all day and went over it foot by foot. The only sequence, which was of any interest, was the last split second in the Federal Building when Ayanna had reached down with her right hand to touch the shelf under the telephone, her left hand on the receiver. Because Sam and Gerry had been at the back entrance, to Ayanna's left as she was facing the phone bank, the camera's vision had been partially obscured. Ayanna appeared to feel under the phone shelf and then reach behind her back.

If she had done anything else, it was not visible because Ayanna and Noonan walked away from the phone almost immediately. A quick trip back to the phone bank in the Federal Building revealed nothing. All of the phones were in working order and all of the shelves had phone books beneath them.

"What did we just see?" asked Sam and he looked around as though expecting the answer to be revealed by some clue on the walls.

"I don't know. Let's find the Facility Manager. Something set off the alarm."

When the Facility Manager saw Gerry, he gave a perfect impression of Dracula looking at a wooden stake.

"What the," the Facility Manager said when he saw Gerry and then broke into the center of the question with a l-o-n-g expletive and finished with ". . . are you doing here?!" The Facility Manager was in his late 60's, dressed like a janitor, had a pasty white head with about six strands of hair over his pockmarked pate and a very vivid memory of Gerry when she did her expose' on corruption in the janitorial trade contract at the Anchorage Pavilion and Symphony Center. Right smack dab in the center of the scandal was the Facility Manager, then a Contract Supervisor for the State of Alaska who was living well beyond his means. As the investigation heated up, he had suddenly resigned from state service effectively ending the legal investigation.

But not the news stories.

Inside information on the contract leaked for the next six months after which two commissioners and two deputy directors also resigned. Then the story died under its own weight.

"Walter!" said Gerry with a broad smile. "What a pleasant surprise," Gerry indicated Sam should shoulder his camera. "It's always nice to see a friendly face in a federal building." She emphasized the word *federal* to indicate she knew she was on public property.

"Turn that *&^%$ thing off," snapped the facility manager as he glared at the camera. "Get the heck out of here! This is a restricted area!"

"Walter, be nice now." Gerry was soothing and indicated Sam could continue to film. "This is your place of work, in a public building. Paid for with taxpayer money and I," Gerry tapped her chest with her right index finger, "am a taxpayer. Now you want to be cooperative with the press, don't you?"

Walter didn't look at it that way. "Get the blazes out of here!"

"Walter," she said in soothing voice. "Be nice. You never know what might show up on the evening news."

"You $%#@&^s!" Walter's face was a beet red and the veins in his temple were throbbing.

"Walter, we don't want to create any problems for you. We're just down here for some information. You tell us what we want to know and we'll be gone."

"Fly away!"

Gerry ignored his fury. She just went right ahead as if Walter was the most cooperative bureaucrat in the history of the federal building. "Walter, the alarms in the Federal Building went off this morning. Who set them off?"

"Why do you care?"

"Because if you don't tell me I'm going to run footage of you swearing at us and say you are stalling a police investigation into the kidnapping of 95 people. Then I am going to ask the FBI why you are obstructing a kidnapping case – *and then* I will ask why a contract administrator who resigned as part of a public funding scandal . . ."

The magic of words did it.

"What do you want from me?" The voice had the air of defeat.

"The fire alarms. Who set them off?"

"No one. It was automatic. Whenever the detectors get a whiff of smoke, the alarms go off automatically."

"Where did the smoke come from?"

"We don't know. There was a strong smell of smoke but we could not locate the source."

"Where was the smell?"

"Everywhere. All floors."

"So the smell of smoke on all floors set off the alarms on all floors. The smell of smoke was on all floors at the same time?"

"Yeah."

"Isn't that odd?"

"Sure is. I can't figure it out."

"Could the smoke have been introduced into the air vents in the basement by someone who wanted to set off the alarm?"

"You're a smart lady. Yeah. That's what we think happened but I didn't say that!"

"Of course you didn't, Walter. You couldn't have said it because we never talked, did we."

"You got that one right!."

"Good. Now, let's see the source for the air vents."

"I can't help you there. The FBI has closed off the room and they are going through it with a fine tooth comb."

"The smoke in that room would have gone to all floors at the same time?"

"Yup."

"Thanks, Walter. You've been a great help."

A filthy word formed on his lips but he stopped himself and had to live with a vitriolic "Don't come back."

"He was *not* a very pleasant fellow," Sam said as they left the basement of the Federal Building.

"No, I suppose not." Gerry grinned. "He was very helpful. Now we know what happened. The first payoff was made in the Federal Building and the kidnappers were clever enough to set off the alarms at exactly the right moment to cover the pick-up. Very, very clever. It would take split-second timing. At least two of them, one to pick up the payoff and the other to set off the alarm."

"I'm not an expert at this," Sam said as he snapped the camera off. "I'd count three. Someone had to be in the basement to get the smoke smell into the air vents. How do you think they got the smell to move so fast?"

Gerry though about it. "Not sure. A flare might do it. There's a lot of air pressure down there. Has to be to get air to blast all the way to the Fifth Floor. I'll bet the instant our two pigeons walked across the lobby the flare was lighted. Then it was stuffed into the air vent system. Might even be a handful of flares, the kind you can buy at a fireworks stand. Lighted them and tossed them into the compressor. Then hit the fire alarm on the way out of the basement. They all had to be talking by cell phones to have the timing so precise."

"Talk about precision," said Sam, getting to like this game of cat-and-mouse with an increasing number of players. "What we've got now is an A-1 news story. We've got 95 hostages, an out-of-state cop, ransom pay-offs and split-second timing for the crooks. All we need is some drugs and sex and we've got a made-for-movie contract."

"And we own the tape," said Gerry as she tapped the camera. "Just remember who you work for, Sam: me. Got it?"

"Yes, Ma'am."

Chapter 14

The expression "not a lot of happy campers," was the perfect description of the 80-odd relatives of the hostages when they gathered in the ballroom of the Anchorage Intercontinental Hotel. The hotel had not been expecting anyone to use the ballroom so it had taken more than an hour before a buffet could be set up. The food was adequate – adequate in the sense no one complained – but not a lot of people were eating. They were just milling around waiting for something to happen. The airport security people who came in occasionally kept telling them the same thing: there was nothing to report. In the meantime, a lot of the relatives were on the phones with friends, newspapers, radio stations and one was working on a reality show deal.

The atmosphere was not pleasant because of the circumstances. It wasn't as though this was a large family of relatives who only came together once an eon because of personal animosities. Rather it was a crowd of increasingly angry individuals who took out their frustrations on hotel personnel, meal servers, janitors and desk clerks. No one was in their good graces.

The situation threatened to get out of hand so a no-host bar was wheeled into the room. When it ran dry management decided some members of the crowd were too wet. Then some of the crowd got nasty – all four of them. These individuals were quietly escorted into a booth in the back of the nightclub – not yet opened – and each was provided with a full bottle of his/her choice of liquid sustenance and a six pack of mix apiece. The refreshments quelled the level of complaints considerably.

What made the waiting intolerable was the press of reporters who kept sticking microphones and cameras into peoples' faces for real time quotes on the ongoing crisis. Twelve hours into the standoff the relatives had run out of polite. Then they were outraged. After the second camera crew was escorted out of the gathering by a collection of family members, the press was banned from the ballroom. If anyone wanted to talk to the press they had to do it in the lobby.

Chapter 15

"You what?" Ayanna's shrill voice was loud enough to catch everyone in the Command Center by surprise. There was a momentary lull in the conversation as Ayanna confronted the FBI Agent in Charge, the AIC.

"This is an FBI operation," the AIC reminded her like a teacher chastising a child. "You and Detective Noonan are only here at the insistence of the kidnappers."

"Look," snapped Ayanna. "What we've got here is what we c-i-v-i-l-i-a-n-s" she spelled it out–"call a very delicate situation. We've got almost 100 lives at risk and we do not need a single screw-up to make anything worse than what we've got right now."

"Ayanna," the AIC was almost casual in his tone—and he used her first name, the only one who dared do that. It was a clear matter of talking down to her. "There's no problem here. This is all procedure. There's no risk."

Ayanna was in a red-hot burn.

Noonan, who had been sitting alongside the two at the Formica table stood up slowly and leaned into the conversation.

"What I think Ayanna is saying," he said softly to the AIC. "Is if there is anything happening which has anything to do with the payoffs, she'd like to know about it. Ahead of time. Not after we get a call from the kidnappers. Yeah, yeah, yeah," Noonan continued as the AIC started to interject a comment. "I know it's your procedure but Ayanna doesn't and she doesn't like surprises. No one does. Next time you do something like put a homing device in with gems, tell her."

The AIC looked affronted. "It's procedure. We don't talk about procedure. We just do it."

"Well," said Noonan casually, "as far as this case is concerned, you're dealing with a civilian. Ayanna is not traditional law enforcement and doesn't have any kind of 'inside information,'" Noonan made quote marks in the air with his fingers. "It's what she doesn't know that can cause real problems for all of us. Let's cut this discussion short and just agree you will tell Ayanna everything you are doing which falls within 'procedure.'" Again he made quote marks in the air with his fingers.

"All right," sighed the AIC, but he did not look happy about it.

"Look," said Ayanna, not willing to let the FBI have the last word. "You should have told me there was a homing device among the gems. I should have been told!"

Noonan spoke faster than the AIC. "It really doesn't make any difference at this point. The bad boys and girls knew it before we dropped off the bag. They expected it. That's why they led the FBI on a wild and merry chase around town. So let's drop it."

"That must have made you very unhappy," Ayanna said to the AIC, a bit of a gloat on her face.

"Yeah, we weren't happy. It was a long shot. We followed the bug for an hour. Where it went, we went. After chasing ghosts around town for an hour we ended up at the Railroad Terminal at the same phone where you got your first call. We found the bug with a note about your next drop."

"Well, let's not have any more trouble!" Ayanna was not going to let the matter drop.

Chapter 16

It wasn't going to take long for the bathrooms to start to stink. You didn't have to be a rocket scientist to know there were too few toilets to handle 95 people. The restrooms had been designed to accommodate mechanical crews, mostly men. There were, what, six men per shift. Maybe. Men didn't spend a lot of time in restrooms. It was in, do your business and be gone.

The women's toilets—all two of them—had been installed because of the sex equality legislation, not any functional reason. It had been easier to install the two toilets, mirrors and bidets than fight a legal battle costing more on paper than the toilets, mirrors and bidets. No one had ever used the toilets, mirrors and bidets. They were just installed and left. Functional, functioning but never used.

The extortionists had planned well. The warehouse in question was a substantial distance from its nearest neighbor. At least three miles. It was hardly in the proverbial middle of nowhere but it was remote. Originally it had been a mechanical shed for a farming conglomerate. It had served its purpose well until Boeing paid more per acre than farm labor ever would. Thereafter it sat empty while, at the same time, its raw value per square foot went up appreciably. The structure was too expensive to tear down so it was mothballed. Its toilets flushed and it was still on the power grid so it was as good a place as any to keep 95 people away from the prying eyes of the FBI, FAA and even the local constabulary.

You could see the warehouse for miles. If you happened to be within a few miles of the warehouse. Which no one was. The hostages had commented on the warehouse on their way in. They didn't yet know they were hostages as they were riding into the compound. They weren't hostages yet. No even captives. There was no reason to be alarmed. No one was carefully watching where they were going. All they had been told was there had been an emergency and they were being taken to a place of safety. It was a matter of national security and it just happened they were in the eye of a maelstrom and it was best if they would not be at the airport. Suitable substitute transportation would be provided along with four–count them, **four,** *one-two-three-four*–round trip tickets to anywhere Unicorn flew. Or its frequent flier partners. Which included Hawaii and Mexico and Europe.

So no one was particularly concerned if they got to Anchorage a day later. After all, **FOUR,** *count them,* round trip tickets were worth the inconvenience. No one was complaining. And no one objected when their cell phones and laptops were collected. National security, you know, all hush hush.

So no complained. No one said a word. They went along with the two men in the TSA uniforms.

When they arrived at the warehouse they had been screened through the front door. It was just like the airport. Looked like an airport screening entrance. No one thought otherwise. It was routine – not there was anything routine about flying these days. You just put up with the inconvenience. So they had freely given up their cell phones and laptops. It was only after they had entered through a one-way door did it become apparent to them something was amiss.

The interior of the massive warehouse had been divided into quadrants. Two of the quadrants had cots, one labeled MEN and the other WOMEN. The third quadrant was an eating area. The last, where Jennifer was now sitting, was the meeting area. It was called the meeting area because that's what the sign overhead read: MEETING AREA.

This was a long way from her desk at the Northern Lights Real Estate Exchange in Anchorage. Though it was only a cubicle there was a lot more privacy than here. The only consolation was she was here with her son, Jason. Jason, all ten years of him, was having a great time. He wasn't in Anchorage and he wasn't in Seattle and he wasn't listening to his father and mother fight over things he knew nothing about: custody, child support, and court appointed administrators. Which was fine with Jennifer too. She needed to get on with her life. There wasn't anyone in her life, except Jason, at this time but who knew?

Jennifer shook out her hair. Growing it long had been a good idea months ago. Now, under these situations, it was not such a good idea. Cleaning up, or *freshening up*, as the expression went, was not going to happen until this was all over. Whenever *that* was. So now Jennifer was stuck with the clothes she had on, far too formal for flying but what she had to wear for the court hearing. Then it was right to the airport, high heeled shoes and all. Now she was here, dressed for success in an abandoned warehouse sharing toilets with 93 other people not one of whom she had ever seen before.

Jennifer and Jason, were sitting at one of the Formica tables. There were six tables set end to end and stretched across the width of the quadrant. Jennifer's feet hurt. They always did when she traveled. There was something about air travel that did not go well with her feet—not as though her feet had a mind of their own. Or maybe they did. They hurt, didn't they? And the high heels were doing her no favors.

The good thing about traveling this time of year was being with her parents. One of the nice things about working for yourself is you could take time off any time you wanted. It wasn't called unemployment; it was called vacation. She saved for it so you could take it. Mom and Dad loved to see her and Jason, their only grandson. Granddaughters they had aplenty but only one grandson. So Jason was special. He would be until he got to be a teenager and then he'd be a problem just like every other boy or girl who turned 14 or 15 or 16. He was ten now, a few years from the "time of trouble" as her father would say.

The only downside to Seattle was Henry, her ex. Or about to be her ex. The marriage had been so good when it started. Then it went bad. South. Way south. It wasn't as though Henry was a bad person or had grown bad. He just wasn't the same person she had married. He had grown small, lost touch with the world. His world had imploded until all he did was legal work, 12 hours a day, six days a week and sometimes Sundays. Yes, the money was good, but he had lost his soul. Now he wanted custody of Jason?! With his work schedule? Henry, she had told him, get real. You want a son you will only see half a day every Sunday? What about his life? Henry didn't think normally way anymore. Half a Sunday was good enough for Henry; why wasn't it good enough for everyone else?

For his part Jason was just a normal boy, if there was such a thing. He was just as sharp as everyone else in his class. Just as mischievous as well.

Good in school, better at baseball. It was all right for Jennifer now but she could see the writing on the wall.

Jason was fiddling with a picture book when the massive screen covering one of the walls came to life. There was a popping noise like fire crackers and then a picture snapped into view on the screen. It was fireworks going off. The popping stopped and was followed by some soothing music. Thereafter the words IMPORTANT ANNOUNCEMENT IN THREE MINUTES ran across the screen, over and over again. At the end of three minutes, everyone was clustered in front of the screen.

Precisely at the top of the hour, indicated by a ticking clock with the second hand arriving at the 12, the image faded to a cartoony character. The character danced across the screen and finally came to a lonely chair in the center of the screen. He sat in the chair as the words PLEASE TAKE A SEAT appeared above him. Then the picture changed to Alaska scenery like a tourism tape. There was scraping as some people took a seat. The only sound from the screen was of an older man with a soothing voice.

"Welcome to our little warehouse. I'm sorry we have to meet under these conditions but it was necessary. Now, if you will sit down, I will do this as quickly as possible."

There was some movement to sit but not everyone did so. The voice continued.

"Please be seated. I say this for two reasons. First, so you know I am always watching what is going on in the warehouse. You, sir, in the three piece suit with the power tie. Please be seated."

The man sat.

"Thank you. Now, if you will look around you will see some security cameras high on the wall."

Everyone looked.

"These will watch you the entire time you are here. If things go as planned, you will be here no longer than two days. I am sure you have guessed by now I am not associated with the airlines or the airport. You are correct. I am not. I am a member of a gang of extortionists. You see, we are holding all of you hostage for $25 million. You should be proud to be worth so much." The voice chuckled.

"Now, to the basics. There is no reason for anyone to panic. All of your needs will be taken care of. First, there will be announcements on this screen at the top of every hour. That way you will always know what is going on outside. I have a selection of movies which will play around the clock along with news coverage when it is appropriate. You will also notice a phone under this screen. It connects you to me. If you have a concern, pick the phone and record a message. I will respond as fast as I can. If anyone has a medical condition which requires a doctor, let me know now so I can anticipate your needs."

There was a murmur through the audience.

"As to food and refreshment, please look at the dining area now."

There was a general scraping of chairs on cement floor as the audience turned to look sideways. As soon as everyone was looking at the dining area, a section of wall moved, sliding. It opened to reveal a bank of refrigerators along one wall. There were a half-dozen microwave machines on the edge of a table on one side of the room and a line of garbage cans on the other. There were some *oohs* and *aahs* and a little girl ran toward the kitchen. When her mother rose to stop her, the voice came back over the television.

"I'd prefer if everyone would sit through my entire presentation but I understand what it is like to have children. I have a few myself. So, allow me to continue. There is enough food in the refrigerators to last you for about two days, all the time we will need. If it turns out more time is needed, we will replenish your food. I will be bringing fresh fruits and vegetables every day. That's the reason the door slides. Every 6 hours I will be taking the trash out of the kitchen and bringing in fresh fruits and vegetables. Please leave all trash from the kitchen in the kitchen."

There was a pause and suddenly the screen was filled with a camera shot of the room in which the hostages were sitting.

"Just to be sure no one tries to slip out through the kitchen, we will be taking roll before the doors are closed. Please do not try anything funny. We have no intention of hurting anyone in this room. We are only interested in the money. As far as the bathrooms are concerned, they will also be cleaned every 6 hours. This will be a bit trickier since there is not a sliding door dividing the bathrooms from the living area. If you will look up above the bathroom . . ."

The voice paused long enough for everyone to look above the bathroom.

". . . you will see a mesh grating. When we want to clean the bathroom we will lower the mesh grating. Since we cannot see inside the restrooms–for your privacy–we will have to assume there is no one in the restrooms. To be sure no one is hiding in the restrooms, we will be entering with gas masks and pepper spray. Anyone caught in the restrooms after the grate comes down will be chained in the restroom for the next 6 hours. If you like it so much, you are more than welcome to spend six hours there."

There was an odd twitter through the audience.

Jennifer pulled Jason close to her.

"Finally, as we are not unfeeling, if you will look in the very back of the warehouse you will see a fume hood with plastic drapes. That is for the smokers."

Jennifer stood up and looked at the television. There was a moment of apprehension when she rose.

"Can you hear me?" She yelled.

"Yes," replied the voice. "I can. Is there a problem?"

"My son has asthma. He has enough medicine now but I need to get the rest of the prescription from our carry-on luggage."

"That will not be possible," the voice replied. "You see, your carry-on luggage in already in Anchorage."

There was a momentary outburst of surprise.

The voice continued. "For your information, after you disembarked, the plane left for Anchorage. It left a little late but it did leave. It arrived in Anchorage with all of your luggage and carry-on baggage. We also messed the interior of the plane a bit, just to fool the authorities into believing you had been onboard. So, in a nutshell, your carry-ons are not in Seattle. I am so sorry. If you will advance to the phone beneath the screen and tell me what you need, I will do what I can to fulfill any need."

"Fine," said a young man in an Army uniform as he stood. "Could I ask you to call my commander at Fort Richardson and inform him I am not AWOL and I'd like a six-pack of beer–per hour?"

The voice chuckled. "Good try. First, all of the names of the passengers who were checked onto Unicorn Flight 739 are available to the authorities. If you are flying under your own name, which I believe you are, your commander will be notified. As for the beer, I will see what I can do. There will be no hard liquor and no wine. There will be no wine because we do not want any broken glass."

The Corporal was not to be outdone. "What if I run out of cigarettes?"

"Borrow some until I get you what you want."

The Corporal thought for a moment and then said, "How about some transistor radios?"

The voice was clearly taken by surprise. "Radios? What do you want a radio for?"

"Well," replied the Corporal. "I may want to listen to a football game while everyone else is watching what you put on the screen."

"Radios," the voice pondered. "More than one. Why more than one?"

"More than one game," replied the Corporal. "I guess I'm asking for someone who hasn't thought of it yet."

"Radios? Not so you can turn one into a transmitter, eh?"

"Come on! You've got to know more about telecommunications than that! Transistors are hard wired so we can't just pull out wires and make a telephone. Even if we could make a telephone, what are we going to tell the world? We're hostages and don't know where we are?"

"Radios?" Again the voice was suspicious. "I'll get back with you. Anything else?"

The crowd was silent.

"OK," the voice continued. "That's it for the moment. It is quite a ways to a store so the sooner you put in your requests, the faster we can get them to you. You will also find diapers and changing materials in the hamper outside the bathroom. Bottled milk is in the refrigerator on the far left and a collection of deodorants, mouth fresheners, tooth brushes and paste, combs can be found in a footlocker in each sleeping area. You'll have to live without showering for a day or two."

The cartoony character disappeared off the screen with a 'pop!' and the screen came alive with the latest Disney film. Jason's eyes went pop too!

"Mommy! I haven't seen this one!"

"Well you enjoy it, dear. Mommy has a call to make." After making sure someone was watching Jason, she advanced on the telephone beneath the screen.

In the back of the room, the Corporal was talking with a man, urging him to follow him into the bathroom.

Chapter 17

Gerry McComber was pissed. Really pissed. The biggest story of her career was happening right in front of her and everyone else seemed to know more about what was going on than she did. Everyone. The scut reporter had scooped her! HER! She was the golden child. The FBI angle and the tracking device had popped up on a radio station–a *radio station* for heaven's sake!–and the evening newspaper was doing a rundown on the false alarm at the Federal building. This was supposed to be her story!

When her cell phone rang, she was still fuming.

"Gerry, dahling, you must be just miffed over the way things have been going."

"You!" snapped Gerry. "You told me I had an exclusive on this!"

"Now I never said *that*," said the voice in an ingratiating tone. "If I did I was lying. I think I said something along of the lines of you having the inside track on just about everything which was going to be done. I haven't lied. You've had the first crack at every part of this matter. You were the only one I called for the pick-up."

"The FBI angle. That was . . ."

"Dahling," the voice was ingratiating. "The FBI is going to do what the FBI does. They are also going to use the radio and television the same way we do. We didn't call any radio station, by the way. That would be, be, *unethical*. You're our lady, Gerry."

"That's not the way it looks from this side of the microphone. I'm sitting here while the other news outlets are running with my story."

"Well, let me give you a lead to make up for you thinking I'm a very bad boy."

"You are a very bad boy."

"I know. I just can't help it. It's in my DNA. I'm hard-wired that way."

"OK. Enough of the gab. Do you have something for me? Something no one else has?"

"Of course! If I didn't, why would I be calling?"

"I'm not sure why you are calling." Gerry stalled for a moment, "Not that I want you to stop. No, I'm not sure why you are calling."

"OK, how about a glimpse of the big picture?"

"OK."

"What do you know right now?"

"I know a lot of passengers were not on a plane they were supposed to be on and the plane landed in Anchorage with no pilot on board. I know there is an extortion attempt for . . ."

"P-l-e-a-s-e, not an extortion *attempt*," said the voice in faux outrage. "There's no *attempt* about it. We *are* extorting $25 million out of the Anchorage International Airport. No go on."

"OK, you *are* extorting $25 million. One payment of about $5 million in stones has already been made. That is correct isn't it? I mean, the amount is correct."

"Close enough," responded the voice. "Gems aren't something which have solid dollar and sense values. A stone isn't worth $4,500. It has a range. Which is neither here nor there. Yes, we have received about $5 million, give or take."

"So what's the next step and when?"

"Ah, if you told you everything at once, that would take all the fun out of it, right?"

"I don't look at it that way?"

"Well, I do. Now, if you remember your ancient history, the Greeks believed the world was made of four elements."

"Air, water, fire and, and, and . . . What's the fourth?"

"Earth."

"Correct. Earth, air, fire and water. So?"

"Well, there are four parts to this puzzle. The first was fire, in the Federal Building. There are three to go, three phases."

"I hate riddles?"

"You didn't just think we'd give away the rugby match, did you?"

"Go on with the earth, air and water."

"The second delivery will involve one of those. I'll give you a call just before the next delivery. When you get the call, think Medusa."

Then he hung up. Gerry stared at the phone for a moment. "I hate riddles. Medusa? Wasn't that the woman with snake heads for hair?" She felt her hair. "I know just how she felt?"

Chapter 18

The weightlifter was a woman and she balked at the idea of going into the men's bathroom with men she didn't know. "Hey! What kind of a fruit cake are you, anyway?"

She didn't look like a weightlifter. Not the traditional weightlifter anyway. They were bulky in the shoulders and swayed at the shoulders as they walked. Almost waddled. This woman was all of a five-foot-two and didn't look to be into pressing iron. She had a presence, the kind of confidence body building gave you. Confidence. The outward appearance of being comfortable with your body. It was something you earned, day after week after month of taking care of your body, inside and out, muscles and brains and poise.

The Corporal was not exactly her cup of tea. He was not the kind of a man she was looking for. Yes, he was young enough for her and she didn't have anything against Army men. Except they were, well, in the Army. Army men went where the Army sent them. Wherever the Army sent them was away. Away from where she was. You didn't love Army men; you missed them. They were here today and gone tomorrow because of Uncle Sam, not because they chose to leave.

So, yes, he was good looking enough for a rodeo but this was not the time or the place for a rodeo. Or a relationship for that matter. All she wanted was for this, this, event to finish so she could get back to Anchorage. Back to the gym. Talk about a bad time to visit a sick friend!

"Look," snapped the Corporal under his breath. "We don't have a lot of time. We'd better have a plan in case things go wrong. With this many people," he waved at the rest of the hostages in the warehouse, "anything can happen."

"Yeah, yeah, yeah," snapped the weightlifter as she flexed bicep. "What's that got to do with me going into the men's room?"

"Because," said the Corporal softly as he leaned toward her, "one of the oldest tricks in the book is the way you defeat listening devices is to talk near running water. The human ear can hear the conversation but electronic equipment cannot. There are no cameras in the bathrooms either."

"We should talk while we can," said the third in the trio, an older man with a Seahawks jacket. He had short cropped hair and wore jeans. "So we're going to go into the men's room and have a little talk."

Number three was definitely not her type. Never would be. Too chunky. Didn't care about his body. He was the kind of guy who sat around the house all weekend and watched football games. Hey, he had a Seahawks jacket on. What did that cost? Say two, three hundred dollars? He was older, maybe 40. Putting on weight, not lifting it.

"That's the best place to talk," repeated the Corporal. "If that's OK with you."

"It's not like we've got a lot of other things to do right now," said the older man. "I'm Sam, by the way. Made too much money, retired too early. Now I've got too much time on my hands. And you are," he said to the weightlifter.

"Gloria. Gloria Susan. Everyone calls me Mittles. Don't ask why."

"Mittles it is," said Jim as he held out his hand. "Jim"

"Inside," said the Corporal. "We've got to talk."

Once Mittles, Jim and the Corporal were inside, the Corporal turned on the two cold water taps.

"Do you think all this is necessary?" asked Jim.

"I don't know that it isn't," the Corporal replied.

"Good point," said Sam.

"Look," said Mittles. "I don't really know why I'm here. You asked to talk to me. Fine. I'm here. Let's make this quick."

"OK," said the man in the uniform. "Right now we have to believe what we're being told. I don't. I have no way of knowing if this guy is telling us the truth. We're only good to him as hostages. Once he doesn't need us, he doesn't need us, if you know what I mean."

"You mean he'd kill us?" The thought crossed Jim's mind for the first time.

"For $25 million, yeah. I think it's a possibility." The Corporal raised his hands and eyebrows to emphasis the logic of the situation. "A real possibility. If there's a chance we could recognize him or his people, yeah, I think he'd kill us all for $25 million."

"Why am I here?" asked Mittles. "Aren't you better off dealing with the pilot and crew? They know more than we do about what's going on."

The Corporal shook his head. "I don't trust them. They could be in on it. Probably are, inside man so to speak. Naw, I don't think I trust any of them. I trust the passengers more than a pilot and crew."

"Even if it's true, what's it got to do with me?" Mittles asked.

"Because," said the Corporal, "we'd better have a Plan B. Plan A is to go along with this guy. We'd better be thinking about an alternative. Why are you here? A couple of reasons. First, because you're a woman. We need someone with the women, in their sleeping area, someone who can talk to them, keep the men informed as to what is happening. Second, you don't just *be* a weightlifter. You work at it. It takes dedication. You are in it for the long haul. I think it makes you a great candidate for someone who cares."

"What makes you think I lift weights? Not that I care?"

"I'm trained to notice things."

"You just like me for my body."

"I'm a brains man if it matters. Besides, I don't see us getting it on in here. All this sex stuff aside, we could be very great danger. We'd better have a team looking for possibilities."

"OK," said Jim, "what should we do now?"

"First," said the Corporal. "Talk to as many people as you can. See who we can count on to do something. We need a plan. We need to know who we can trust. You," he pointed at Mittles, "see if you can find out who the female trouble-makers are. What I mean is, I find it hard to believe these guys are going to stick us in a room for two days to make $25 million and not put a sleeper or two in the group."

"So you think there are some traitors in the group, spies so to speak?" Jim looked the Corporal intently. "How do you know I'm not one of them?"

"I don't. I'll find out as the day progresses."

"What about me?" asked Mittles.

Before the Corporal could answer a man wandered into the restroom. When he saw Mittles he stopped suddenly and looked around. When he spotted the urinals, he looked from the urinals to Mittles to the toilets to Mittles to the urinals and then at the group.

"Can we have a little privacy here," snapped Jim.

The man slowly backed out of the restroom, but not before taking a close look at the sign reading MEN on the door.

"What about me?" said Mittles again. "I want an answer."

"I don't know," said the Corporal. "I'm taking a chance. I don't have a crystal ball to tell me the truth. I just know I," he paused for a moment, "we, don't have much time. If things don't go well, we won't know it. We don't have a lot of time. Why you two, I don't know. It was just a feeling you were OK. I could be wrong."

"How do we know you aren't one of them," snapped Mittles.

"Good point," said the Corporal. "You don't. But if I was, I wouldn't be plotting on how to escape, would I?"

"Only if you really were with them and wanted to see what we would try," said Jim. "Right now I don't give a hairy rat's left hind leg. You have said one thing that is true. People will kill you for a lot less than $25 million. If there's one chance we could monkey up their parade, we're dead. End of story."

"OK," said Mittles. "For the moment, and just for the moment, I'll buy off on what you say. Only for the moment. It's not that I do not trust you, it's that I just don't know. Anyway, I've got nothing better to do."

The Corporal turned off the water faucets. "For the moment, just listen to what people have to say. See if you can find people who will work with us, quietly. We need sharp people, clever people, not gung-hos who will charge the machine gun nest types."

"That's odd coming from you, a man in a uniform," said Mittles. "I would have figured you'd want heroes." Mittles kind of liked this guy.

"Heroes are for Hollywood. They get killed. The people who survive are the clever ones. We don't need heroes. We need survivors. That takes guile and craftiness. No, look for the quiet clever ones."

Mittles really liked this guy so she said "I don't know how I'm supposed to find them but I'll look. When should we meet again?"

"Whenever," said the Corporal. "When the time is right, we'll know."

The three started to leave when an evil thought crossed Mittles' mind. As the other two walked out the door, Mittles stalled for a moment and then flushed both toilets and both urinals. When she came out, the man who was waiting to go in gave her a confused look.

"It's OK now," she said as passed the man. "I'm the urinal inspector."

Giving her an indescribable look, the man entered the restroom watching her over his shoulder out of the corner of his eye.

Just before the three parted, Mittles asked the Corporal. "Why'd you really ask for the radios?"

The Corporal smiled. "Because we can't keep meeting in the toilet room. With a radio we can meet anywhere. Playing the radio is like running the water. It screws up the recordings."

"Where'd you learn that," ask Jim. "Spy school?"

"I spent a year in the Mideast," said the Corporal. "You can learn a lot when you're forced to."

"A year?" Mittles looked at him strangely and then at his rank. "You're a corporal."

"I am not always a good boy," he said slyly. "It makes some people very unhappy."

"Kissing butt ain't all it's cracked up to be either," said Jim. "It can be profitable. When the two of you get older and have kids you'll find out just how much fun it is."

Chapter 19

"Well, what do we do now? Ayanna scratched a brassiere strap beneath her blouse unconsciously. "I'm not used to this kind of a thing. Waiting and all."

"No one is," replied Noonan. "It comes with the territory."

The two were sitting at the end of a solid oak table in the Command Center. The table top was littered with used coffee cups, plates with half-eaten sandwiches, some doughnuts and empty pop cans. There were several piles of napkins, most of them unused, and a heap of plastic silverware at the far end of the end of the expanse. The AIC was speaking quietly to a covey of law enforcement personnel near the window overlooking the runway.

"At least he knows what he's doing," Ayanna said and indicated the AIC with an inclination of her shoulder.

"He doesn't have a clue," said Noonan quietly. "Not a clue. Hasn't had since the gems were picked up. He's just trying to look like he's in charge."

"If he doesn't know, who does?" Ayanna looked concerned.

Noonan smiled at her. "Ayanna. No one knows. This isn't usual police type business. That's exactly why the thieves are doing it this way. They have all the cards. They won't make a move until they're ready. We're the ones who have to sit and wait."

"So we sit and wait?"

"For the moment, yes. We should be gathering those gems as slowly as possible. There are still a few things we can do. We just have to be careful how we go about doing them."

"Why be careful?"

"Because," said Noonan said quietly, "we are not all on the same team."

Ayanna immediately went from concerned to conspiratorial. "We're not all on the same team? You mean . . ."

Noonan cut her off before she finished her statement. "What I mean is, the thieves have a pipeline into what we are doing. They know what we are doing. Which means they have someone on the inside. Their movements are too confident *not* to have an inside source."

"Are you sure?"

"For $25 million I'd be sure. This is a tight knit group, these extortionists. They know airports, they know police procedure, and they know terrorism-prevention procedures. They didn't just pick unique knowledge up by reading *Time* and *Newsweek*. Nope, they've got an inside man. Or woman."

"It could be someone in this room, right?"

"Could be but I don't think so. See, everyone is this room is working so close with everyone else if there was leak, everyone would know where it came from. No, I think it's one level down. Probably within the Police Department. Police know airport procedures. Airport people do not know police procedures."

"You seem pretty sure of yourself."

"Nope. Just a guess. I don't have the slightest idea what I'm doing. I'm just waiting for events to offer me an opening to try to solve this crime. Until the hostages get released, I have to play it cool. There's always time to track down a thief after the crime but you can never bring a dead man back alive."

"Kind of makes us a secret team, doesn't it?"

"Always was. It just took you until now to realize it. Just you and me."

"OK, partner. What do we do now?"

"Now, partner, while we have time, we track down the loose ends. I don't trust the police to do it. I don't want the police doing it. For the moment, let's just keep what we are doing as our little secret."

"Fine with me." She leaned forward conspiratorially, "What are we doing?"

"First we talk. What are the loose ends we can play with? I think we've got four solid threads to follow. First, we have the names of the passengers and crew. Every one of those names should be run through NCIC, the national crime data base. Who knows what we might find?"

"I'm pretty sure that's already been done."

"I am too. I just haven't seen the read-out. Second, some of those passengers had lap tops and cell phones. I doubt the perps let them keep the electronic equipment but, who knows, we might get lucky. We need the cell phone numbers for the passengers. With them we can find the issuing company and then locate the phones using GPS."

"Too late. The AIC has already done it."

"Nope," said Noonan as he pulled out a sheet of paper. "He only did it for the passengers who have relatives in Anchorage. Not for the passengers who have no relatives here. This is a list of the cell phones of Seattle residents who were on the plane. There is probably some crossover, but the AIC doesn't have this list."

"Where do you get it," whispered Ayanna quite impressed.

"No matter what business you are in, my dear lady," Noonan said in an avuncular manner, "you should always be thinking ahead. As soon as the ransom demand came in, I called my office. They traced all the passengers they could and called every contact number in Seattle. We got six cell phone numbers. Six are still in Seattle."

"Fantastic! Where are the other six?"

"The other six are why," Noonan said sadly, "I didn't bother to bring this up before. The six cell phones were on the plane with the passengers. Two of them were located here, in Anchorage, probably in the carry-on luggage or in the luggage compartment."

"The other four?"

"These guys are really good, Ayanna. They are really good. One is on an Hawaiian-bound flight. It took off an hour after Unicorn 739 landed here in Anchorage. Another is in Juneau. The third is moving north slowly, probably on a ferry, somewhere on the Inside Passage. The last one, and this is rich, was actually located in Seattle. It was in a Special Delivery package to the President of Unicorn Airlines."

"The President of the Airlines? Brutal. Had it been sent from Seattle?"

"We assume so but we don't know. It was delivered to the front door just like a regular delivery. A temp signed for it and opened it. She passed the phone along upstairs. By the time anyone realized whose phone it was, the delivery man was long gone. All the temp could say was he was 'not white.' In Seattle that can mean anything."

"How about the . . ."

"Envelope." Noonan cut her off. "You're getting good at this. Yes, there was an envelope. It was an Air Rapid Delivery envelope from Nome, Alaska."

"Nome? Do they have a . . ."

"No. Nome doesn't have an Air Rapid Delivery office. The label was a fake. The phone had a note on it: 'Don't lose this. You'll never know who's calling."

"I hope someone dusted for prints?"

"The whole forensic ball of wax. Inside and out of the envelope. No fingerprints. No hairs, just some fibers."

"I'm afraid to ask."

"Walrus whiskers."

"How the . . ."

"The Seattle PD has some Alaskans. One of them is a Native. He recognized the whiskers. Everyone thought he was kidding but they compared them anyway. They were walrus whiskers."

"So what's it all mean?"

Noonan shook his head. "The same thing we knew when we started this case. The thieves are very, very clever people. So far they have thought of everything."

"So there's nothing for us to do? Sounds like you've done it all."

"No. I've only done the easy part. I just made a phone call and let loose the hounds. The hard part is what's next. Here's where you can do your fair share. What I need you to do . . ."

Chapter 20

To say the fire alarm took the extortionist by surprise was an understatement. He made it from his cot to the bank of monitors still naked, trying to pull on his underwear. When he remembered he was alone, he didn't bother to try.

The first thing he did was cut the power to the alarm. Then he scanned every inch of the warehouse he could see with the cameras. Other than the fact everyone was milling around wondering what was happening, he could not see a puff of smoke. Flicking on the microphone he asked if everyone was all right. He actually didn't have to ask. Just by looking at them there was no a sign of panic.

"The alarm must have cut in because of a short in the wiring," he said into the microphone and then re-started the movie.

Then the phone rang.

Looking up at the screen display of the area in front of the screen, he saw the Corporal on the phone. He let the tape run and watched the lips of the Corporal trying to guess what he was saying. When the Corporal hung up, the extortionist replayed the tape. The message was short: "What about those radios?"

Something gnawed at the extortionist. The fire alarm should not have gone off. Those wires had been disconnected to avoid an unexpected alarm. What had made it go off? He scanned the interior of the warehouse through the lenses of the six security cameras and did not see anything out of place. Strange.

When the alarm went off a second time an hour later, he was sure there was something amiss. Why had the alarm gone off again? Weren't the wires disconnected? What was going on here? He'd have to spend a lot more time watching the monitors. This was rapidly turning into a two-man job but until his partner got back with the medicine, it would have to be a one-man job.

It was not starting out as a great day.

Chapter 21

Gerry didn't think it was such a great day either. She knew who Medusa was. After all, she did have a college education. A good college education. Not one of those you get by taking Mickey Mouse classes. She was a journalism/English major. No Mickey Mouse classes for her. If you wanted to be the best, nothing but the best education was necessary. So it was San Jose State? So what? A quality education doesn't depend on where you went to school; it's what you forced yourself to learn.

She punched up Medusa on the Internet and read everything she could. There were lots of links to earth, air and water. There were lots of links but none appeared meaningful. She did discover Medusa was not a stand-alone demon–if that was the term the Greeks would have used to describe her. Actually she had two sisters, known as the *gorgons*, the root of the word "gorgon." Of the three sisters, only Medusa was mortal. Perseus, the man with the winged sandals, killed her.

Winged sandals? Was this the answer to the 'air' part of the riddle? It seemed a good bet until she read a little further. Since whomever looked in the face of the Medusa turned to stone, Perseus had slain the Gorgon with a trick. He had buffed up the inside of his shield until it shown like a mirror. Then he slew Medusa by guiding his sword toward the death blow by looking in the mirror located on inner face of his shield. She also learned Perseus slew Medusa while she was sleeping. Gerry hadn't known that before. She also hadn't known that when the gorgon was slain, Pegasus and a man whose name she could not pronounce leapt out of Medusa's severed neck. They were both children of Poseidon.

There was another air reference. Even from her rudimentary knowledge of Greek mythology, she knew Perseus didn't ride the winged horse. He got away by making himself invisible with a *kibisis,* a helmet giving invisibility. He didn't need to ride Pegasus to get away.

Who rode Pegasus? A few clicks of the keyboard and she discovered it was Bellerophon. Bellerophon tamed Pegasus and used the winged horse to kill the Chimera – a beast part lion, goat and dragon – and then had tried to ride to the top of Mt. Olympus. This apparently pissed off Zeus to no end so he put an end to Bellerophon. Zeus sent a lightning bolt to knock the headstrong mortal off his mount. The fall didn't kill him but it left him crippled and blind for the rest of his life.

"Another Greek mythological consistency," she mused. "Everyone who ticks off the gods ends up wandering the countryside alone, blind and crippled."

Pegasus got the better end of the deal. He ended up as Zeus' thunderbolt carrier.

"Well," said Gerry as she logged off the Internet. "I've got air images with Pegasus and Perseus and Bellerophon. I've got earth images from Bellerophon. And I've got water images with Poseidon. I went from no clues to too many. Do I hate riddles."

Chapter 22

It took Ayanna all of about ten minutes to get a complete cargo manifest for Unicorn 739. It was just a matter of printing a readout. As far as locating the owners of most of the property, it was even easier. She didn't have to go looking for them. They were looking for her. Almost every one of them. They wanted their cargo off Unicorn 739.

Checking with the AIC, the answer had been simple. "No way. Not until this case is resolved. We're not talking cargo here; we're talking crime scene."

"Do you have any objection if I take a look at the cargo?" Noonan had asked.

As far as the AIC was concerned, Noonan was a fly in the ointment. No one knew what was going on which was fine with the AIC. It made him as good as anyone else. He was the AIC, in fact, and when this matter was resolved it was going to be his office taking the credit. Actually, he was going to take the credit. All of it. He'd thank a laundry list of locals, of course, but the single mention would be as far as it went. Any crime is only good for one press conference. The rest of the coverage is called "background" or "follow-up." No one reads background or follow-up articles. They are like where-are-they-now stories. Who cares? News is a here-and-now medium. It is the here-and-now coverage which gets you the promotion and star status. No one cares what you did last year; they want to know what have you done for me lately? It was pure politics but without the election.

Noonan, the AIC sensed, was bad news. He was not in any chain of command so he was, basically, a freelancer. The AIC hated freelancers because they could not be contained. He could not tell or order them to do anything. They didn't have to do what anyone told them. He couldn't fire them either.

Worst of all, freelancers had no stake in the game. The police, airport security and the troopers pretty much had to follow the AIC lead. They didn't have a choice. He was the man in charge. EOS: End Of Story. If the AIC said the sky was orange, everyone would agree because that's the way the system worked. He said it *ergo* it was true.

Freelancers were a sunrise of a different color. They didn't have to say the sky was orange. The AIC couldn't make them say the sky was orange and if the sky wasn't orange, the freelancer was going to say it was blue. Or some other darn color. Or any color. Freelancers are not team players and should be kept as far away from the command structure as they could be moved.

But they have to move carefully. Freelancers have one thing the police, airport security and trooper do not have: a mouth. They do not have to play the game and a lot of times they did not. They were not necessarily the kind of low life who would throw a dead rat into the punch bowl at the cotillion but they would certainly point out the dead rat. This was a problem because no crime was ever completely solved. There were always people who get away with it, whatever *it* was. Some crooks were just unbelievably lucky, that's all there was to it. Everyone in law enforcement knew it. You couldn't catch them all. You wouldn't catch them all. The one thing you sure didn't want was some freelancer shooting off his mouth to the press saying some of the bad people actually walked away clean and dry. The inside expression was "coming out of the water dry." No one used the expression outside of the office.

No one *in* the office, in the chain of command.

A freelancer might and then *everyone* would be using the term.

Curse those freelancers!

So the AIC had no trouble giving Noonan permission to get as far away from Command Central as possible. Ayanna, desperately running all over town picking up loose diamonds, couldn't join Noonan in the cargo bay so the Chief of Detectives from some rat's nest town in North Carolina was free to do whatever he wanted on his own. It was fine with the AIC. Noonan on his own was a lot less trouble than with someone on the inside. And Noonan was not on the inside. Was not going to be on the inside. He was only in the mix at the personal request of the extortionists. Which was a public relations brickbat the AIC could use if things went bad.

Why *they* wanted Noonan in the mix was not clear. The AIC only knew Noonan as a detective from North Carolina. He was in Alaska on vacation. How convenient, eh? Too convenient. The head office said he was sterling. No blemish. Good cop. Long track record? How good was that? There was no reason for Noonan to be here and no reason for the extortionists to know he was here but they did know he was here. Why? What was the angle? Synchronicity? The AIC didn't believe in synchronicity.

He didn't have the time or manpower to keep Noonan under surveillance. So he did the next best thing: he moved him off the field of play. If he wanted to snoop around far away from where things were happening, fine and dandy. Let him go. Best wishes and don't come back too soon. Not at all would be best but the longer the better.

Noonan had no problem with being away from Command Center. All of his years of experience told him the last place anything important was going to happen was in the Command Center. The Command Center was pure politics. The stench was overpowering and Noonan knew the extortionists had planned well. They were playing the political card p-e-r-f-e-c-t-l-y.

So he followed his instincts. If you do not know what you should be doing, go back to square one and look around, kick a few cans and then scrounge for cigarette butts and theater ticket stubs. You never know what you will find.

The closest he could get to Square One was the airplane. So it was back to the airplane he went. He flashed his badge to the airport security people to get onto the apron. No one stopped him. Security may have been tight in the terminal but out here on the apron it appeared just like a normal day. Ground crew and baggage personnel were shuttling back and forth. The trucks which had been blocking the plane were gone, which made sense. The plane wasn't going anywhere. Watching it was a waste of time, like guarding the barn after the horse had been stolen. There was a solitary woman in uniform at the base of the back stairs and she gave Noonan's badge a perfunctory glance. That was it.

The passenger compartment was exactly as he had left it the previous day, eerie and silent with every indication people had been here and left suddenly and unexpectedly.

Suddenly and unexpectedly were exactly the terms to use when he stepped into the cargo area where a large Doberman instantly accosted him. It was both large and a Doberman, neither of which was good news.

Not quite the killer of a late night thriller, the animal was still, nonetheless, formidable because of his size. When Dabney the Dog Man arrived from the cockpit, the dog, quite literally, rolled on his back and exposed his belly as if to say, 'Hey, I've done my part. Now you do yours!'

"Back again!" Dabney said when he spotted Noonan. "You're that out-of-town detective up here helping us?"

"I'd like to think so," replied Noonan. "I talked to you yesterday, right?"

"Could have been. Things have been crazy around here, you know."

"I'll bet. I came down to do some work. Got a couple of extra minutes?"

"For the forces of law and order I always have time."

Dabney leaned against one of the crates and spread his hands. "What can I do for the forces of truth, justice and the American way of life?"

"Did they ever find video footage of our mysterious pilot?" Noonan leaned against some of the cargo boxes.

"Naw. She was too good. The only thing the big boys with the clean uniforms could figure out was she was wearing a uniform of some kind and just blended into the crowd when everyone came rushing out. Her timing was perfect. She knew where the cameras were so even if she could have been picked out of the crowd her face was never exposed."

"So she pulled a fast one, eh?"

"Ab-so-positive-lootly." It suddenly dawned on Dabney he should not been familiar–or out-spoken with Noonan. "That is, I mean . . ."

"I know exactly what you mean, son. Don't worry about the enthusiasm. The crooks have been very clever. So far, anyway."

"Yes, sir, they have been."

"You have any ideas how they did it?"

"Did it, sir?" Dabney was still not sure he should trust Noonan.

Noonan pulled the man aside an avuncular arm around the man's neck. "Let's just have a talk between the two of us. I'm not your boss. I don't know your boss. I don't care who your boss is. I'm just one of those so-called interested parties. You're a bright guy. You know what's going on. Tell me, how did they do it?"

"You mean, suck the passengers off the plane?"

"Part of it, yeah. How did they do it?"

"You really want me to guess?"

"As Elvis Presley is my witness!" Noonan put a hand over his heart.

Dabney laughed. "Elvis Presley. Rich. Very good. OK. What do I think? I don't believe in ghosts. I don't believe in little green men from Mars. I don't believe in the President's foreign affairs policy and I don't believe 89 passengers and 6 crew members were part of an alien abduction."

"I don't either," confided Noonan. "But where are they?"

"Oh," replied Dabney. "An easy answer. They're somewhere in Seattle."

This candid assessment took Noonan by surprise. "Why do you think so?"

"It's the only place they could be. From what I've heard the plane could not have been on the ground anywhere else long enough to get the passengers off and then back to altitude without the FAA knowing about it. The only logical answer is they never got on the plane in the first place. So they are in Seattle."

"Where in Seattle?"

"Good question. Answer: I don't know. But I'll bet the FBI in Seattle has hit every building large enough to house 100 people anywhere near the airport so they have to be somewhere else."

"Did you tell your boss what you told me?"

"Old Poop for Brains?" Dabney looked sideways at Noonan. "Have you ever worked in Alaska?"

"No. Why?"

"Alaska," Dabney said looking sideways, "is the last place in America striving for the highest standard of mediocrity. People from the Lower 48 do not get jobs here because they are competent. They get them because they are incompetent. Frankly, confidentially, this was the best possible airport in America to hit. There isn't a qualified person from mid-management up. This airport was a disaster waiting to happen – and it did."

"You don't have a lot of faith in your superiors," Noonan said wryly.

"They aren't my superiors," Dabney responded. "They're my supervisors."

"Point well taken. Let's play a game. Do you like games?"

"Maybe." Dabney was suspicious.

"Just between you and me. What's going to happen?"

"Nothing. That's the beauty of this crime. Nothing is going to happen. The Airport is going to pay. The police aren't going to stop them. The FBI is going to diddle until it's too late to do anything. The only people who might do something are the airport security people because their jobs are on the line." Dabney sighed and stalled, "But I doubt it. Three-quarters of the people working for airport security could not find an elephant in a bath tub. The only reason this hasn't happened before is no one knew how incompetent our security really was."

"You mean in Anchorage or across the country?"

"Well, I work in Anchorage so I know how bad we are. I can't imagine any other airport is better."

"All this being said, you really think these guys are going to get away with it?"

"Who's going to stop them?"

A point well taken, Noonan thought. "Let's take a walk."

Wandering down to the end of the cargo bay, Noonan wanted to know as much as possible about the cargo procedures.

"Let's talk cargo."

"This is a joke, right?"

"Not really. Does all of the cargo get picked up right away?"

"Hey, for what people pay per pound, believe me, they pick it up right away. Time is money. The minute the plane lands there is a line of people to get their cargo. They paid big bucks to get it here. The last thing they want is to be delayed."

"So no one waits very long to get their cargo?"

"Not a minute. That's why there's such a mess right now. There is a lot of cargo on Unicorn 739. *Is* as in it *is still* on the plane. A lot of people want their cargo to go to work. The longer the FBI holds it up, the angrier the people will be."

Noonan handed him the print out of the cargo manifest. "Of these names, how many want their cargo now?"

Dabney looked over the list. "Well, I can't tell you about all of them but I'd say about 80 percent of this list want their cargo right now. The rest is bypass."

"Can you show me which ones are bypass?"

"Maybe. Have a pen?"

Over the next 15 minutes Dabney slowly went over the list, checking the customers he knew to be bypass. As Noonan sat and watched him, the Doberman jumped up, putting his paws on Noonan's chest. The Chief of Detectives scratched behind the dog's ears, a motion the dog appreciated.

"He loves that kind of thing," Dabney said without looking up. "Darndest security dog I ever worked with. Most ferocious looking animal when you first see him and the friendliest dog on the planet when you get to know him. Cats frighten him and he'll lick a burglar to death."

"I guess there isn't much of a call for security here."

"You got that right," said the Dog Man. "Now over at the International Terminal it is a whole other ball of wax. Even the bell caps are surly. Here's your list."

"How do you know all these customers are bypass?" Noonan asked as he looked at the check marks.

"I don't. You asked me if I could identify them. I said maybe. These are good guesses though."

"How do you know?"

"Simple. Look at where the cargo is going. If the cargo's not destined for Anchorage, it's bypass. As an example. See this hospital bed. Its eventual destination is Lime Village. Lime Village is about 300 miles from here. This bed is going to be taken over to the Post Office and mailed. It'll end up on a Northern Air Cargo flight. No one from Lime Village is going to be driving down here to pick up the bed. Primarily because you can't drive here from there. I'm guessing anything for the pipeline is bypass. I happen to know this company is in Fairbanks." He tapped the list with his index finger. "So is this one and this one." I'd guess the rest are Anchorage area customers.

"How sure are you?"

"Real sure. If you want to be *real* sure, just walk over to that desk," he pointed at a desk at the far end of the cargo bay where a group of people were clustered around a harried clerk. "That's the poor women who's got to tell the Anchorage customers they can't have their cargo."

Noonan looked at the desk and then back to Dabney. "Got a few more minutes?"

"Sure. Whatcha need?"

"Let's take a walk."

Stepping out of the cargo area onto the runway apron, Noonan led Dabney a dozen feet away from the building, until he could see the security cameras on the roof. "Do all those security cameras work?" He pointed at the cameras on the roof.

Dabney looked at him nervously. "Who's asking?"

"Well, let's put it this way. Cameras like those are not good for very much. They are old, too high on the building to offer much detail of someone on the ground, are in a very bad place for wind and ice and snow. Those cameras are not made to pick up people. They are made to pick up vehicles which are not supposed to be on the apron."

"A fair statement. In answer to your question, *yes*, they do work. But they are in the process of being moved and upgraded. Which ones have been deactivated, if any have, was a decision made by management to move them. They all worked the other day when Unicorn 739 came in. I know because I and every other employee who was there when the plane came in had to look at the footage of all cameras over and over and over again."

"And there was nothing unusual? Even something you might not think related to the crime."

"Not a thing. It was like watching a normal day until the flight came in. I didn't see anything odd, even after the turmoil in the cargo area. I didn't see the pilot or any suspicious characters until the police showed up. Then there were too many people moving too fast to be distinguished."

Noonan nodded. "One more thing. I notice the cargo on the plane was in front of the bulkhead, between the passengers and the pilot. Since the passengers cannot get out of the plane by stepping over the cargo, they exited out the back. Is it unusual to have a plane with cargo pull into a terminal gate and then have the passengers disembark from the rear?"

"Not for Alaska. I'd say it would be unusual for a carrier like Alaska Airlines or Northwest because they have passenger flights carrying nothing but passengers. Let me revise what I just said. If Alaska Airlines and Northwest flies into Anchorage or Fairbanks, their planes won't have cargo. Northwest probably all the time but Alaska Airlines services Nome, Kotzebue, Bethel and Dillingham. Those cities are . . ."

"I know where they are," replied Noonan. "Alaska Airlines will fly bulkhead cargo to those areas?"

"Depends on the season and flight. In those airports, there isn't a terminal like Anchorage. The plane just rolls up to a building and people get out. Sometimes they get out the front, sometimes the back, sometimes both."

"So having a passenger plane with cargo at the front forces the passengers to get out the back is not unusual, even if the plane is nose-in a terminal and there is a corridor to the plane and the corridor can be opened into the terminal?"

"Not for Unicorn Airlines."

"Is Unicorn the only one?"

"It's probably the only big airlines coming in here. The smaller, regionals do it too. They don't pull into the terminal. They park outside the terminal and let the passengers get out and walk into the building."

"How far out are we talking about?"

"20, 30 feet."

Noonan walked to the building and paced off twenty feet, the Doberman trying to catch up with him for another series of ear scratches. Noonan obliged. When he finally made the 30 feet, Noonan turned around and looked up at the cameras again.

"As old as those cameras look, they appear to be doing the job."

"They are. Like I said, I watched every running inch of the video tape on all the cameras including those," he indicated the cameras. "They may be old but they are doing their job. There was no suspicious person, vehicle or activity I or anyone else could spot."

Noonan took a long look up and down the terminal. Then he looked across the runway and into the trees on the southern side of the air field.

"Forget it," the Dog Handler said.

"Eh?"

"I know what you're thinking."

"What am I thinking?"

"You're thinking it might be possible for whomever it was flying the plane to have left the airport by heading south, toward those trees. No. I looked at the tapes. No one left the plane headed across the runway. Nothing left the cargo area and went any further than the edge of the runway apron."

"So this side of the airport is secure?"

"We'd like to think so. Even the moose have a hard time getting through. There's a solid fence over there – expect for some moose gates. Someone walked the length of the fence looking for anything suspicious right after the plane landed. Zip. Nada. Goose egg."

"It was a thought."

"Since you've searched my brain, let me search yours. How did the guy do it?"

Noonan smiled. "If I knew I'd be in Vegas. The pilot didn't disappear, she wasn't abducted by aliens and she'll be back before this case is closed."

"Hear! Hear!" The Dog Man raised his fist twice. The moment he did, the Doberman jumped up and placed his paws on the Dog Man's chest.

"He loves you," Noonan chuckled. "There's no substitute for the loyalty of a dog."

"They don't have a mother-in-law, get the mumps or force you to go to church."

"Ah, the joys of married life!" Noonan smiled. "Is the cargo document handler as approachable as you?"

"She's a vicious, unpredictable, disreputable individual whose husband is even worse."

"She's your wife?"

"You see through me like glass. Yes. She's actually very nice." He paused for a moment and then added "most of the time."

"I know just what you mean. All wives are nice (pause) most of the time."

In fact, she turned out to be exceedingly helpful even though she was under tremendous pressure.

"Sorry to pull you aside on a busy day like this."

Dabney's wife was as tall as he was. Both had played basketball in college but she was the one who got the scholarship. For biology, not basketball.

"How did you end up doing cargo?"

"Have you ever worked in a laboratory?"

Noonan scratched his head. "I've been in and around laboratory, crime labs most of my life but I never worked there."

"Don't," said Dabney's wife. "You get to mix chemicals all day come home smelling like formaldehyde. The beakers have more personality than your coworkers and the thrill of the year is naming a new chemical no one will ever use."

"Frustrating, eh?"

"Hey! I'm here. I get to deal with people all day here. Real people. There are some pills but by and large it's entertaining. Today's a bit different because I'm telling people they can't have their cargo. Usually they are telling me they want their cargo."

"You look busy."

"Busy? I'm not busy. Other than Unicorn 739 it's a normal day. Cargo in and cargo out. I'm not allowed to move anything off Unicorn 739 so I'm spending my time telling those customers 'no,' 'no,' and 'What part of *NO* don't you understand?'"

"Pushy?" asked Noonan.

"Yeah, but I can understand why," she said. "Those companies paid a lot of money to have their cargo brought up quickly. Now it's sitting around the airport for no apparent reason."

"Which brings me to why I'm here. Can you look over this list of customers and tell me which ones are trying to get their cargo out now?"

She looked at Dabney the Dog Man. "He's with the Police," he said authoritatively. "Out of North Carolina but working with the locals. Working on the Unicorn 739 case."

Assured, she looked over the list. "What exactly are you looking for?"

"I don't know," Noonan responded. "Anything unusual, out of the ordinary."

"This is Alaska during the summer. There isn't anything ordinary about the cargo we get. I've off-loaded an elephant, sent cows to bush villages, medevac'd a Santa Clause and spent half a day getting a swarm of bees back in a hive. What exactly do you think is unusual?"

Noonan smiled. "I'm thinking too much like an Outside detective. I forgot I was in Alaska. OK, let's do this backwards." He handed her the cargo manifest print out. "Which of these names are regulars?"

"Do you want me to mark them?"

"Please."

She went down the list meticulously, checking off customers. As she handed him the list back, she asked "What do you know about the air cargo business?"

"Air planes carry it." Noonan smiled.

Dabney the Dog Man's wife smiled. "It's a good start. I don't know what you are looking for but it might help if you knew some of the basics."

"Go ahead."

"You might be making a mistake concentrating on the cargo. There are all kinds of cargo but there are only a few kinds of customers."

"What do you mean?"

"Before 9/11 anyone could ship anything anywhere with no problem. 9/11 changed the way everyone does business. Cargo restrictions came out of Washington D. C. in a river."

"All for the better, of course," Noonan said.

"In this case," she replied, "yes. Cargo regulations before 9/11 were worthless. The new regulations make the skies a lot safer. The restrictions are a lot tighter, particularly at the big airports."

"What do you mean?"

"OK. Right now, if you want to ship something from, say, San Francisco to Denver by air, no one is going to take the cargo unless you are an established customer. If you are a new business starting out, you have to jump through a lot of hoops to get your cargo onto the plane. If you can't meet every single requirement – and I mean *every* **single** requirement – your cargo does not fly."

"If it doesn't fly, how does it go?"

"Truck, train, boat. It just doesn't fly."

"That must make it hard for the rural airlines and places like bush Alaska."

"There's a bit of discretion allowed with the new regulations but actually the new regulations didn't change much of what was actually happening. Alaska has bypass mail so a lot of cargo came – and is coming – through as mail. We don't process the mail. The Post Office does. The only thing I can tell you about the mail on Unicorn 739 was it weighed," she paused for a moment and then flicked through some paperwork on her desk, "1,865 pounds."

"You don't know what's in the mail?"

"No. I'm not allowed, we're not allowed, to touch it. Privacy act. Only the Postman knows for sure."

"So, excluding the mail, or what the United States Post Office calls mail in Alaska, what are we talking about in terms of cargo?"

"This," she replied as she held up the cargo manifest. "This is a list of everything which came in on Unicorn 739 including the mail. Taking out the mail and regular customers you have six, no seven, unusual customers." She tapped the paper five times. "Here and here and here and here and here. Five of them. The other two I've seen before. They are erratic shippers. *Erratic* as in not regular, not *erotic* as pornographic."

"What makes them erratic?" Noonan asked.

"They are not regularly scheduled clients. They might get six crates in one month and then nothing for three months, a crate one week and then five crates the next week but then nothing for six months. It's unusual considering the usual, regular customers get a crate a week, for instance, but these guys have been doing it for as long as I've been here."

"How long has that been?"

"Five years."

"This one," she tapped on the paper, "is unusual because of the product. It's a meat packaging plant, wild game, kind of product. Usually his heavy weights are going out, not coming in. So it's unusual in that sense. I've seen him before."

"OK." Noonan looked over her shoulder at the five remaining names on the list. "These are absolutely new people."

"Yup. Never seen 'em before."

"Can you tell me anything about the five?"

"Let's see," she pulled open a drawer and searched for, and found, five folders. She read through the first one and set it down, "this one is for magazines coming in. It must be a news service or publisher or a similar business."

"Why didn't they send the magazine through the Post Office and save on the cargo bill.

"Because bypass mail is only mail that is mailed in Alaska for Alaskans in Alaska. This company had no choice but to send it Anchorage as cargo. There's a street address meaning the publisher will probably break apart the pallet and distribute the magazines. Some will be sent out as bypass mail."

"The others?"

"Four to go." She picked up another folder. "This one is for a church and it's an organ part. Weighs about 30 pounds. I've got another for a motorcycle for a man by the name of George Sampson in Talkeetna. Supposedly the motorcycle is an antique and had to be shipped as a motorcycle and not crated. It's unusual, first because it's a private individual, second because it's expensive and third, he's a newbie."

"Do you have a name and phone number for him?"

"Yeah, here." She handed him the file.

Noonan wrote down the name and phone number and returned the file. "How about the other two?"

"One is a ten-pound box of some medicine and," she looked at the last folder. "The last is a strange one too. It's an igloo – do you know what an igloo is?"

"If it's not a *barabara* it's a cargo container shaped like an igloo."

"Right. I don't know what's in the igloo, just that it's been inspected. Weighs 136 pounds and was transferred from New Orleans and before that New York."

"New Orleans and New York? Sounds odd to me. Sounds like it's been bouncing across the country."

"Let's see what we can come up with. Humm, it's also been losing weight as it crossed the country. It was 200 pounds in New York and 163 in New Orleans."

Noonan shook his head. "Does that mean people have been taking things out of it as it went along?"

"No. Once cargo is put on the plane, no one can get into it. The definition of cargo is a package loaded at Point A and offloaded at Point B. In this case, the on load was in New York and the offload was Anchorage. It went through New Orleans because, because," she stalled as she pulled up her computer and slipped through the maze of numbers. "It went through

New Orleans because the shipper wanted it to go there *originally*. Once it arrived, the shipper changed his mind and sent it on to Anchorage."

"Who's the customer?"

"Harrison, Johnson, McDonagle. A firm in New York."

"Great. Just what we need is a pack of lawyers involved."

"Then you're in luck," she said. "According to this they're not lawyers. They're a cargo forwarding company." She punched a button and the printer next to the computer came to life. "Let's give them a call. I want to know why the cargo is losing weight."

"How do you know it's losing weight? Do you weigh everything as it goes onto a plane?"

"Yes we do. It's too easy to overload a plane. Had the crate gone from New York to Anchorage directly, it would have only been weighed once. In New York. Even if it was transferred a few times along the way it would have only have been weighed once. The difference here is the crate was sent with New Orleans as its final destination. When the crate arrived and was re-routed, new paperwork had to be issued. So it was weighed again."

"Why didn't someone in New Orleans notice the weight difference?"

"No reason to," she said as he stared at the screen. "It was offloaded and sitting on the warehouse floor. When it was re-routed, the airlines treated it like a new, incoming crate. The paper work was filled out and the crate was weighed just as if it had come through the front door in New Orleans. There was no reason to compare the weights. In fact, if we hadn't had this problem with Unicorn 739, it would have made it out the door here in Anchorage with no one asking at all. It's only by chance I caught it. You did, actually. If you hadn't asked, I wouldn't have checked."

"Let's get those guys on the phone."

Chapter 23

It took Mittles less than a heartbeat to snap the bolt on the warehouse bay door. It wasn't really hard because the Corporal and Jim and been working on it for three hours. Somehow the Corporal had scrounged up a sturdy piece of wire. Then he and Jim had gone to work on the bolt. They had chosen the warehouse bay door bolt because it was on the only doorway partially hidden from the security cameras. The fume hood for the smokers was in front of it.

In actuality Mittles was proud of the fact she had been the one to snap the bolt. Working with weights did count for something. Only she could have done it. The Corporal might have been good with his brains but brawn was not his strong point. Brawn was her strong point because she worked at it. It didn't mean she was stupid because she was strong. It just meant she was in good shape. The Corporal noticed such things.

It was too bad he was in the Army, Mittles mused.

Then she snapped the lock.

The Corporal was impressed.

There had been quite a bit of complaining when the Corporal and Jim had told all of their growing ranks of escapees-to-be everyone was going to have to take a turn in the smoking area. There had only been six smokers on the plane but the three conspirators needed a wall of flesh between themselves and the security cameras. The ex-smokers were the worst. Even just standing under the fume hood with a cigarette and pretending to smoke caused them to shake.

"I gave up smoking so I could live to see my grandchildren grow up," snapped an older woman. "Now I've got to start smoking to see my grand-children at all?"

"Could be the size of it," Mittles had whispered. "Right now there are no guarantees. We don't know what's going to happen."

"Let me tell you, young lady," the old woman leaned forward conspira-torially, "I'll tell you one thing that will happen. If we don't take care of ourselves no one else is going to do it."

It seemed to be the attitude of just about everyone else in the ware-house. It was like a prisoner-of-war camp coming together complete with the speaking out of the side of the mouth and distractions. The airline crew immediately established itself as the liaison for the hostages. Mittles dealt with the women; Jim with the men. The Corporal was the scavenger.

Of the 89 passengers, only a dozen were excluded.

"What do you mean I can't get involved?" snapped Jennifer when she was told she could not join in the ranks. "I'm good enough?"

"That's not it," Jim told her. "You're not the problem. Your kid is. We don't want anyone with kids involved."

"You don't like kids?"

"Love 'em. Too much, as a matter of fact. No. Kids talk. We don't want anything to get blown because a kid doesn't know to keep quiet. Second, if we make a break for it, the women and children, in this case, go last. The best chance of survival we have is to get people out and running. If we can get a dozen people out, one of them is going to find a phone. Kids will slow us down. Besides, we've got more important things for you to do."

"Like what?" Ayanna said suspiciously.

"Keep the main man busy. Off balance. Ask for things. Diapers. Medicine. Tampons. Whatever. Start a Women-With-Children's group and keep him busy. Give us time to try something."

"I guess I create some problems."

"Good. Get the other mothers to help you. Have the kids upset an apple cart here and there. Kids are good at screwing things up. Provide a distrac-tion. Many of them. All the time."

"If there is any one thing Jason is good at," said Jennifer with the voice of exasperation, "it's being a distraction."

As it had worked out, the WWC group, Women-With-Children, had done better than expected. It included six women and two men. They encourage the kids to knock over a trash can in the kitchen scattering used food all over the floor. Another child skinned a knee allowing his mother to stand in front of a security camera with blood all over her hands. A father encouraged his son to jerk the phone out of the wall while the extortionist was speaking and then stood with a KIDS!-what-are-they-going-to-do-next? look on his face.

All the while, the Corporal and Jim were working on the bolt to the combination lock.

"What do you think we'll see when the door comes up?" asked Sam.

"I don't know," replied the Corporal. "All I want to see is five or six people through the door and running by the time the alarm sounds."

"You think there is an alarm?"

"It would surprise me if there wasn't."

When the bolt almost severed, Mittles took a look at it. She didn't like being in the smoker's area but liked what she saw with regard to the bolt. "You guys did a good job. I'm impressed," she gave the bolt a pull.

"How much longer before you can snap it?" Jim was nervously looking over his shoulder.

"None." Mittles handed him the padlock. The wire and her strength and been enough. "When's the great escape?"

"Let's adjourn to the men's room." said the Corporal.

Chapter 24

"Have you been a good girl and done your research?" The voice was on her phone again. Ingratiating. Patronizing. Smooth on the outside and choppy in message, like the ocean before a storm.

"If you mean the Medusa connection, yeah. I found lots of earth, air and water images."

"Good. Good. You won't have to worry about earth. Save it for another day. Like tomorrow. Concentrate on the other two."

"You know I hate riddles."

"Oh. Well, I think I could find another reporter who does."

There was silence for a moment.

"I can live with the indignity."

"I thought so. Now as this caper winds down, Gerry, dear, it's going to get a bit messy. Things happening fast. So you won't have the luxury of time you've had so far. Do you understand me?"

"Meaning?"

"Meaning wear your tenny sneakers all the time. The next drop," he chortled, "this makes me so excited! The next drop is going to be for another $5 million in gems."

"Numbers are going up."

"I love it when you talk that way. It excites me. Yes, the numbers are going up. $5 million so far, $5 million today, $5 million tomorrow and the balance shortly thereafter."

"If you can get away with it, it's going to pay very well."

"It's not *IF* we can get away with it; it's *when* we get away with it. For a journalist you have a problem with your adverbs."

"Ooh, an educated man. Not many of them left. OK. Where do I go for this one?"

"You had such a terrible time with the evil Chief of Detectives last time I'm going to take you right to the end of the chase so you'll be there for the crowning moment."

"Where will that be?"

"I'm not going to tell you now. I'll call you with ten minutes to spare. You and your cameraman best be ready to roll when I call, Jah?"

"Jah, we'll be ready to go."

Chapter 25

Ayanna dropped into the chair at the Command Center as though the weight of the world was on her shoulders. She had snagged six hours of sleep a day earlier but she felt as though she had barely closed her eyes when she was up and moving again. She even tried an old college trick, sleeping in her clothes, but hadn't seemed to work. She was exhausted and had still spent the last four hours collecting the next ransom payoff, $5 million in stones.

She was getting her 76th cup of coffee when the guards from the armored car came into the room with the $5 million in gems. The AIC spread them on the table and everyone oohed and aahed them. The AIC called Ayanna over.

"Ayanna, I want you to see this because you're making the delivery. What do you see?"

Ayanna looked at him strangely. "I hope I see about $5 million in precious gems."

"That you do," the AIC said. "What else do you see?"

"A leather bag?"

"Good." The AIC tossed her the leather jewelry bag. "What's inside of it?"

Ayanna dug her hand into the bag and felt around. There was nothing there. "What was I supposed to find?"

"You found it. Nothing. I just wanted to show you there is no directional device with the stones. Do you want to check the stones individually?"

"No. I want you to catch the people who are extorting us."

The AIC smiled sickly. "We're all in this together. The FBI just works a little differently. We'll be behind you the whole way. You just won't see us."

It was the 'we'll be behind you the whole way' statement causing Ayanna concern. It was one of those clichés meaning exactly the opposite of what was intended. People who were *behind you the whole way* were not there at all. You were one your own. Until you succeeded and then you were part of the team. If you failed you were on your own. In the wilderness. 'We'll be behind you the whole way' and 'We're all in this together' were code words for 'be sure and cover your butt because we will only be there to share in the glory.'

"The extortionists will know you are there even without a tracking device." It was an honest assessment.

The AIC dodged the comment. "We've got agents on the ground all over town, cars will be tracking you with this," he held up a directional device. "You will carry one on your person. We've got a speed boat in the Inlet and a chopper ready to fly. Wherever they go they are going to have a hard time staying ahead of us."

This did not sound good to Ayanna. What did they know she didn't? She was going to carry the directional device on her person. On her *person*? That sounded a lot like they were expecting her to be taken hostage. This was definitely not good news. Speed boat and chopper? What kind of a drop off was this going to be? This was not turning out to be a good day.

"I don't know if I like walking around with a directional device on me," she snapped. This wasn't just unexpected; it was unacceptable. "What happens if I get searched?"

"So what if you do?" The AIC was not pulling any punches. "They don't care about you. All they care about is this bag," he pointed to the leather gem bag bulging with $5 million in stones. "One other thing."

"I'm breathless with anticipation." Ayanna was not looking forward to a surprise.

"The thieves did not specify this Noonan character was to accompany you. So you're going alone."

"But, he's . . ."

"He's not part of the show," the AIC flatly stated. "He went on the first drop because he was requested by name. There was no such request this time. He stays; you go."

Ayanna was still arguing with the AIC when Noonan made his appearance. He arrived as in he was suddenly there. One moment Ayanna was fighting to have him on the drop team and the next instant Noonan was right beside her agreeing with the AIC.

Agreeing with AIC!

What kind of garbage was this?

Agreeing with the AIC?!

Her partner in crime-stopping?

"This is quite a surprise," she said snidely to Noonan. "I thought we were a team."

"We are and the AIC is correct. They wanted me to be there for the first drop. Now they're getting serious. Besides, I have other things to do."

"Do you know anything I ought to know?" The AIC used the penetrating stare FBI agents practice in front of mirrors every morning.

Noonan returned the stare with a mild *who knows?* look. "I looked into the disposition of all the cargo on Unicorn 739."

"I didn't authorize any cargo to be released," the AIC was instantly animated.

"None of it has been released," returned Noonan. "There are at least two suspicious packages. One is an antique motorcycle which doesn't look much like an antique and the other is a freight igloo which has been losing weight since it was shipped in New York."

"Losing weight?" The AIC clearly wasn't sure he had heard correctly.

"Odd but correct. It weighed 200 pounds in New York and is down to 136 here. I've put in a call to the company which sent the package, a freight forwarder in New York, but I haven't gotten a call back yet."

"Losing weight as if someone is taking something out of the crate?"

"I asked but, no, you can't do that. Cargo goes in and gets shipped. No one gets into the cargo after it has been logged in."

"The FBI does. Harry!" A man with a flat top virtually snapped to attention when his name was called. He walked over to the AIC with the gait of a weightlifter.

"Sir?"

"Go with this man, Chief of Detectives Noonan from the Sandersonville Police Department. He is going to show you an igloo. Get a warrant to open it."

"Yes, Sir." Harry stuck out his arm to Noonan as if he were saying "Shall we go?"

"Is there anything else I should know?" The AIC was not going to let anything slip his attention.

"You know everything I know."

"Fine. That will be all." Then he turned abruptly toward Ayanna.

To Harry, Noonan said, "I guess that's my cue to go downstairs."

Harry didn't say a word; he just stood with his arm extended toward the door. "And the gesture," Noonan said to Ayanna as he turned to leave, "is about as friendly as the FBI ever gets."

Chapter 26

The ramp had not been difficult to construct. It had not been difficult to construct because it was not going to be a permanent structure. It only had to be stable for two seconds. No longer. Then it had to have the ability to self-destruct. No loud bangs, puffs of smoke or anything dramatic. Just a simple pull of a cord and the cement block footing would collapse into the water. No wood here. Wood would float.

The Fisherman jumped from the shore back into the boat. Nosing his way out of the thicket carpeting the shoreline, he headed toward Anchorage. He was going to his favorite fishing hole: Sebastian Seafoods.

Chapter 27

This was getting ridiculous! If it wasn't the fire alarm it was the plugged toilet or the spilled trash can. He'd been to the pharmacy twice in the last ten hours – once at three in the morning – for bandages, tampons, aspirin, and cigarettes. How could there be so many smokers? There were more smokers on this flight than in every waiting room on the West Coast! What the Sam Hill was going on? There had to be something going on. There was too much activity for these people. Yes, there were close to 100 of them but they all wanted something different. A lot of different. All the time.

There were only two of them to watch the hostages. This was supposed to be the easy part of the caper. After all, how hard was it going to be to keep 95 people happy for two days? Everything they needed was in there! Food, pop, entertainment, games. What were they asking for? Radios, cigarettes, hair brushes, Windex and paper towels, Lysol and paper towels, diapers, pampers, Pop tarts, batteries for hearing aids. The list just would not end. Not a lot of repeats either. Right after he made one trip, the requests would start again. Cigarettes?! What were they doing, eating them?

When the door alarm went off, the extortionist was prepared for yet another disaster. What was it going to be this time? By the time he got to the screen and flicked on the security cameras, the alarm had gone off.

Gone off?

What?!

Panning the room by letting his eyes rove from screen to screen, all he could see was people milling around and looking at the television screen.

Nothing seemed to be out of place. He gave special attention to the doors. All three of the conventional doors were secure. He could tell by the light over the doors. There was no way anyone could have gotten out those doors. He could still see the bracings which welded the door shut. The double doors were still secure too. The outside camera showed the truck backed up to the double doors just in case.

That only left the massive warehouse door. It had been bolted too. He stared at it trying to see the lock. He couldn't because it was behind fume hood and there was a wall of people between his view and the door.

This was not good.

When the warehouse door went up again, this time without the alarm going off, he was more than distressed.

Chapter 28

"I think you're right," Harry with the FBI said flatly to Noonan as they looked over the motorcycle. This was about as excited as an FBI agent every got. "It doesn't look like an antique to me."

"I don't know why it makes any difference," Noonan responded. "Nothing is coming off the plane anyway. It is interesting."

"You said you contacted the owner?" Harry looked at the shipping label, "George Sampson?"

"I left him a message. His recorder said he was on his way into Anchorage to pick up his motorcycle. He might be in the crowd of people downstairs waiting for something to happen."

"It's worth a check. Now, what about this igloo."

Noonan took a step sideways and tapped an igloo. "This was originally shipped out of New York by a freight forwarding company. When it was loaded in New York it weighed 200 pounds. When it arrived in New Orleans it weighed a little over 160 pounds."

"New Orleans? What's it doing here?"

"It was originally shipped to New Orleans. After it had arrived, the freight forwarding company called and ordered it shipped to Anchorage on Unicorn. It was weighed in New Orleans as if it were new, incoming cargo. No one looked at the old manifest because, technically, it had arrived. It was not technically a transfer. It was a new shipment."

"So no one knew the weight differential."

"When it arrived here it was weighed again?"

"No it hasn't been weighed here. Just in New York and New Orleans. Logically it should weigh less now. Why don't we just open it?"

"It could get sticky if there's evidence in there. A good lawyer could say it was an illegal search and seizure." Harry was a by-the-book man.

"A better prosecutor would say it was reasonable to assume it was intricately linked to a crime in progress in which about 100 lives were at stake."

Harry looked at him or a moment. "Just a second," he said and whipped out his cell phone like he was drawing a revolver. He walked into the corridor to get a better connection while Noonan looked over the cargo one more time. Nothing seemed out of the ordinary. Then Harry came back.

"We're going to open it," he said flatly as he pointed at the igloo. We've got Airport Security on their way now. It's in their chain of command. We'll be professional witnesses."

"I've always wanted to be a professional," said Noonan.

Chapter 29

Eighteen seconds after Ayanna left Anchorage International Airport, there was not a single reporter—print, tabloid, radio, television or public broadcast—who was not following her. The entourage, which included the FBI undercover and the Anchorage Police out of cover, was more of a parade than a kidnapping payoff drop. There was even a line of cabs, already retained, ready to follow wherever Ayanna went.

The only reporter absent was Gerry McComber. She was sitting in a car staring at her cell phone, waiting for a call she was praying would come. She knew Ayanna was on the move –every radio station in town was tailing her. Gerry was stuck where she was. She had no control over the voice on the cell line. He had obviously called every news outlet in the city so where did that leave her?

Chapter 30

For Ayanna, the day had started badly and it was so much worse now she shuddered to think what the next hour would bring. She was wearing her tennis shoes so she could run; at least the pouch with the diamonds didn't weigh much. She didn't have her gun either. She went out the door of the Command Center and into a cab. Her instructions were to be at the telephone booth at the Railroad Terminal at exactly 2 p.m.

She was.

So was the crowd, not even staying far enough back to give the appearance of being unobtrusive. When the phone rang, Ayanna picked up the receiver slowly.

"No small talk," came the voice. "Your entourage is expecting something."

"Franz Kafka would have loved you. Why are you doing this?" said Ayanna calmly. "This may be a joke to you but there are 95 people whose lives are on the line. One screw up anywhere along the line and we are talking mass murder here."

"Naw! It won't come to that, dear lady," said the voice. "We have everything well in hand. Besides, this is America. How can you tell the press no?"

"Well, let me tell you something you haven't thought of. You can take the money and go to a lot of places on earth, places where no one will send you back. If one person dies, there's not a country on earth where you'll be safe."

"Love! It's all in the plan! Now, here's what you are going to do. Take a cab to the Aurora Borealis Mall. Go into the Parking Lot. It should stall a few of your friends. Then take the escalator to the Fifth Floor. Do you know where the Ladies' Room is up there?"

"Yes."

"Right down the hall from the Ladies Room is an emergency exit. Go out the exit and then down the stairs to the second floor. Go back into the Mall and head for the Williwaw Steakhouse at the other end of the Mall. Go directly through the Steakhouse to the Emergency Exit there and down the stairs. Go across Fifth Avenue and go into the Knik Inlet Bookstore. There's a payphone in the back. Be at the phone in ten minutes."

"What you are asking for is a tall order."

"What I am asking you to do is lose our friends with the press. They've had their taste. No one ever said this would be easy. Now, be a good little bird and do what you've been told."

The line went dead.

Ayanna turned around to find a cab. The press was a mob on the sidewalk. Television cameras were being set up and newspaper photographers were snapping like crazy. She hailed the only cab in downtown Anchorage someone from the press had not already hired and headed for the Aurora Borealis Mall.

The perp had been correct. There were so many reporters following her they had a hard time finding their own cabs much less following hers. The road from the Railroad Terminal to city center angled up a hill and Ayanna was well up the hillside before her entourage was in gear. Bumper to bumper they followed her through the downtown and then up into the Aurora Borealis Garage, parking for the Aurora Borealis Mall.

If Ayanna had been walking with a baton she would have called the progression a parade. It looked like a parade. It moved like a parade or a convoy, everyone headed in the same direction. It did not have a route, every car simply followed the one ahead with the second car following Ayanna's cab. Where she went they followed.

The joyous procession followed her a whole two blocks before life got complicated. Getting *to* the Aurora Borealis Garage was not hard. Getting *in* was another matter altogether. The automated gate created the first obstacle for the press of the press. Cars could only enter one at a time, every car being required to wait for the vehicle in front to pluck a ticket from the dispenser before the gate would go up and the car would enter the garage.

The wait was made even longer because the gate came down behind every vehicle as it went through. The proceeding vehicle then had to wait for the gate to come all the way down, then the driver had to push the entry button, wait for a paper ticket to come out and then wait again for the gate to lift. It was a time consuming process.

It took the reporters less than five seconds to see what was going to happen. If they had to sit in their cabs to get into the mall parking garage, they'd lose Ayanna. If they left their cabs, they wouldn't be able to get back to them to follow Ayanna if and when she left the Mall. The only alternative for the reporters was to leave their cabbie with a cell phone and call when they knew where Ayanna was going.

It was as though everyone came up to the same conclusion at the exact same second. Instantaneously all cab doors opened and reporters flooded out, chasing Ayanna up the incline into the skywalk to the mall. The plug of humanity clogged the walkway and jammed the escalator. Everyone in the Mall looked toward the head of the pack expecting to see a celebrity in town. All they saw was a small woman with a leather fanny pack who could easily have just been a member of the public caught up in the frenzy.

With a determined step, Ayanna headed for the hallway leading to the Women's Restroom on the fifth floor. Unless someone had actually been in the hallway, it was deceptive. From the food courtyard, it appeared to be a long hallway with Men's and Women's Restrooms at the back flanking a bank of phones. The phones were clearly visible from the court yard but there was not enough room in the hallway to accommodate the reporters. The moment Ayanna headed into the hallway, it was assumed she was going to be using the phones. By the time she had made it halfway down the hall, the television cameras were set up, peering unblinkingly at the bank of phones. Ayanna snapped into the focus of the collective lens just as she reached the phones.

Then she did something totally unexpected. To the shock and horror of the reporters, Ayanna walked right by the phones, pushed through the emergency exit and headed downstairs.

Then the alarm for the entire mall went off.

Mack Sennett could not even have orchestrated what happened next. The Keystone Kops had been graceful compared to the stampede to make it to the stairwell. The crush of reporters did exactly what the extortionists had expected them to do: plug the hallway and Emergency Exit. By the time some of the reporters were able to extricate themselves from the mob pushing on the door, Ayanna was on the second floor re-entering the mall.

In the meantime, the alarm had not raised a single eyebrow in the mall among the shoppers. There was a moment of indifference among shoppers and then, finally, at the urging of all retailers, the customers were asked to leave the building. By the time Ayanna entered the second floor, there was a general migration underway moving toward the exits. She made the front door of the Williwaw Steakhouse well ahead of the press. By the time the first of the reporters made it onto the second floor, all anyone could be see was Ayanna's back as she disappeared into the restaurant. With so many people headed out, there was no way for the press to catch up with her. She was out the restaurant's Emergency Exit and across the street before the press made it to the front door of the restaurant. By the time the press got down to the street, the mass of humanity from customers having to leave the mall was so great she could easily have been swallowed by the mob.

She wasn't in the mob. She was across the street in the Knik Inlet Bookstore.

As she approached the pay phone in the back of the bookstore, the phone was ringing. This time there was no small talk. She was told to exit the back of the store, cross the alley and come out on Fourth Street and take a cab.

"Where do I tell the cabbie to go?" asked Ayanna.

"I'll call you on your cell phone," said the voice. "Now move. We don't want any reporters now, do we?"

This time Ayanna didn't argue. She went out the back door of the book store and cut across the alley and emerged on Fourth Avenue just in time to catch a cab.

"I wonder who gave him my cell phone number," Ayanna mused as the cabbie looked at her, waiting for instructions. "The airport," she said. "Just take it slowly."

Chapter 31

"Gerry, my dear, are you ready for your rendezvous with destiny?" Gerry nearly jumped out of her shoes with relief. "I thought you'd forgotten me!"

"Not a chance, love. This game is far from over. Now, be a good little girl and take your cameraman and go to the Park Strip. Set up on the 9th Street side somewhere between H and I streets. Make sure you are set up because things are going to happen very fast so don't delay."

This time the voice did not stay online to banter.

Chapter 32

"I need some salmon in the round," the Fisherman said as he stood at the counter. "I know it's a little odd but my wife's family is from the Philippines,"

"I understand perfectly," said the clerk. "I think we've got two in the freezer right now."

The Fisherman opened his wallet to pay cash. "I'll pick them up tomorrow. Can you take them out of the freezer so they'll be thawed by then? Then I'll pick them up, OK?"

"Not a problem. Do you want them in plastic bags?"

"Nope. I'll have an ice chest."

"Fine with me. What time?"

Chapter 33

The instant a line of outside light from under the massive door pierced the gloom of the warehouse interior, there were 89 passengers and a crew of 6 ready to exit. Not just ready to exit, quite literally chomping on the bit. This was not just an escape in the romantic sense of the term. It was a life-or-death matter. It also might be, again quite literally, a once-in-a-lifetime chance. It was more than escape; it was survival.

The instant the door rose to waist level the crowd surged out of the warehouse, those in front dipping their heads as the door came up. By the time the door was six feet and rising, the crowd was half out of the door.

Chapter 34

C hief of Detectives Heinz Noonan was dressed as if he were exactly what he was. He had an old uniform in Anchorage, in the days when he weighed less, his hair was browner and his crow's feet shallower. It had been for some kind of a law and order conference or speech and Lorelei had insisted he leave the uniform at her parent's house.

"You never know when you might need a uniform in Alaska," she had said but both of them knew full well what she really meant. The bulky uniform in an Alaska closet was more space for her clothes in their Sandersonville closet. Noonan had not cared one way or the other, particularly since it had always been hard for him to throw out old uniforms. He wasn't sure what he was going to do with the collection he had, but someday he would figure it out.

Today, however, the uniform was a blessing. After he had left Ayanna to make the drop, Noonan had put in a call to his Department and gotten the green light to visit the Alaska Crime Lab. The Lab, barely a decade old, was the pride of law enforcement community. Prior to the crime lab, every piece of evidence needed for trial was sent to the FBI laboratory in Quantico, Virginia. Because Alaska had a 45-day rule, every piece of evidence being used in a trial had to be processed within 45 days of its seizure. This meant a bloody towel had to be sent across the United States to Virginia, examined, processed and analyzed then make it back to Alaska within 45 days. With other states sending their evidence as well, the lab was more of a criminal evidence train station than a crime detection superstation.

As each state established its own crime lab, fewer and fewer pieces of evidence had to be sent to Virginia. Alaska, the last state to build a crime lab, was pleased only the most arcane of evidence actually had to leave the state now. DNA and ballistics were sent out of state, of course, but even the most sophisticated tox screens could be done locally.

"We are quite proud of our crime lab," the public relations flack told him.

"You should be. It's a fine facility." Noonan said in spite of the fact he was still sitting in the Visitor's Room. To himself, Noonan thought, *I guess I can't be important since I'm meeting with Public Relations, not the Director.*

"You come highly recommended, Chief," the flack went on. "Your request went straight down our food chain."

"Well," Noonan feigned a look of concern, "I'm helping the Anchorage Police on an important case. I'm a food chain kind of guy. I just want to make sure my boss knows what I'm doing. He gets very angry when he gets taken by surprise."

"I know the feeling well," said the flack as he rolled his eyes. "Your Commissioner called our Director and he called me. Directly. I was ordered to provide you with what you wanted."

"Did he tell you what I wanted?"

"This." The flack handed Noonan a very small plastic pill bottle. "I was specifically ordered to give it to you and ask no questions. So I won't."

"Ask questions or give it to me?"

The flack quickly handed Noonan the bottle. "Oh, you are funny, sir. Here's the bottle. I do need you to sign a form, however."

"Always the forms. Not a problem. Do you have a pen?"

The flack handed Noonan a sheet of paper and a pen. Noonan looked at the paper and signed.

"I'll bet there are at least 100 people a week who wished it would be this easy," said the flack as he poked the sheet of paper with the pen.

"It would save a lot of money," replied Noonan, "but it would upset the legal system like you would not believe."

Chapter 35

"I don't like this," said Ayanna into her communicator. "We're being set up again."

"Where are you to go?" asked the AIC, his voice a buzz on the cell phone.

"9th and F," she responded. Ayanna was sitting in the back seat of a taxi, hunched over so no one could see her. By now every one of the reporters she had ditched at the Aurora Borealis Mall would be out scouring the city streets for her. Unfortunately she would not be hard to find. Already she could hear the chatter over the taxi radio as the reporters tried to pin down which cab she was in and where it was at that moment. Her cabbie, a black woman, oblivious to the chatter, didn't know who Ayanna was but assumed she was hiding from an angry husband.

"I can take you to the AWAIC Shelter," the cabbie had said as Ayanna slipped in the back of the cab and lay down on the seat. "They help women in trouble with their boyfriends and husbands."

"No," she had said. "Just take me to 9th and F."

"That's the park strip, girl."

"Just drive."

Now, over the radio, Ayanna was hearing the cabs, one at a time, confirm where they were and who their passenger was. When her cabby's turn came, he looked at her over her right shoulder. "I won't give you away, girl" she said. "You get your life together, hear? No need to take guff from no man and then hide in the back of a cab."

"Are you there yet?" the AIC came over Ayanna's cell phone.

"Not yet."

"That's on the Park Strip. Get out and I'll get the chopper airborne."

When she got out at 9th and F the cabbie was still concerned. "You sure you don't want to go to AWAIC, girl?"

"No," Ayanna said as she handed her a twenty. "I'm fine. Just don't tell anyone I'm here."

"Your secrets safe with me." The black woman shook her head and left.

The cab hadn't covered more than a dozen feet when Ayanna's phone buzzed to life.

"This is the end of the trail for you, Ayanna. Listen very carefully. I want you to cross the street and take the bike path across the Park Strip. That's *across*, Ayanna, not along. I want you to take the bike path *crossing* the Park Strip. Got it?"

"Got it."

"Do not hang up this phone. Do you understand me?"

"Yes."

"Good. You are being watched. Now progress down the bike path. Good girl. You are doing just fine."

"You are not going to be fine when I catch up with you."

"First things first, love."

Anchorage, by United States standards, was a very young town. It was so young, there were people still living in town who had been born in the tent city alongside Ship Creek. The city itself had been founded in 1915. There weren't a lot of them, but enough the Chamber of Commerce or Rotary could always find an old timer to talk about the good old days and how Alaska had gone down the drain with oil and drugs and children who didn't get to school on time.

Until the Second World War, Anchorage had a population of a little more than 4,000, almost all of them clustered between 9th Avenue and Ship Creek, the latter being the equivalent of First Street.

When the city had been laid out, it was designed so even a Norwegian could get around. To accommodate the large population of Scandinavians who had come to Anchorage to work on the railroad, the city planner had specifically not included the letter "J" as a street because of the confusion the letter would cause to Scandinavians. Starting at the base line of the tent city, all streets running north and south to the west were letter streets: A, B, C, D so on with the exception of J. Streets running north and south to the *east* were alphabetic: Barrow, Cordova, Denali so on with a "J" street included: Juneau. Streets running east and west started with First Street, in essence, Ship Creek, and proceeded to grow in numerical to the south.

The numbers did not grow very far. Only to 9th where the city's landing strip was located. Because the city had so many pilots, the landing strip was necessarily lengthy. At both far ends of the landing strip were tie downs for the planes, mechanical shacks and, with the coming of the Second World War, Quonsets simply erupted from the earth like mushrooms on a wet lawn.

Because all land beyond the park strip was federal, there were lots of squatters. Some homesteaders but lots of squatters. It was an idyllic moment in Alaska history and then, with the surprise bombing of Dutch Harbor and the Japanese seizure of Kiska and Attu – the only square inches of American soil held by a foreign power since the War of 1812 – Alaska became the front lines. Overnight the Territory was on a war footing. Army and Air Corp personnel by the cargo plane full landed and turned Anchorage into an armed camp. When the Alaska-Canada Highway was completed, the in-migration flow increased fast enough for Anchorage to triple in size in five years. It went up by a factor of four the next decade. Between 1940 and 1960, the population went up ten times, to 44,000. Over the next 20 years, the population went up four times again and by 2000 had doubled again.

One of the growing pains Anchorage had to face was the desperate need for more land on which to build homes. The first and most obvious place to construct was the already cleared landing strip. This was quickly nixed by the City Council because moving the strip would mean an increase in cost to get cargo to local businesses – a constituency near and dear to the publicly-elected members – and it made sense to have the landing strip in the center of the growing town so passengers would be conveniently close to the strip whether they lived on the north or south side of town.

It was not until the 1950s the modern airport was built. Even as the last of the bush planes left the landing strip, the city's founding Fathers and Mother's did not want to see this last vestige of Alaska's heritage be swallowed by claptrap, sheetrock and fly paper. So the old landing strip was preserved as the Park Strip, a ribbon of land one block wide running from L Street on the south to Barrow Street on the north. Over the years an elementary school was built on the eastern end of the park strip and, gradually, tennis courts and a hockey rink began moving from west from the school. A massive flag pole was erected midway down the strip and there was a sprinkling of small buildings, flower gardens, a monument and some pathways the linked 9th Avenue with 10th. There were only three streets cutting the park strip.

Unlike the rest of the city, the Park Strip do *not* have one thing in common with every other street in Anchorage: overhead wires.

When Ayanna reached the center of the park strip on the walkway, she was told to stop.

"Face due west," the voice said on her phone. "If you are not sure which way west is, put your back to the mountains."

Ayanna did as she was told, vaguely aware there was at least one camera set up a block from her on the 9th Street side of the strip.

"Now. When I say **go**, you are to start running right down the center of the strip. Due west. Do not stop and do not look back. About twenty yards in front of you is a white handkerchief on the ground. You will gently place the bag of gems on the handkerchief as you pass. Make absolutely sure those gems do not spill and only slow down long enough to drop off the bag. *Directly on top of the handkerchief.* I repeat, *directly on top of the handkerchief.* Do not stop. I repeat, do not stop. You are to keep running as fast as you can until you come to the end of the Park Strip. Only then can you turn around."

"Run?"

"Correct. At top speed. The only thing you have to do is put the bag of gems directly on top of the handkerchief. Then you are to increase the speed of your run and do not stop until you reach I Street. Then take a cab away from the area."

"What if I . ." she started to say.

"**Go!**" said the voice and the line went dead.

It was only then she saw the reporters start to tumble out of cars on F Street and start to clog the 9th Avenue corner.

Chapter 36

It was probably the first press conference in history where no one showed up. With hindsight it was to be expected. The only press people not chasing Ayanna around town were secretaries and salespeople. They didn't do hard news. They did a nine-to-five. Everyone else was playing gumshoe.

The lack of press didn't bother the Director of Homeland Security for Alaska, Anchorage Office. As a matter of fact, he liked it better than way. He could use his own people to film the press conference, take nothing but friendly questions from the crowd of family members who were concerned about the safety of their loved ones and then splice the tape into department-friendly public affairs spots which his staff would personally deliver to the radio and television stations. It was canned. It was perfect. It was exactly what news should be if you were with Homeland Security.

Standing as if he were Richard Burton about to give an Academy Award winning performance – except Burton never won an Academy Award though he was nominated seven times – Henry Harrison looked every inch a Richard Burton. He had the perfect visage for a United States Senator or, at the very least, a Governor. With a mesomorphic six-foot-two frame topped with salt-and-pepper hair, he was the prototypic politician. Even if he wasn't, his staff and the video camera would make him seem so. And they were very good at this job.

"I have a few announcements," he said, pleased his sonorous voice quieted the small but milling crowd so quickly. This was going to be a good video clip for the news – all channels and FOX. Maybe even CNN? "As quickly as possible I'd like to give you an update of what has happened to this point."

Someone started to speak but Harrison raised his hand in a casual gesture working magic in silencing the questioner. "As I'm sure you can understand we are midway in this matter and I can only tell you what will not endanger your loved ones. I would also ask you not to speak to the press until this is over. We have to assume the kidnappers are watching the news and we don't want to give them anything they can use to aggravate an already dangerous situation."

This was true but it was like locking the barn after the horse had been stolen. Everyone who had wanted to talk to the press already had and there was no way he could keep anyone else from talking to the press after his conference. The comment was for show, not for go.

The room was deathly silent.

Harrison turned his good side to the camera. "For those who did not hear me earlier, my name is Henry Harrison, just like the former President, and I am the Director of Homeland Security for Alaska. At the present time, though both I and you are loath to do it, we are paying the ransom demands for the kidnappers."

He smiled inwardly as he said the words "I and you." It made him one with the audience. It would be a great sound bite on the evening news.

"Our first obligation is to the living. We will sort out the financial responsibility later. What I can tell you is the kidnappers have asked the ransom be made in four payments. The first payment was made yesterday and it was picked up successfully. As we are speaking the second payment is being made. We do not expect any difficulties as we are following the instructions of the kidnappers to the letter."

He paused for a moment. Then he repeated and emphasized the last three words, "to the letter."

It was pure theater and he loved it. He raised his hands and spread them, a practiced gesture which made him Moses-like. "I will be more than pleased to answer any questions which you may have as long as the answers do not pose a threat to the hostages. Yes, Ma'am." He pointed to an older woman in the front.

"How much longer is this going to last? Do we know the people are all right?"

"Did everyone hear the question?" He looked over the crowd and no one yelled for the questions to be repeated. "The kidnappers have indicated they want everything done within two days, 48 hours. We have met their timetable so far. I am hopeful we will be out of this jungle within a matter of hours." He paused for a moment and then, dramatically, leaned forward and said in a soft voice, "As far as I know, Ma'am, there has been no trouble with the hostages and we are all praying for their safe return."

This was basically a lie. No one had heard from the hostages. Or, for that matter, from the extortionists about the fate of the hostages. It was not going to make Henry Harrison any friends by telling the relatives the truth.

So he lied.

He didn't look at it as a lie.

He looked at it as pragmatism.

Or politics.

Either term would have been correct. Both were lid holders, something to hold over the simmering pot until the heat went away. Until the hostages were freed, he was the man on the hot seat. Then he wanted to be the man in the limelight.

A man from the back yelled, "I've heard we're going to have to pay those slime balls $25 million!" There were some very unpleasant murmurs from the crowd.

"It is true, sir." Harrison craned his neck majestically as if he straining to hear the voice. "Unfortunately it is true. As I mentioned before, we are paying because we want the hostages back alive. When they are safe, then we'll see about getting our money back."

"I don't have $25 million," snapped a voice from the center of the crowd. "Neither does my mother. You are going to have a hard time getting $25 million out of me." There was general approval among the family members.

Harrison smiled like a Dutch uncle. "Not to worry. We're not going to ask you to re-pay the ransom. Who actually pays the $25 million will be debated between the City of Anchorage, State of Alaska, Anchorage International Airport, Unicorn Airlines, the Seattle-Tacoma International Airport and the insurance companies of all parties I just mentioned. In the unlikely event they cannot pay, the Office of Homeland Security will handle the matter. All we want from you are your prayers and cooperation until this matter is resolved."

He loved this last line. It just *came* to him. Was he *good* or what? The only thing he left out was the American flag. He couldn't use the flag yet because he didn't know if the extortionists were terrorist or not. If they were Muslim they were terrorists. Or skinheads. Until he knew for sure he had to be careful not to wave the flag. Then again, just let one hint drop they wore turbans and he planned to flap the flag from every flagpole in the 49th state.

There was a moment of silence and Harrison chose this moment to end the conference. He had enough footage with good questions. Now he needed a gem of a wrap-up, which, as it happened, he had been working on for hours – right down to the facial twitches and warble in his voice.

"It is truly sad day in the annuals of our nation when innocent Americans can be snatched off American airlines in America. Once this has been peacefully resolved," he leaned forward, toward the camera with a sincere look in his eye and a waver in his voice, "the Office of Homeland Security is going to make absolutely certain this never happens again. The perpetrators will be chased all over the planet if necessary. They can run but they cannot hide." He paused again. This time, not for emphasis, but to give a second of dead air on the video tape to make the next sentence the noteworthy sound bite of the conference. "In civilized societies there is no room for terrorism, no excuse for kidnapping and no reason to put innocent lives at risk anywhere in the world."

He gave another second of dead air to the video.

"Thank you and God bless."

The camera snapped off the Harrison was out of the room as if he had been sent on a mission by God.

Chapter 37

Ayanna's first clue something was happening was when the growing gaggle of news reporters started yelling and pointing behind her. Even though she was running as fast as she could she dared a quick look behind her. Just as she half-turned, an ultralight hit the ground and rolled to a California stop beside the handkerchief and the bag of gems she had just left on the Park Strip. In the next instant the ultralight was reaching for the sky. The craft was fifteen feet above Ayanna when it passed overhead – and the pilot gave her a goodbye wave.

Chapter 38

"You are not going to believe what I just saw," said the pilot of the Alaska State Trooper chopper as he looked out his side window. He had been on patrol in the downtown area for the past hour, following the elusive Ayanna as she was sent from pillar to post by the extortionists. He had always known where she was. Once she had been separated from the gems, he was to watch the spot like an eagle eye in the sky.

What he had not expected was an ultralight.

"I've got a pickup on the package," he said into the microphone as he banked toward the departing ultralight. "It is an ultralight flying low and fast. I am in pursuit."

"Just keep the suspect in sight," were the instructions over his headset. "Let us know where and when he lands and we will apprehend. We have the downtown covered like white on rice so wherever he lands we will have an officer on the ground within a block. He will have a hard time getting out of town. We've got him in a box."

"Affirmative," snapped the pilot and gave chase.

Using the ultralight for the pickup was an excellent idea. It was small, maneuverable and could land just about anywhere there was a short landing area. Those advantages were counterbalanced by the fact it had to come down somewhere. Wherever it landed, the police would be on the landing area in a matter of moments, even seconds. The city was locked down with police and troopers at all points of the compass so it was hard to believe the ultralight was going to be able to set down anywhere and not be taken within a *very* short period of time. The ultralight had taken the gems and was in the air. Now it had to come down.

It was not a long chase. Either the ultralight anticipated the arrival of the helicopter or planned for it. Most likely it was the former for the small aircraft waited for the helicopter to get close and then it veered steeply to the right, heading due north directly into the downtown area. The trooper chopper took more time to make the bank and by the time it was heading north, the ultralight had several blocks on its pursuer. Then the ultralight took another bank to the right, now going due east, and blasted down Fifth Avenue at the third story level. All along Fifth Avenue tourists looked up to watch the small plane whip by.

This was dangerous for an ultralight and suicide for a chopper.

So the chopper rose, putting lots of air between itself and the ground. By the time it had risen above the tops of the downtown structures the pilot could see the ultralight start a 180 degree turn over the old City Hall and double back on Fourth Avenue. The ultralight was moving so fast by the time the trooper chopper started its turn, the ultralight was already passing beneath it, headed due west now.

"He's headed for the Inlet," the pilot said as he rose and looked over his shoulder. "Right down Fourth Avenue like he owns it! I'm watching people wave at him as he blasts down the canyon!"

The trooper pilot could not make a steep banking motion this low so he had to rise to 500 feet before he could bank. As the chopper strained to make the turn, the pilot looked up and over his left shoulder, now parallel with the ground, trying to spot the fast moving ultralight.

"I've lost him," the pilot said.

"Fine. OK," said the Command Center. "We've got cars on the ground all over downtown and a fixed wing moving into position over city center."

"I can't see him!" The pilot desperately scanned the horizon looking for the ultralight.

"Keep on your vector," Command Center ordered. "Wherever he comes down, we've got him."

The chopper rose to 1,000 feet and the pilot scanned the horizon. "Still have no visual," he said, the anxiety rising in his voice. "I am headed 270, due west for any cars listening. Due west. I see no ultralight. It is not over the Inlet and I do not see it over Knik Arm on the North and I do not see it fleeing city center to the south. He could not have passed me moving east. I cannot see the ultralight. Repeat. I cannot see the ultralight!"

"Keep looking," the anxiety now rising in the voice of the operator at Command Center. "He couldn't have disappeared. We've got cars all over city center. He has to land somewhere."

What everyone in uniform knew was the basic rule of pursuit: do not run from the police. If you must, make the run as short as possible. Once a pursuit has begun, the longer it lasts the more likely you are to be caught. There is no end to the amount of manpower and technology which can be focused on the pursued. The wisest course of action, which the ultralight had taken, was to make the pursuit as short as possible. It had made the pick-up, shaken off the helicopter and disappeared before the fixed wing could make it over the downtown area. All the pilot had to do was land. He wasn't in the air so perforce he had to be on the ground.

But *where* on the ground was he?

There was a moment of stunned silence. Then Command Center came back on line. "We are checking with all cars on the ground. Maintain your altitude." There was another long agonizing moment. "Bear One this is Command Center. We have no visual of the ultralight on the ground. Repeat. No visual. It has not landed. It is either still in the air or has landed on top of a building."

"Copy," stated the chopper pilot shaking his head. "Unlikely ultralight has landed on a building. There is no roof long enough for a landing strip."

"Affirmative," continued Command Center. "How about the parking garages?"

"There is only one at this end of town," came the voice from the trooper chopper. "I can see it from here. It is clear on top, no ultralight. Do you want me to check the other two?"

"No. Remain in the western sector. The fixed wing will over fly the other two parking garages. Over-fly the Alaska Railroad yard just in case our cars on the ground missed something."

The chopper banked to the north, headed for the Alaska Railroad switching yard but the chopper pilot knew he'd been snookered. There were too many troopers on the ground at the rail yard for an ultra-light to land unnoticed. It had not landed on any street, any roof top or the Park Strip.

Where in the blue blazes had it landed?

Chapter 39

It was a heartbreaker. After all the work, the subterfuge, the smoking – particularly the smoking – to come up this short.

The Corporal had been the first one out under the warehouse door. Jim had done everything he could with the alarm system, which wasn't much. He had disabled what he could from the inside but there was still the problem of the electric eye on the outside. The inside alarm was set to announce the arrival of someone on the outside, a truck on its way in. When the movement of the truck hit the motion sensor, the warehouse door would open. With the opening of the door, an alarm would sound, not to alert security but to make sure everyone in warehouse knew to get out of the way of the incoming vehicle.

There were no fire alarms on the inside of the warehouse. They had been disabled, most likely to keep the hostages from setting them off in hopes of attracting attention. It was a vain hope if you were outside and knew the nearest structure was well beyond ear shot. If you were inside the warehouse you would not know how far away the next building was. Or if the fire alarm was hooked up to a fire station. So it was worth a chance setting off the fire alarm.

If the fire alarms inside the warehouse worked.

Which they didn't.

Which left the alarm system outside the warehouse.

Which made it a problem.

There was only going to be one way to get the warehouse door open without setting off the alarm. It was to slip one person outside to disable the electric eye – or motion detector – whichever one it was. It was risky because the instant the door went up, the alarm would go off. Mittles had come up with the suggestion they slip one person out to disable the alarm and have the rest of the hostages wander around and look at the ceiling stupidly. This should give the outside person enough time to disable the system. Then, after a sufficient period of time had passed, assume the extortionist was not watching and make a break for it.

The first half of the plan had worked well. The Corporal made it out under the door and was able to rip the wires from the electric eye quickly. It silenced the alarm.

Then there had been an unexpected problem. A human problem. Until the Corporal actually made it out under the warehouse door, all discussions of escape among the hostages had been more academic in nature than a real life possibility. It was a theoretical concept, this escape. Only three people believed it was possible: Jim, Mittles and the Corporal. No one else did. The job of distracting the extortionist was an interesting sidelight to their captivity, something akin to poking a stick in a tiger's cage to see it move. It was not looked upon as a prelude to escape. It was a pleasant way to pass the time.

Then came a change. The instant the warehouse door went up enough to let the Corporal slide under, **escape** changed from a theoretical concept to a reality. Seconds after the alarm shut off, the door was harmless. Now, rather than mill around like sheep looking at the alarm system to fool the extortionist, the hostages felt it was, as the Southern expression went, 'time to get gone while the getting was good.'

En masse the hostages raised the warehouse door and flooded out.

But they didn't rush far.

Though the warehouse had been built in the 1970s, with the advent of 911 it had been retrofitted with security fencing. The wide open entrance has been narrowed with chain link fence to form a channel to the front gate. Razor wire topped the fence on all sides of the warehouse as well as above the gate. The entrance had two gates in sequence, 20 feet apart. The design was to allow a truck to enter the first gate, close it off and then open the second gate after the truck had been inspected – going in and coming out. Both gates were controlled by an electronic switch located behind a bullet proof glass room in the top of the warehouse.

There was no place for the hostages to go.

Then it started to rain.

Chapter 40

"Which one was this?" asked Gerry when the voice called to gloat. "Air or earth?"

"Gerry, dahling. A bit of both, actually. Earth for the pickup and air for the escape. Two for the price of one."

"This is not funny."

"I think it is. What we have here is a clean getaway. Again. Two out of two. Not a bad batting average."

"I haven't heard you got away with anything yet."

"Of course. You have footage of the takeoff. Why not get footage of the landing as well: air and earth. Like I said."

"The police don't know where your pilot came down. I'm listening to them on the squawk box. I don't know either."

"Oh, but I do." The voice chuckled. "Zip over to the top of the Wickersham Hotel garage and see what you see."

"You think the police are going to let me in?"

"They don't know to look there yet."

Gerry was already moving. She indicated by waving her hand the cameraman was to load up. As he was packing, Gerry asked, "By the way. When are the hostages going to be released?"

"You don't trust me?"

"The police don't."

"It's their job, Gerry, dear. The hostages will be released right after the final payment of $10 million. Five and five and five and ten is 25."

"That's a lot of money."

"Cost of doing business."

Chapter 41

To say Ayanna was not pleased to see Gerry McComber at the scene of the landing before the police got there was a grotesque understatement.

"You can't be here," snapped Ayanna as she put her hand over the camera lens. "This is a crime scene."

"I'm press!" Gerry was reaching for her press credentials when Ayanna stopped her.

"You can be Santa Claus for all I care. Beat it!"

"Hey, you can't be here either. You're not the cops. You're a state worker. Out of my way!"

Gerry might have tried to face down Ayanna who was, after all, simply security personnel who had no more right to be on a crime scene than she, but with the arrival of the Anchorage Police, Gerry retreated. She had her footage. No one else did. She'd beat the rest of the press corps. All she had to do was make it to the station without losing her tape.

"I'll take that tape." An Anchorage Police lieutenant she did not recognize blocked her path, extending his hand toward the camera.

"Not a chance." This time Gerry did pull out her press credentials. "Press."

"I don't give a rat's patootie who you are. The tape is called *evidence*."

"This tape," Gerry said as she tapped the side of the video camera, "is press footage. If you don't like it, get a lawyer."

"I just might do that!" The lieutenant leaned forward menacingly.

Gerry smiled. She loved men like the lieutenant. They were a dime-a-dozen. She leaned forward while she said, "Roll it!" Nose-to-nose with the lieutenant she looked down at his name tag. "Lieutenant Hardingfield, are you telling me you are going to violate the First Amendment of the United States Constitution and steal a tape legally shot by the press?"

The lieutenant stalled. The color drained from his face but his eyes were alive with rage. "That's, that's evidence! You're not leaving her with it!"

Evidence it may have been but confiscate it he could not. He was gently informed of the unfortunate fact when the public relations flack for the Anchorage Police Department made his appearance. Ten minutes of shouting later. He had a rather hasty conversation with the lieutenant after which the lieutenant left – quickly.

"Gerry! It's so good so you!" He was all smiles as the flack approached Gerry. "Sorry to hear there was this little misunderstanding. Tempers are running a bit high. You can understand things are a bit tense now."

"Sure can," Gerry played her cards carefully. "And I've got the tapes to prove it."

"Gerry, Gerry, Gerry. There's no reason for a hot-under-the-collar lieutenant to spoil a perfectly good relationship."

"What's in it for me?"

"Cold-blooded, eh? Well, there could be something but frankly, at this stage of the game, I don't know what to offer you."

"How about an exclusive on the next drop. I get the tip. Me and my cameraman."

"You know I can't do that, Gerry!"

"Sure you can, Sid. Just think how you can spin it." She put her hands up as if reading the words in lights, "Anchorage Police Enlists Aid of Reporter to Solve Crime."

"I still can't do it."

"Well, consider this news story then." She puts her hands up again. "Anchorage Police Threatens Reporter, Violates First Amendment."

The flack gave a supercilious smile. "Now, you wouldn't do that, Gerry. Oh, you could but you'd never get another lead out of the Department. No plates run, no files, no reports. I'll tell what I'll do. You forget about this unfortunate little incident and I will do what I can to involve you in the next pickup. I don't know what I can do but I'll try. It's the best I can do for you."

"Sid, you'd better be good for this."

"I will be as good as I can. No guarantees. Now, about the tape." He held out his hand.

"I'll hang onto it for a while," Gerry smiled, "just in case. You know, Sid, just in case things don't work out well."

"Gerry," the Flack smiled. "I've always been fair with you."

"Fair," replied Gerry, "is what happens every Labor Day in Palmer. This is just good old fashioned horse trading. You do for me; I do for you."

Chapter 42

The Fisherman picked up his two fish in the round from the back of Sebastian Seafoods. He rolled the dolly with the ice chest right up to the back door and rang the bell. This made the clerk very happy. He didn't have to lug the two salmon out to some customer's car. He just lay the two salmon into the ice chest and slide the back door down.

The Fisherman had parked his truck half a block away, behind the cinderblock fence separating the front of a gun store from the street. As an added precaution, the Fisherman had removed the front license plate and slathered the back plate with mud. Mud made it hard to remember even one letter or number.

If anyone was watching.

Which they weren't.

Then the Fisherman wadded the receipt and stuck it in his mouth. You couldn't be too careful for a one-sixth share of $25 million tax-free dollars.

Chapter 43

"What kind of Mickey Mouse outfit are you guys, anyway?" Henry Harrison was not in a good mood. "Jez Louise! You are making Homeland Security look like a joke!" He was so close to the AIC he might as well have been in the man's shirt. "Some yahoo on an ultralight picks up $5 million in gems from the Park Strip in full view of every blasted television camera lens in Anchorage and he gets away! GETS AWAY! What kind of message does *that* send to our enemies overseas?"

"It's not as if we *let* the man get away." The AIC was in an awkward position, but not an uncomfortable one. His directive, straight from the glass tower in Washington D. C., with regard to Homeland Security was in three parts: Be Respectful, Be Cooperative, Be Silent.

Nothing was said about Homeland Security being in charge. That made it simple. Again the rule was in three parts: defuse, deflect and delay. *Defuse* the anger so something productive can happen. *Deflect* the anger from what cannot be done to something that can be done. *Delay* making any decision in haste.

There was also one letter the two men had in common: "H." For the AIC, the H was for hostages; for Henry Harrison, headlines.

Harrison then started right down the law and order food chain; the Alaska State Troopers and then the Anchorage Police. Last and most vociferously to Airport Security and their *pro bono* consultant, Heinz Noonan, Chief of Detectives of the Sandersonville, North Carolina Police Department – wherever in the universe was *Sandersonville* was anyway.

"You are an embarrassment to your uniform," Harrison said to Noonan as he shook his finger at the Bearded Holmes. "I should call your Chief, the *real* Chief, and tell him what a miserable job you are doing."

"Well, sir," said Noonan, faking a slow Southern drawl, "you could do that, of course. But you see, sir," and he accented the word 'sir' so it was more of an insult than a title of respect, "the fact of the matter is, technically, you are in charge. That is, according to the President of the United States, the Office of Homeland Security is supposed to be coordinating all matters of security. Which means you, sir," again the ingratiating use of the term. "A lot of people are going to want to know what you, personally, have done to ensure 89 passengers and a crew of six can make a trip on an American airliner from two secure American cities. And those same people are going to want to know why you, personally, agreed to pay $25 million in tax payer money to secure the release of hostages who never should have been taken in the first place."

This clearly gave Harrison a moment of contemplation. Noonan plowed right on. When it came to playing politics, he was a master at getting people off his back. So he continued. "Then those same people are going to want to know why you insisted on trying to capture the people responsible for picking up the ransom without securing the safe release of the hostages first. All 89 passengers and six crew members. Now you can go ahead and make a big deal of the FBI, Alaska State Troopers, Anchorage Police Department, and Anchorage Airport Security forces who are doing their job exactly the way they have been trained to do their job. If you do, I'll be forced to talk to the national newspapers which are, I might add, read by say, ten times as many people as the Anchorage papers. I'm just on loan here. I'm not in the administrative food chain."

This clearly did not sit well with Harrison, as evidenced by the snarl of his lips falling to a frown. Harrison tried a comeback. "I will also have to check in with the Special Assistant for the Mayor for Homeland Security who is, I believe, your immediate superior while you are in this city. He, also, is going to be very interested in knowing what you are specifically doing to secure the safe release of 89 passengers and the crew of six who have disappeared."

If Harrison was hoping from reaction from Noonan. He didn't get it. Mixing faux humility with a soft Southern drawl, the Chief of Detectives from Sandersonville, North Carolina – which was just up the coast from Nags Head – was the very soul of avuncular discretion. "In that case I'll have to contact the Special Assistant for Eastern District of the Homeland Security who is, I believe, your immediate superior's superior. With all of the publicity he is going to be very interested in knowing what you are specifically doing to secure the safe release of 89 passengers and the crew of six who have disappeared on your watch and what you are going to do to keep future abductions safe in your region of the country."

Noonan then tilted his head toward Harrison as if to say, "and what do you have to say to that?"

Harrison didn't know what to say so he did the worst thing he could do. He threatened. "You, you, you" he said to Noonan and then looked around the room, "all of you! You are only working because I let you work!"

"Not exactly true," said Noonan softly. "The only reason you are working is because you couldn't find a job on your own." What tittering there had been in the room dropped. There was a hushed silence. Noonan went on. "The only reason you're keeping this job is because we are doing ours. Now why don't you be a good little boy and run along and find some butt to kiss."

Harrison stood rooted to the ground. No one had ever talked to him like that! No one! "I'll see you're fired for this," he snarled.

"Fine with me," Noonan says. "I'm past retirement age anyway." He brightened as if a thought suddenly crossed his mind. "I know. I've got the connections to get a job with Homeland Security!" He extended his hand toward Harrison. "Maybe we'll end up working together."

That was too much for Harrison. He was off in a huff. But he knew he couldn't just leave; he had to exit with a parting shot. Weak though the parting shot was, it was, blessedly, a parting shot. "You haven't heard the last of this!"

Then he was gone.

The door to the Command Center slammed behind him.

There was a moment of stunned silence and then thunderous applause.

After a moment the AIC called the room back to order. "OK. Enough. Technically, as the good Chief of Detectives from North Carolina – and our hero for the hour – has stated, Homeland Security is in charge. So let's all keep that in mind. Now, if everyone will take a seat, we'll have everyone give us an up-to-date on what has happened to date."

There was a shuffling of chairs as the Command Center staff, such as it were, found seats and sat down.

"Well," said the AIC looking at the main door, "now that everyone who should be here is here . . ." He let the rest of the sentence hang. There was a shuffling of feet and murmuring as the AIC continued, "I, for one, would like to say I am pleased our unpaid, *pro bono* consultant is on board for both his experience and his, how shall I saw this, 'quickness of wit.'"

Again there was thunderous applause. Noonan simply waved one hand as if say, "Aw, it was nothing."

Once it was said, the AIC got down to business. "It's been a while since we've all been together with 13 seconds to talk. So let's do a rundown of where we are. Chief Noonan, you've been following the cargo that lost weight. What the latest?"

"Let's talk about the hostage first. That's our top priority."

The AIC nodded assent.

Noonan got to his feet and set his fingers delicately on the table. "As of this moment, I, like you, have no idea where the hostages are. The last I heard from my department was there has been and continues to be an ongoing search of large structures in the airport area. The Seattle Police Department assumes, and I agree with them, the passengers and crew were somehow taken away from the flight line under a pretext a terrorist attack was anticipated."

"What makes you so sure the passengers are in the Seattle area?" The hostage negotiator for the Alaska State Troopers asked.

"There are only three possibilities," Noonan stated. "The hostages are in Anchorage, Seattle or were taken off the plane somewhere in between. We know they are not in Anchorage. If they had been sucked out of the plane by some alien force I doubt they would be held for ransom. Also, there was not enough time for the plane to land anywhere between Seattle and Anchorage to let off the passengers and then take off again. Ergo, the only place the passengers could be is Seattle."

"That's where they probably *were*," replied a hostage negotiator in the crowd of law enforcement personnel. "That might not be where they are now?"

"True," replied Noonan. "We are talking about 89 passengers and six crew members. That's a lot of people to keep hidden. They have to be fed, kept warm and dry, away from phones. It means they are in a large structure, like a warehouse converted into a barrack. There are not many in the Seattle area and the Seattle Police are checking them as fast as possible."

"What's this about the cargo losing weight?" Noonan could not place the question to the questioner.

"There are a number of leads still being explored," Noonan said. "One of the strangest is an air cargo igloo. It was checked in at the Unicorn cargo bay in New York where it was weighed at 200 pounds. It was sent to New Orleans where it was off-loaded. Then the New Orleans Unicorn office received a message to forward the igloo to Anchorage via Seattle. It was treated as a new shipment where it weighed in at 136 pounds."

"136 pounds?" Said the same voice. "What happened to the odd pounds?"

"We didn't know there was a weight discrepancy until it arrived in Anchorage. When we did a cross check of the cargo, the weight difference was noticed. When we opened the igloo, it was empty."

"Empty? As in the igloo had nothing in it?"

"Correct. The seal on the igloo still had the New York imprint. The FBI broke the seal to enter and examine the cargo except there was no cargo to examine."

"Who sent the cargo in the first place?"

"We don't know that either. The shipment was placed and paid for by a cargo forwarding company, Harrison, Johnson, McDonagle. We contacted them and they checked the records. An electronics supply company in New Jersey had made the shipment. The supply company is a regular shipper so there was no reason to suspect the shipment."

"Wouldn't someone be suspicious when an electronics supply company sent cargo in an igloo? It should have raised some suspicions." The man asking was wearing a trooper uniform.

"Not really," Noonan replied. "The supply company has no record of the shipment other than the billing. Someone stopped off at the Unicorn air cargo terminal in New York with the igloo and checked it in as a late shipment. No one cared because the supply company was a regular shipper and the paperwork was correct. The supply company has the paperwork but it's a forgery."

"This is all very confusing," said the trooper. "We have a shipment with a phony billing for an air cargo igloo losing all its weight between New York and Anchorage and yet nothing had been taken out?"

"Correct," said Noonan.

"Do you have any idea what was in it?"

"I'd guess dry ice," said Noonan. "It would have evaporated to gas and thus the weight would have dropped with no indication anything had been taken out of the igloo."

"I'm even more confused," said the unidentified voice. "So we have a shipment of dry ice and nothing but air in the cargo igloo. Does this have something to do with the case?"

Noonan sighed sadly. "We don't know. I did a check of all cargo just in case there was a glitch. We ended up with three packages, which was odd. One was this igloo. Then there was an antique motorcycle which isn't an antique and a box of medical supplies."

"Let me get this right," said another voice. "What you are saying is out of a ton of cargo, there are only three shipments which are odd. Is there a definite link between any of those packages and the kidnapping?"

"Not that I know of," replied Noonan.

"We could be grasping at straws," the AIC said. "Just in case we have put a hold on all cargo so whether those packages were significant or not, they are still under lock-and-key, so to speak."

"Is there anything else we should know?" The question had a tinge of satire and was aimed at Noonan.

'Yesterday's hero is today's lackey,' Noonan thought as he responded, "As we speak, the Seattle Police have no solid leads on where the hostages are. My office in Sandersonville is tracking this case around the clock and working with the Seattle authorities. All cell phones from the hostages have been accounted for and email to the three lap tops owned by three of the hostages have not responded. The hostages are not in any warehouse near the airport. There is no cargo which links directly with the hostages. So, in a nutshell, I have nothing but negatives to report."

There was a moment of silence. "Ayanna," the AIC said after seeing no one had any other questions. "What about the ultralight?"

"All I can say at this time is the ultralight picked up the gems. I saw the perp as she flew over – yes, it was a 'she'– and she waved at me as she flew by."

There was a soft groan from someone in the crowd.

"That's enough," snapped the AIC looking toward the command table. "We've got a long way to go before this is over." Then he looked back to Ayanna. "Describe her."

"Small, petite. I'd say she was about five feet tall, weighed close to 100 pounds. The ultralight looked gargantuan. She rose fast indicating the ultralight had no trouble with her weight."

"She landed on the top deck of the Wickersham Hotel garage?"

"Affirmative, "continued Ayanna. "I'll let the Alaska State Trooper helicopter pilot tell of the chase."

Ayanna started to sit down but the AIC had another question.

"How did you know where to go to find the ultralight?"

"I didn't. I just guessed. There was only one reporter at the far end of the Park Strip. She'd been the one who tracked us for the first drop, Geraldine McComber. When she and her cameraman started to beat feet to the Wickersham Hotel, I followed them. I got there just a bit ahead of her because I didn't have to wait for a cameraman to catch up to me."

"Where'd she get the lead?"

Someone in the audience cursed.

"That's such a good question," replied Ayanna hastily, "I don't have an answer."

"We all know now the ultralight landed on the roof of the parking garage at the Wickersham Hotel." The AIC addressed the group. "What a lot of us do not know is why there was a special landing area for the plane. Someone had closed off the top floor of the parking garage about five minutes before the pick-up. Then they stretched some strong bungee cords between the parked cars on the roof. The bungees slowed the landing of the ultralight. The plane still hit the back wall, but at quite a reduced speed. Then the ultralight was hand-pushed around to the down incline. Once around the corner it couldn't be seen from the air. The Alaska State Trooper helicopter was searching the ground level areas of the eastern end of the city while the ultralight was being pushed down the incline into the cover of the upper deck of the parking garage. When the trooper chopper made it directly over the top of the garage for a look, the ultralight was already on the second story down."

"Are there any security cameras on inside of the structure?"

"Yes," replied the AIC. "And they were operating. They showed a perfect picture of the landing and the moving of the ultralight down the ramp and around the corner. Security made the call to the police. Not much to report. The woman was wearing dark clothing and a ski mask. After the ultralight was no longer visible from the air, she walked to the Emergency Exit and stripped off her jacket and ski mask. There aren't any security cameras in the stairwells. She kept her face away from the camera on the skywalk. We followed her across the bridge, into the lobby and then out the back door. That's where the security camera coverage ended. She knew where every single security camera was and did not give us so much as an odd angle for a profile. She was very, very good."

"How about the bungee cords and the ultralight?" There was a hopeful voice from someone.

"No fingerprints if that's what you mean. The cords could have been bought at any sporting goods store anywhere in town. We ran the ultra-light registration and found it had been stolen from the Oshkosh Air Show last year. We placed a call to the Oshkosh Police and all they could say was the ultralight disappeared during the show. The owner wants it back. Seems it was specially designed for power and maneuverability."

"What a surprise," someone said caustically. "So we have nothing?"

"Butkus is what we've got. We do have two mores drop to make. Maybe we'll get lucky with one of those."

Chapter 44

The room smelled like a wet dog. The hostages were standing around, soaked to the bone, and none of them were happy. Jim and Mittles took the brunt of the abuse. The invectives thrown their way were on par with favorite line of Oliver Hardy, "This is another fine mess you have gotten me into."

"Well, we tried," didn't cut it. Everyone was shivering and angry.

The escape attempt had been an absolute failure. All 95 people rushed out of the warehouse and ran right into the cyclone fence. Then they fanned out in both directions, running along the fence as far as they could, trying to find a gate or a break in the fence. It didn't take them long to realize they were in a fenced compound of abandoned buildings. There was razor wire on top of the fence so climbing was out of the question.

As far as attracting help was concerned, they were out of luck. There was forest on all sides of the fencing and no structures of any kind could be seen through the trees. The only break in the forest was a frontier road, double ruts in deep mud running to a doublewide gate. The gate was padlocked shut.

Then came the rain. It was a downpour. With no place to go, everyone went back into the make-shift barrack. They passed around what towels there were and everyone sat on their cots cursing Jim, Mittles and the Corporal.

The voice behind the screen was bordering on the hysterical. Apoplectic would have been a better description. He was so angry at times his voice was so loud it distorted the sound system.

Raging about how stupid their escape attempt had been, he demanded they close the bulkhead door. At the very least it would keep the rain out. For their safety, he told them, they were not to try to exit again. He, like them, was also a prisoner. He was alone in one of the buildings within the compound. He could not come out until his partner came back from a drug store run. When his partner did come back, the bulkhead door would be locked from the outside again. They were all warned his partner would be armed and there was surely going to be deaths if there was any interference in the re-locking of the door.

Then he ordered everyone to stand on one side of the room. As he read their names off the passenger manifest, they were to cross to the other side. This was to make sure everyone was present and accounted for. It was a clever way of doing it since no one could double count themselves.

Name by name he went down the list. Those who were called walked across the room and lingered on the far wall. All was going well until the voice said, "Randall McFerson."

No one walked across the room. There was a stunned silence. Everyone looked for this Randall McFerson, whoever he was. "Don't be shy, Corporal," snapped the voice. "I'm sure you were the one behind the escape attempt. I know you are there."

Still, no one walked across the room.

"This is not funny, Corporal," said the voice, irritated now.

Still no one walked across the room.

"OK," said the voice. "We'll play it your way," and he continued to read names off the list. When he came to the last name, no one was left on the near side of the room.

The Corporal had vanished.

Chapter 45

Even as the Command Center was shaking from its second failure, it got a call for the third delivery. The call came in on Ayanna's cell phone. The texting read "Unknown Number."

"I hope you have recovered from your little jog," the voice said pleasantly.

"Oh, I have. You'll be spending a lot of time in a place where there is no jogging," she snapped. "At least not any cross-country jogging."

There was laughter on the other end of the line. "You need a sense of humor, Ayanna. If you don't have a laugh every now and again, life can be so droll."

"I can't find anything funny about what you are doing."

"Ayanna! My love! You don't see the humor in all of this? We've made 95 people just up and disappear. We've snarled every rule in the book for law and order for over 2,000 miles, snagged $10 million in gems, made the front page of just about every newspaper across the country and half of America has their radios on waiting for the next drop. I'd say we've done pretty well."

"This game is not over!"

"Right you are. Right this is a game. Right now we're winning it."

"You've been lucky so far!"

"Luck has nothing to do with it. Skill, Ayanna, skill. There's a whole new world of entrepreneurs out there. We're the vanguard. Plan well, focus on the prize and strike. It's all in the sleight of hand."

"You've done well twice. Your luck is going to run out."

"Not likely. Now let me speak to Captain Noonan."

Ayanna looked up from the phone with questions in her eyes. The rest of Command Center was staring at her. They knew she was on the phone with the extortionists, they just didn't know what she was talking about. The AIC was reaching for the phone but Ayanna just shook her head.

"He wants to talk to Captain Noonan."

Noonan just smiled. He looked at the AIC and said, "I sort of knew this was coming." Then he took the phone. "Noonan here." He hit the phone button with the loudspeaker imprint to put the conversation on speaker phone. "You are on speaker phone."

"Well, well, well," said the voice. "We meet again."

"We have met before?"

The statement took everyone in the room by surprise.

"Oh, yes. We have met before. The last time was many years ago."

"I was very young then."

"So was I," said the extortionist. "I've waited a long time for this moment."

"Should I remember you?"

"You will. It will take a while but you will. It was a long time ago. You interrupted a caper of mine. Took all my comrades. But, as the saying goes, 'Ha, Ha, Ha, He, He, He, you got my brother but you didn't get me."

"You were the lucky one?"

"Yes. My brother died in prison."

"Well, my condolences. He earned his trip to prison I suspect."

"The price of our business."

"Heck of a business. Are you going to tell me who you are or is this just a casual trip down Memory Lane?" Noonan listened intently.

"Oh, no. This is just a courtesy call. I want you thinking about who I am for a while. I don't think you'll figure it out in time to stop me. I want you to know I have been waiting to pull this caper for years. I was waiting for the stars to align so you would be here – so I could walk away with millions and tarnish your career at the same time."

"Well," Noonan said, "the stars must have aligned properly. But you are a long way from home free."

"Not so far. But you are a long way from stopping the wheels we have been set in motion. We're about half-through and so far you haven't so much as touched us."

"Every worm has a tendency to turn."

"Shakespearean still, eh? Good for you. Haven't changed in years."

Noonan looked at the AIC and made a motion with his hand he wanted a pen or pencil. One of the officers at the table slid a pad in his direction. Noonan started taking notes, everyone at the table either reading his handwriting upside down or craning their necks to see what he had printed. Noonan looked at Ayanna as he wrote, "Have my office pull up my arrest record."

"Are you still there, Captain?"

"Of course," replied Noonan. "I was just indicating to the gathered throng you are gloating over your successes."

"I am modest, I must say. Now, you are going to make the next drop."

"Me? Why me? I don't know the town. How are you going to make sure I can hot foot it to the phone booth where I'm supposed to be?"

"I'll be kind. How's that?"

"You are gracious as well. How about a hint as to who you are?"

"The hint will be when you see me. My parents say my brother and I looked alike."

"Twins?"

"Five years apart."

"You sound English. A clue or are you just a good actor?"

"Performer! Captain! You should know better! *Actors* are people who pretend to be doctors when they advertise Seltzer on television. *Performers* are professionals. They can become Claudius at the drop of hat or quote Prince Hamlet at a cocktail party. *Actor!* I think not." Then the voice of the extortionist changed to a deep throated, boom. "*All the world's a stage, And all the men and women merely players: They have their exits and their entrances; And one man in his time plays many parts.*"

"AS YOU LIKE IT, well done."

"Well done, indeed. Now, on to more important things, the next drop. You will be making the next drop."

"I am giddy with anticipation."

"Don't be. I'm going to add a bit of turmoil into the mix."

"Oh?"

"You see, I know you. You are, and I am loath to admit it, very good at what you do. You are so good you are the one cog in the law and order machine which needs special handling."

"Dare say."

"Yes. But, as it happens, I have a natural advantage here. You see, the way to dilute quality is to mix it with inferiority."

"A bit of a mixed metaphor, don't you think?"

There was silence on the line for a moment. "Maybe. Word games again, Captain. OK, let's cut to the chase. You will be making the next drop but the man who will be organizing the drop is not going to be the Federal agent who thinks he is in charge. I'm going to go right to the top."

"The top of what?"

"The lines of authority. The man who is going to organize this drop is going to be the Head of Homeland Security for Alaska, Henry Harrison."

The blanching of Noonan's face was so clear everyone around the table held their breath. "You are kidding, of course."

"On the contrary I am quite serious. In fact, I have his personal number right here. After I hang up from you, I'll be calling him. I will expect the next drop to be made no later than 4:15. No time for shut eye. Keep this phone, by the way. I know the number."

Then the cell phone went to buzz.

Everyone looked at Noonan with questioning eyes.

"This," he said shaking his head and smiling at the same time, "is going to be very interesting."

Chapter 46

"Gerry, dahling, how are you?"

"Well, you did me well the last time so I'm happy to hear from you now."

"Good, good. I hope you are ready to travel?"

"Of, course. Where are we going this time?"

"Gerry! You know I don't reveal state secrets! It's been a busy day for you. I hope you're not sleepy."

"Not yet. It's still early in the afternoon."

"Well, you be ready to go at 4 p.m. You won't have to put on running shoes this time but you will have to be in your car in the downtown area when I call."

"In the downtown area?"

"Correct."

"Any particularly place in the downtown area?"

"Not really."

"It is not a good idea to be *just anywhere* in the downtown area at 4 p.m.," Gerry said. "At 4:30 every federal, state and city worker gets off. Ten seconds later the streets are clogged."

"Exactly why I chose 4 p.m. It will give you ten minutes to get in place."

"So the action will happen at 4:10?"

"More or less. As long as you are in place by 4:10 – and I mean exactly 4:10, you'll be able to capture some a-m-a-z-i-n-g footage."

"Amazing as in Pulitzer Prize winning?"

"I'd like to think so."

"Then I am your girl."

Chapter 47

Henry Harrison was giddy with excitement. Had he been alone he would have been jumping for joy.

The extortionists were calling him!

Him!

HIM!

The Head of Homeland Security for Alaska!

Henry Harrison!

He was getting the call!

Not the FBI!

Not the Anchorage Police!

Him!

The extortionists clearly didn't think the FBI was up to the job of doing it right!

Now it was his turn.

Why, he'd show 'em.

"Yes, that is correct. And you are?"

"I am the extortionist but you already knew that. Hoping for a clue to my identity?"

"It would be nice," said Harrison.

"OK, I'll give you a clue."

Harrison smiled, "Give me a moment to get a pen and piece of paper."

"Of course."

Harrison dug around in his desk for his personalized stationery. This was the kind of a tip which made history! He wanted to make sure he got every drop of legacy he deserved! On his own personal stationery! With a time and date stamp!

"OK, I'm ready."

"Anaktuvik"

"What?"

"Anaktuvik. It's spelled A-n-a-k-t-u-v-i-k. It's an Inupiat Eskimo word. Just like the Pass."

"The pass?"

"Anaktuvik Pass. It's in the Brooks Range north of Fairbanks."

"That's the clue?"

"Half of it. There was an organization in Anchorage in 1964 by that name. That's your clue."

"That's not much of a clue."

"It's not the clue that's given that's important, Mr. Harrison."

[**Mr. Harrison! It was Mr. Harrison! They knew him by name!**]

The voice continued. "A clue is something you follow to find something more important."

"How should I follow this one?"

"Well, if it were me, I'd go down to the National Archives. It's on Third Avenue just up the hill from the new state office building. They've got a whole bunch of really smart people working there who would know how to find out about Anaktuvik."

"National Archives, eh? I wasn't aware there was such a place in town."

"You might want to keep the clue under your hat," the voice said confidentially. "You know how the FBI is when it comes to sharing credit."

"Oh, yeah!" snapped the Director.

"Now let's get to the reason I called, Mr. Director."

"I'm listening."

The Director *loved* to hear his voice. He even loved it more when the person used the term "Mr. Director." His grandchildren and their children's children were going to be so proud of him!

Chapter 48

As soon as the bulkhead door was secured from the outside, the two men assigned to guard the hostages began the painstaking search of the compound for the corporal. At first they assumed he was hiding in one of the empty buildings. Where else could he have gone? 30 seconds into the search, it ended. Just beyond the line of sight of the electric eye over the bulkhead door they found a pair of blankets tossed over the razor wire. The blankets were punctured and ripped.

"Son of a . . ." snapped one of them.

"Not so fast," his partner said. "We check everywhere else first. This could be a ruse."

"It doesn't look like a ruse to me. How long before he finds a telephone?"

"It'll be couple of hours. If he's smart he'll follow the road but stay in the trees."

"Do we have a couple of hours?"

They both looked at their watches.

Then they looked at each other.

"I'll make the call," the taller one said.

Chapter 49

At 3:30, the Command Center went from professional to tumult the instant Henry Harrison – "just like the President" – came storming through the door. It wasn't so much anyone was doing anything important at the moment, save waiting for the clock to reach 4 p.m. The functional web of agents on the street and squad cars on patrol had already been established. Everyone was primed for the next drop.

Then Harrison showed up.

Worse, he showed up with his minions. Eight of them. All political appointees.

"What's going on here?" The AIC was not pleased to see Harrison.

"I'm in charge here," snapped Harrison. Then, to the assembled law enforcement and security personnel, all of whom were looking at him he said it louder. "I'm in charge, now. We're not going to any more fu. . ." he caught himself just in time, "screw-ups."

There was a moment of deathly silent. Then, to a man (and woman) everyone's gaze shifted from Harrison to the AIC. The AIC's face was ashen for a moment. Then it went purple.

Chapter 50

Noonan pulled Ayanna out of the Command Center just as the proverbial excrement came in contact with the rotating metal blade. She half-stumbled rather than walked out of the room, Noonan pulling her by the elbow.

"Aw," she complained. "It was just about get fun!"

"*Fun* we don't need now. Let's go to your office!" As they moved down the hallway away from the Command Center they could hear the ensuing uproar.

"I just love it when men fight," Ayanna sighed.

To have called Ayanna's office small would have been an overstatement. To have called it an office would have been an overstatement as well. What it actually resembled was a large table with a single drawer pushed up against a cement wall–in a hallway. There were three other tables alongside hers, all with single drawers and there was a single phone on one of the tables. All of the tables were obviously desks because they had blotters and personal items.

"This is Airport Security?"

"From the moment. Homeland Security snagged our regular offices. We ended up down here. It's not as bad as it looks."

"Could have fooled me."

"We aren't really in our office much. We don't need the phone because we all have cell phones. It's actually a blessing. The Homeland Security people now have to put with all of the bureaucratic garbage while we can actually do our job. Do you know much paperwork the department requires us to fill out?"

"I can imagine."

"No you cannot. Not in your wildest nightmare. Well, we let them fill out their own paperwork. If they can't find us, we can't fill out the paperwork."

Noonan sat on the edge of one the tables. "Well, while they fight the turf war," he indicated the Command Center with a shake of his head, "we've got to do the heavy lifting. The bad boys have deliberately included Homeland Security."

"That's stupid."

"No, it's smart. What they have done is added one more bureaucratic layer of confusion to the crime. With the FBI in charge, there was some semblance of order. The FBI can get things done," he paused, "eventually. Then there is Homeland Security and it does not have a clue."

"How did the bad boys light the fire under Homeland Security?"

"I don't know – yet – but they did. We were told they were going to muck up the next drop with Homeland Security. I just didn't know how they were going to do it."

"Any special reason the dimwits are coming into the ball game this late," Ayanna paused, "I mean Homeland Security. Usually they let everyone else do the work and then grab the headlines."

"No idea. I do know three things we have to work on. First, the extortionist who talked to me on your cell phone said his path and mine had crossed many years ago. Apparently I arrested his brother but not him. His brother died in prison and there was a five year difference in their ages. The extortionist also said he had been waiting for years for the time to be perfect to pull off this heist when I was in town. I assume he wants to embarrass me. It gives the perp an Alaska connection. Since I am going to be making the next drop, what I need you to do is coordinate with my office in Sandersonville and the Anchorage Police. Have my staff go through every one of my cases, starting with the oldest first and look for an Alaska connection. When we find the connection it will be the clincher on who he is. I've arrested a lot of perps who had younger brothers. See if you match the names of those arrested with those who have died in prison."

"Could be hard."

"In reality, no. Just get the names of those who were arrested and run them through the Social Security Death Index. It's on line. In my career I've arrested, maybe, 200 perps. You can zing through the Death Index looking for 200 people fairly easily."

"How will the Social Security Index tell me which ones died in prison?"

"Look at the place of death."

"OK. What next?"

"I hate to ask you to do it but someone has to."

"Am I going to like this?"

"No but we need to get it done. The perps told Homeland Security something. Something important. Important enough to want them to take charge. Usually Homeland Security just tags along and claims credit. This time we've got what's his name . . ."

"Henry Harrison."

"Yeah, just like the President. Harrison. He's really worked up. Means the perps have told him something motivating him to really get in charge. We can't have a split command. You have to find out what motivated Homeland Security to get involved."

"So you want me to spy on the spy masters?"

"Use your feminine wiles. Something put a burr under their butt. Go visit them in your old office."

"So you want me to go into the lion's den as well?"

"Think of it as the call of duty."

Ayanna shook her head. "OK, but it seems like a waste of time. You said three things. What's the third?"

"We're up to drop three. This means we've got one more to go. The next one is going to be the big one, a $10 million drop. Once they have the diamonds, the hostages have no more value. I don't see the perps killing the hostages. They are not going to release them until they are in the clear. We've got to be prepared for anything. Open a back channel to the Seattle Police."

"Back channel?"

"Right. You call them from here. Make sure you know everything they are telling Homeland Security. Right now we're clearly not being told everything Homeland Security knows. In a nutshell, it's not good news."

"You really want me to go to the wall."

"Only you can do it. The FBI and Homeland Security are in the middle of a cat fight over who's in charge, just the way the perps want it. Somebody's got to solve this crime. It's up to us because we're not the FBI or the Homeland Security."

"All right. What are you going to be doing in the meantime?"

"Going back to Command Center and wait for my phone call."

"Aw. You have all the fun!"

Chapter 51

"Gerry, dahling, are you ready to rumble?"

"I've been waiting for your call for hours."

"Are you in the downtown area?"

"Just like you told me to be."

"Good. Now listen carefully. You have to set up your camera in one particular spot. I've put a mark on the sidewalk for you. The camera has to be set up in the *exact spot*, not five feet to the left or right. On the spot. On the exact spot. With the camera pointing the way of the arrow. Do you understand?"

"I understand. Where is the spot?"

"I will tell you at 4:10. On the nose. It will be in the area of the old courthouse. Be in your car ready to move."

"I'll be there."

Chapter 52

Back in the Command Center, Henry Harrison and the AIC were both on phones. From the dual conversation it was clear both were talking to superiors somewhere up the administrative chain of command. Everyone else in the room was standing around with the classical stern, professional law-and-order look. It was easy to tell the agents from the Homeland Security people. The former were around the desk of the AIC and the latter were standing shoulder-to-shoulder like the front line of an offensive team protecting their quarter back.

Then Ayanna's phone in Noonan's pocket started buzzing. Noonan answered it.

"Time for our little rendezvous, Captain."

"I have been waiting for you call."

There was a deathly hush in the room – with the exception of Harrison and the AIC on their respective phones.

"Do you have the diamonds?"

Noonan looked up from the phone. "Just a second." He looked at the FBI agents. "Are the stones ready to go?"

There was a general murmur of indicating yes.

"Yes. Now don't you have me running around too much. I'm an old man."

"Not to worry. Since you don't know Anchorage I'll have to give you all the directions you need. Do you know where the old courthouse is?"

"On Fourth Avenue?"

"Correct."

"Yeah."

"Of course, you know where the new courthouse is."

"A couple of blocks away."

"Good. There are a number of buildings sharing the same side of Fourth Avenue as the old courthouse. There's one building known as the Blankenship Building. It even says it on the outside."

"Blankenship building?" Several of the FBI agents nodded. So did two Homeland Security people.

"What do I do when I get inside the Blankenship Building?"

"Go to the Third Floor. At the end of the hall you will find a janitor's closet. Open the janitor's closet and you will find a note with instructions. Make sure you follow the instructions on the note. Precisely."

"Precisely."

"Take Ayanna's phone with you."

"Exactly when am I supposed to be at the Blankenship Building?"

There was no answer. The phone was dead.

"I'd say you mean right now," Noonan said to the phone receiver.

Chapter 53

To anyone in the law enforcement business, the entourage escorting Noonan to the Blankenship Building in downtown Anchorage was more farce than force. Since it had not been determined whether the FBI or Homeland Security was in charge, both were. As neither would bow to the authority of the other, neither was in charge. Rather, neither was not. Thus neither was in charge, it was a split command at the top.

With a split command on top it also became a split command beneath. The Anchorage Police, who took their instructions from the FBI, maintained a loose net of patrol cars around Anchorage. Not being privy to the inner workings of the Command Center, their function had not changed at all. This was a federal case and therefore the Anchorage Police were an appendage of the federal system and the FBI represented the federal system.

Sort of.

Maybe.

Then again, no one had told the Anchorage Police Department boo so the men and women in blue were following the old orders which were to support the Feds – whoever those Feds happened to be.

The FBI agents who were not actually at a command level were told to "follow procedure." In this case, however, there were no procedures to follow. In most cases, and particularly in areas of low population like Anchorage, the FBI, in essence, looked over the shoulder of the local police. It didn't have enough agents on the ground to run an operation of this size and never expected to. So, with the top of the food chain in turmoil, the agents on the street were told to maintain a thin surveillance screen around the Blankenship Building but to be prepared to move as the drop off point was moved.

The real difficulty from the law and order standpoint was Homeland Security. Most important, it was not a law enforcement entity. Since it was populated with individuals who were political appointees few of whom had any law and order experience, it was bull in a China shop. Its minions did not understand crime scene protocol, undercover work or the black arts of crime prevention.

Further, the Homeland Security at the top was split as well. Henry Harrison had left his Second-in-Command in charge of the operation with strict instructions to seize whatever square footage was necessary to capture the extortionist. This was in direct contradiction to the instructions under which the FBI operated. In cases of kidnapping, the FBI will track and follow the perpetrators until the hostage or hostages are released and then wrap up the case. Homeland Security, in the *persona* of Henry Harrison, clearly believed the best way to resolve the matter was to seize one extortionist and then hold him or her – her if she were the ultralight pilot – as a hostage as leverage with the gang.

Harrison, in the meantime, to the shock of the AIC was not even going to be on the streets when Noonan went into the Blankenship Building. He was going to be two blocks away, at the National Archives, on a mission he would not discuss with the AIC.

The chain of command was thus one of blunder and bumble with no one person in charge.

The block on which the Blankenship Building stood was the last city block on Fourth Avenue to have survived the Great Earthquake in 1964 and the subsequent renovation. Because of the unstable ground beneath Anchorage generally and Fourth Avenue in particularly, the entire north side of Fourth Avenue had slipped outward and downward during the quake. Further east on Fourth Avenue, the buildings had fallen six or seven feet and collapsed under their own weight as their cement foundations were snapped and twisted to rubble. The damage was less severe on the west end of Fourth Avenue where the Blankenship Building stood. Here the earth only dropped about three feet and the foundations of the buildings, though cracked, still supported the weight of the buildings. As money being tight in 1964, the buildings were simply patched and re-used.

Originally a bank, the Blankenship Building, was so named because it had been bought for a song by Herman Blankenship for pennies on the dollar after the earthquake. Its vault had been in the basement and the offices on the first floor. The vault was both a blessing and a curse. It had been so well constructed it supported the weight of the building even as others on the same block were coming down. But, at the same time, the cracks in the basement were so severe the bank did not feel comfortable with a vault it did not deem burglarproof. So the bank moved across the street and Herman Blankenship ended up with the habitable building. A second, third and fourth floor were added over the next 30 years. As the Blankenship family knew, it was only a matter of time before the value of the downtown property became so inviting the building would be destroyed. So repairs were at a minimum. It was a tawdry building on one of the most expensive lots in Alaska. It was only a matter of time before some multinational corporation with very deep pockets snapped it up.

Noonan, wedged between two Homeland Security minions in the back seat of a limo, was escorted to the front of the Blankenship Building where two of the three men in the front seat were let out. Their job was to secure the front door, make sure one came out until Noonan did. Then Noonan was driven around to the back entrance.

The back door to the Blankenship Building opened onto a parking lot, which had formerly been the old Princess Theater. The Princess was one of the structures not surviving the quake. Herman Blankenship had bought the property for $1 under the agreement he was to remove the rubble of the old theater. He did and transformed the land into a parking lot for his building, a parking lot which was the second most valuable half-block in Alaska.

Though it was a hard concept to consider, Herman Blankenship had been the Alaska equivalent of a slumlord. This is hard to consider since Anchorage does not have slums in the same sense as New York, Philadelphia or Los Angeles. What it did have in the 1960s were ramshackle cabins, eroding Quonsets and deteriorating railroad housing units. Built because they were cheap and not expected to last much beyond the Second World War, Blankenship bought them for a dime. In this case, a dime is accurate. Proof was the properties exchanged hands for ten cents.

At the time it was a good but modest deal. By the end of the century it was a great deal. Blankenship had initially made his money by filling those derelict structures with "working girls" who serviced service men during the war and thereafter the canners and fishermen. As the population of Anchorage increased, there was an effort to move The Line further out of town. In those days The Line was the collection of structures–all owned by Blankenship under a variety of business cover names– at the end of the landing strip. That wasn't far enough out of town for the city alleged-to-be blue Alaskan bluebloods. So Blankenship sold the structures to morally upstanding individuals who believed once the houses where the working girls did business were emptied the moral problem would be solved. The working girls would move away.

They did.

Downtown.

Into buildings Blankenship had purchased for a dime.

It did solve the problem of working girls on The Line. It brought them downtown where they built the Blankenship fortune one trick at a time. In no other town in America could this have happened. But then this was Alaska. It was not until after Old Man Blankenship died that his heirs moved the girls down to Spenard where the police were more *understanding*. This was because Spenard was part of the Anchorage Borough, not the City of Anchorage. The Borough needed income and turned a blind eye to how some of its properties were being used – as long as the property tax was being paid. More important to the Blankenship sons – who operated under the business name Acme Corporation which was taken from the Roadrunner cartoons because they believed it gave them anonymity – the Borough had a police force of about five while Anchorage had them by the score. Thereafter the Blankenship Building was rented by the room, again, to small businesses, most lawyers, because of the proximity of the building to the courthouse. When the new courthouse was built, the lawyers moved and were replaced with accountants, insurance agents and small corporations involved in dubious or unprofitable ventures in Anchorage.

With Homeland Security in charge, Noonan had no choice but to play along with them. Even he was appalled at the lack of understanding of its minions. With 95 lives at stake there was every reason to be cautious. This, however, did not concern Homeland Security. They just drove up to the Blankenship Building and opened the door for Noonan to step out.

Into an open parking lot.

In broad daylight.

Knowing full well one of the extortionists was in the building.

Looking out any one of the three floors of windows overlooked the parking lot.

"This is not a good idea," Noonan said as he got out of the car. "You've got so many people around the building no one is going to approach it. When I get the run around, you're going to have all the people following me. They're going to be in plain sight."

No one in the car said anything. Then one of the men who wedged him in the back seat of the limo said, "You just do your job. We'll do ours."

"Oh, I am so comforted," snapped Noonan. "There are 95 lives on the line here."

If it mattered to anyone in the car no one said so. Noonan closed the car door and watched it pull away from the back door – and park 20 feet further away. So much for discretion.

The car following Noonan remained at the back of the building. According to the plan, three men were going to cover the back entrance. Two of them were going to use the car as cover and the third would be on a cell phone. How this was going to give the extortionist confidence was beyond Noonan and he had so stated when he was told of the arrangement. Henry Harrison said he, Harrison, was in charge and that was the way the deal was going to go down.

So that was the way the deal was going down.

Noonan took a long look at the circus in the parking lot, shook his head sadly and entered the structure.

Inside, the Blankenship Building was a basic, 1960s Alaska commercial structure. It had a single hallway running down the center of the building with small rooms on either side. The carpet was of 1970 vintage, threadbare and dusty. There was an elevator midway down the hallway. Noonan took it the third floor and started looking for the janitor's closet. It was not hard to find. It had no door and there was a sign above the door which read JANITOR. Inside was a single folding metal chair with a note with bright red letters stating: "Take this note to the basement using the elevator."

Noonan returned to the elevator and hit the B. When the elevator doors opened up he was in a dark hole. There was a single patch of light coming from an open doorway at the end of the hall. He left the security of the elevator and walked toward the light.

"Ah, Captain Noonan. It's so good to see you. I trust you brought a small package with you."

The perp, wearing an Elvis Presley mask, was seated on a folding metal chair behind a grated steel door. This room had clearly been the vault of the bank. The safe and its massive metal door were long gone but the corpse of the vault with its shelving and file cabinets were still there, now filled with office supplies instead of cash. Where the safety deposit boxes had been were cubbyholes, some of them filled. There was a pair of skis leaning against the wall behind the steel door and a piles of cardboard boxes with names written in broad ink slashes. What had been the vault was quite obviously now a storage area.

Between Noonan and the perp was the last vestige of the bank, the metal grate dividing the vault from the work area.

It was locked. The perp was on one side and Noonan the other.

"This is when you gloat?"

"Not yet. First, I'd like the pouch you have for me."

"This one?" Noonan held up the pouch.

"Absolutely. Just slip it through the bars."

Noonan juggled the bag in his hand. "You seem pretty confident you can get away with this. How are you planning on getting out of this building without being spotted?"

"I have a secret plan. The pouch if you please."

Noonan continued to juggle the pouch. "You made a big mistake by having me come directly here. The building is surrounded."

"I expect it is. The FBI is expecting you to be run all over town. They're waiting for you to come out. Homeland Security would be out of their depth in a puddle of water on the street."

"There are still 95 hostages to be concerned about."

"True. This is all coming to an end rather quickly. By this time you should have collected all of the diamonds we have demanded. This collection," the perp pointed at the pouch, "was just a courtesy call."

"So you could gloat?"

"So we could meet face-to-face."

"You're wearing a mask. It's hardly face-to-face."

"It will have to do. Now, I'll take the pouch and then I'll have my little say and then the games will proceed."

Noonan pushed his hand with the pouch through the bars.

"Just drop it. That will be fine. I trust it does have diamonds in it?"

"$5 million. Just like you wanted."

"I'll take your word for it." The perp opened the pouch and let the diamonds trickle into his hand. He rolled the diamonds around on the surgical glove. Then he poured them into a cloth bag he had in his lap.

"Don't trust me?"

"I don't trust the FBI. I'm looking for a tracking device."

"Find one?"

"Nope. Not this time." He tied the cloth bag shut and flipped it inside the waist band of his pants.

"Do I get to know who you are now and why I'm involved."

"Our paths crossed years ago. You busted my brother on a robbery, a small one. He should not have gotten caught in the first place, but he was nabbed. Got a five year sentence and was stabbed to death into his third year."

"I'm to blame?"

"I think so. He was put in for hard time. First offense so he should have been in medium security at best."

"If he got hard time there must have been something more than just a dash and grab."

"There were a number of them involved. Hit a pedestrian as they made their getaway. Old man. He died."

"Deaths change things in the eyes of the law."

"Well, the old man's dead and my brother's dead. Now I'm going to even the score. I'm going to pull off the greatest jewelry heist in American history right under the nose of the great detective Captain Heinz Noonan. You're even going to be part of it! Ironic, eh?"

"You know you can't get away with it."

"So far I have. Within a handful of hours I'll be gone. You're a smart cookie so you'll eventually figure out who I am but by then it won't do you any good. Once I'm out of the country I won't be coming back."

"The FBI will follow you forever."

The perp stood up and stretched. "Let them. I'm pushing 65 now. If it takes then 20 years to get me back, fine. With my cut of the take I can live very well for 20 years. Average life span in the United States is now about 75. I've got a ten good years left." He waggled the empty pouch in front of the bars. "No need for Social Security either." The perp tossed the empty pouch to Noonan through the bars. "Here's a memento for your files."

"So you are not going to tell me who you are?"

"You'll figure it out. I just wanted to confront you in person."

"How are you planning on getting out of here?" Noonan pointed around to the vault. "You don't have a lot of options."

"I am a man of many talents, Captain Noonan. One of the them is the ability to disappear at will."

Noonan pointed around the vault. "Well, you had better be very, very good because vaults are made to keep money inside and the burglars out."

"True, true." the perp leaned forward and made a mock whisper, "I have a secret plan."

"I'm dying to hear about it."

"Just wait outside and see. Now, Captain Noonan, we've have had our little chat and it's time for you to go. You've been down here just long enough to make Homeland Security nervous. The door is already locked from the inside so just close it as you leave."

"You seem pretty confident."

"If I were you I'd worry about how you're going to look in ten minutes." The perp looked at his watch. "It's 4:10 now. You've still have Ayanna's phone?"

"It's upstairs in the car."

"Fine. Be on it at 5:30 for final instructions."

"If you haven't been caught by 4:30."

"I have great faith in the incompetence of Homeland Security. It's one of the few things dishonest fellows like me can count upon." The perp stood and pointed toward the door. "This is your cue to exit. Please make sure the door latches shut on the way out."

Noonan turned and left. As the door latched shut, he could hear the perp on the phone.

"Gerry, dahling. This is your moment."

Chapter 54

Henry Harrison was harassing two of the historians at the National Archives when he got the call from his Second-in-Command. Noonan had just left the building and the perp was inside. No one else had exited. Harrison ordered the building sealed and they were to search the building room by room, detaining everyone. Then Harrison called the AIC and ordered him to support Homeland Security in the search of the building.

Chapter 55

The Corporal was hunched down behind a bush as the Humvee came slipping and sliding up the muddy frontier road. His shoes, top and bottom, were a thick goo of mud and he was not making good time. He didn't know where he was but at least he was not back in the warehouse barracks. He was cut and scraped but still in good shape. But he was soaking wet. That was going to have to change soon or he was going to catch one hellacious cold. He would have to keep moving to stay warm. This wasn't Iraq but the danger was just as real. He didn't have an M-14. All he had were his instincts and, so far, they had not failed him.

It paid to be prepared. In the split second the warehouse door had been open earlier he had seen the razor wire. So he had planned for it. He assembled an escape kit. If there was no gate he'd have to go over the razor wire. It would be tricky and it would require a lot of muscle which, in fact, he had.

As soon as the plug of hostages ran out, he grabbed his escape kit and headed away from the electric eye. He could hear the yells of frustration and figured they had discovered there was no way out. So it was time for Plan B. He climbed the cyclone fence as high as he could and tossed two blankets over the razor wire. Then he put on two hot pad mitts. His grip was not good but it did get over the hump. He fell over the other side and made it into the forest just as it started to rain.

Now he was going for help. Where, he did not know. He figured his best bet was to follow the road. It had to lead somewhere. So he followed the frontier road a dozen yards inside the forest. It as a Herculean task. If he wasn't stumbling over roots he was sinking into ooze or being batted by low hanging branches. He wasn't making good time but, then again, he was making progress.

He tried to get a license plate from the Humvee when it went by it there were no plates. He did see two men in the vehicle. The number matched with what he, Jim and Mittles had figured. One to watch and the other to do the errands. Two coming out meant no one was left at the barracks. It wasn't a good bet but it was a safe one.

It also raised a troubling thought. If there was no one at the warehouse, those hostages were stuck inside. There was no way out. If he could not find help it might be days, weeks before the hostages were found. If it was a week, not all of them would make it. None of the older ones for sure. They'd be stuck with the food and water on hand which wasn't much.

When the whine of the Humvee faded, the Corporal left the security of the forest and began walking along the side of the frontier road. The grass was wet here and he was able to wipe off some of the mud on his shoes. The going was better here. Less mud but he was still walking in a down pour.

Chapter 56

Gerry and her cameraman had no trouble finding the spot on the sidewalk where she was to set up her camera.

"X marks the spot," she said. "With arrow pointing south. How original. Make sure the camera is facing south." She indicated the camera would be focused due south, exactly like the chalk arrow on the sidewalk.

"What are we filming?" asked her camera man. He set up the camera and looked south.

"I have no idea."

The X, a bright red, was about 15 yards back from the corner on Third Street. South of the X, half of the entire block was the parking lot servicing the Blankenship Building and the two other high rise structures opening onto Fourth Street. There was a squat, two-story building to the east and a three-story parking garage to the west. The other side of Third Street was a steep hill, created by the 1964 Earthquake and too unstable for any structure. At the bottom of the hill was a massive parking lot for the new State Office Building, SOB, which had been built at the bottom of the hill.

"What time is it?" asked the cameraman.

"4:20. Joint time if we weren't on duty."

"Stifle it. Pot's not legal yet."

"Not yet," the camera said wistfully.

"Well, we're where we're supposed to be."

They both turned when they heard a commotion across the parking lot. It appeared about a dozen people were clustering at the back entrance to the Blankenship Building.

"Maybe that's what we're supposed to film.

"Shoot it," said Geraldine.

As the cameraman was focusing the lens on the disturbance Gerry got a call.

"Look up," the voice said.

"Eh?"

"Up, Gerry, dahling, up. Look up. The top of the building."

Gerry looked up and there, on the top of the four story structure next to the Blankenship Building was the figure of a man on the roof. He was waving at Gerry.

Gerry nudged the cameraman. "Up there," she pointed. "On top of the building."

The cameraman swiveled his equipment and zoomed in on the figure on top of the building.

"The dude's got an Elvis mask on. Sure he's our man?"

"Do you have an Elvis mask on?" Gerry said into the phone. "He's our man," she said an instant later. "He says to follow him."

Gerry snapped her phone shut. With the cameraman she watched as the figure walked to the edge of the roof where he fiddled with something on the ledge. Then, with a sudden movement he jumped off the roof.

"Jezz," snapped the cameraman.

"Tell me you got that on film," Gerry said holding her breath.

"Ab-so-positive-lulty. You won't believe what he's . . ."

"I can see him from here."

The figure only fell about four feet and suddenly he was whizzing down from the four-story building to the top of the three-story parking garage across G Street.

"That better be a rope," said Gerry. "I don't want to believe he can fly."

"It's a rope all right. Now he's untying the end of it and letting it fall. No one is going to be following him using the rope. He's left everyone behind him on the top of the building. Clever boy. They can see him but not do a darn thing about it."

Gerry looked back to the roof top. "There isn't anyone there."

"Gerry. Look!"

Gerry turned back to the parking garage and there, on the upper most precipice, the figure had jumped up onto the ledge. He was looking directly at them, a dozen yards down the street and three stories up. The figure gave them a salute and then cat-walked to the northeast corner of the parking garage.

"What's he doing now?"

"He's got another rope."

"What?"

"Yup. And there is goes!"

As Gerry watched, the figure dropped off the roof of the garage. Again, he fell only four or five feet and then plummeting down the steep hillside toward the State Office Building. It was another rope slide. But this one was a zip line.

It was at that very moment Gerry and the cameraman realized why they had been required to set up the camera at exactly where X marked the spot. It was the only spot with a clear view of the front door of the State Office Building. The rest of the hillside was bushy but someone had gone to great deal of effort to make certain there was no visual obstruction between the precise location of the television camera and the front door of the building. Half a foot forward or back and the doorway would have been obscured by brush.

"Keep shooting."

"I am, I am."

The distance to the State Office Building was so great Gerry could not see what the figure was doing.

"He made it all the way down, right?"

"Right down to the big tree next to the entryway. Now he's unhitching himself. He's turning this way and waving. Still got the Elvis mask on. Waving again and now he's gone. Inside."

Hearing the sound of voices, Gerry turned and saw a passel of personnel on the top of the adjacent building. "Get a shot of those guys. Run the camera up the slope for effect."

"Don't tell me how to do my job."

Chapter 57

Other than Gerry and her cameraman, the only person to see the figure plummet from the top of the parking garage down the hillside to the State Office Building was Henry Harrison. He was hurrying down Third Street from the National Archives toward the back of the Blankenship Building when he heard a whizzing sound overhead. He looked up just in time to see a figure with an Elvis Presley mask sliding down a rope less than a dozen feet overhead.

Harrison immediately picked up his cell phone and dialed the AIC. "Why aren't your people watching the State Office Building?"

"We are!" came a voice over his cell phone. "He's inside!"

Two minutes later, just before two unmarked cars and six squad cars arrived at the front entrance to the State Office Building, the four double-wide doors were flung open. It was 4:30, on the nose, and every bureaucrat in Anchorage flooded out of the building.

Gerry caught it all on tape.

Chapter 58

The Fisherman lugged a cement block out of the back of his car and loaded it onto the boat. He strapped a rope around the inside brace and tied it off with a bowline. He didn't want to have it popping free when it hit bottom. He left out about six feet of rope and cut it. To the free end he tied the drawstring of a cloth mesh bag.

Next he loaded a plastic bag of clothing and tossed a pair of tennis shoes under the boat's seat. He dragged the ice chest along the pavement and levered it up to the gunnels and then plopped it inside the boat. Finally he took a half-full tank of gas and loaded it aboard. He attached the hoses and gave the engine a quick start. It popped right to life. He smiled as he looked at his watch.

"Almost Showtime!"

Chapter 59

"What kind of bozos do you have working for you?" Harrison was almost dancing with anger. "We had our boy! He was in a vault in a basement with no way out! We had the building locked down! Locked down! And **your** bozos **let him get away**!"

The AIC was just as livid. "You sent your people in way too early. There was no way the perp was going to come out the front or back door. What do you think he is, some novice?! He's a professional. He never intended to go out the front door! Or the back door! He knew the basements were connected! While your men," the word *men* was said with derision, "were slamming their way through the metal grate, the perp was into the next building, the building you **had not** secured."

"The building was not secured because it was your job!" yelled Harrison. "You were told to cover the area, do the things the FBI is supposed to do. You didn't do your job. We did our job! You didn't do yours!"

"Oh, we did our job all right. Your people don't even know what their job is!"

Back and forth the two went at each other. It was like a tennis match where the ball was being batted back and forth viciously. One man would throw a charge and the other would bat it back. It was giants in conflict and no one else in the room said a word.

Noonan was about to interrupt when Ayanna came into the Command Center with a Manila file. The sly smile crossing her face indicated she would enjoy sticking around and watching the political pyrotechnics.

"Apparently I'm the only one here who knows time is short," Noonan said as he pulled Ayanna out of the Command Center.

"Again! This is happening *again* and I can't watch?"

"Those two are doing exactly what the perpetrators want them to do: fighting among ourselves. They are very clever people. This is going to come to a conclusion very quickly and we don't have a lot of time. So far we don't have much to work with. What's with the paper work?" He indicated the folder under her arm.

"Probably a lot more nothing. After I contacted your office I tried nosing around Homeland Security. I got nothing but as I was leaving I saw Harrison headed in the opposite direction from the Blankenship Building. I wondered what he was doing so I followed him."

"Good girl."

"Thanks, I needed the encouragement. He made a beeline for the National Archives where he started harassing the historians there about a business active in Anchorage in 1964 called Anaktuvik."

"Anaktuvik?"

"Yeah. He even spelled it for them."

"That's what he wanted?"

"He wasn't very nice about it. They told him they couldn't help him since Alaska was a state in 1964 and any business in Anchorage would be a state business. He left in a huff."

"Anaktuvik?"

"Right."

"What's this?"

"After he left I asked the historians if there was anything he hadn't been told. They said Anaktuvik is a Native village in the Brooks Range – way north of Fairbanks – and they didn't know of any business in Anchorage with the exact name."

"And?"

"I asked them about city and state records and they told me to go to the Anchorage Museum. I told them it was an emergency and they placed a call for me." She smirked, "They said I was a lot nicer than Homeland Security."

"I can imagine."

"There is a list of businesses licenses on the Internet and there are some businesses with the name Anaktuvik in them but none as far back as 1964. The earliest were in the 1970s and were Native businesses." She held up the folder. "I've got a list here but I don't think there's anything for us. There are two interesting things about Anaktuvik. First, it was not a traditional Native village. It has an odd history. It wasn't established because it was near a resource like a salmon stream, berries or a good hunting area. The Wien brothers established it as a refueling place for their bush planes. They moved people into the area."

"And the second thing?"

"It's famous for its masks. Natives make a unique mask in Anaktuvik Pass. You can find them all over town." She showed him a photocopy of a mask. "There's a glitch, though. No one started making those masks until long after the earthquake." She showed Noonan a FAX copy of an Anaktuvik mask.

"I've seen these around town. They're from Anaktuvik, eh?"

"Yeah. That's it. Nothing else."

"Why was Harrison burning jet fuel to find out about Anaktuvik?"

"That I don't know. Just that he was."

Noonan thought for a moment. He looked at the mask and then held it up. "Does this look like Elvis Presley to you?"

Ayanna laughed. "Not a chance."

"Well, I don't know what Harrison was looking for and neither does he so it makes us even. Ask the Alaskan who works for the Seattle Police Department, the one who identified the walrus whisker, if it means anything to him. Make sure he reports back to you first, not to Homeland Security."

"Roger."

"Make it quick. I expect the next call from those perps to come any minute now."

Chapter 60

Henry Harrison cleared his throat. It was for effect only. Everyone was already quiet, waiting for him to say something. He had come into the room of relatives like an emperor – because he had allowed three television cameras into the room. The camera people were under strict orders to allow questions. That was the way Harrison liked it. Lots of camera shots and questions. Then he could edit out the bad questions. The good ones he had already salted. Relatives had been hinted at what questions were best to ask. All in the name of security. National Security. It was what he had told them. For security reasons. Had a nice ring to it. It was the nice thing about working for Homeland Security. Security was in the title. He didn't have to say why security was necessary. Only that it was 'security.'

Harrison turned sideways for a good profile shot. He was talking on a cell phone, listening actually, and occasionally saying something official. The person at the other end of the line did not acknowledge a thing he said. She was the weather person and every ten seconds she gave the time, weather and advised her listeners to shop at Safeway or Walmart or the other local businesses paying for the advertising time.

Harrison said "Yes, Sir," and hung up the phone. Then he turned to the audience, placed his hands on the sides of the podium and said, "Thank you for being here."

It was dead silent.

"I want to let you know everything is going to be wrapped up within two or three hours, four at the outmost. I cannot tell you very many details except arrangements are being made as we speak to make certain all of the demands of the extortionists are being met. The safety of the hostages," he leaned forward and emphasized "your loved ones" and then he returned to his majestic presence, "is our first concern. We have been assured there have been no injuries and all hostages are in good health and being taken care of. All I can say now is to be patient for another two hours." He looked around the room, "Any questions?"

There was a hubbub but no one said anything. Then a single hand went up in the back. "Do we know where the hostages are located?"

The single question Harrison had been hoping someone would ask.

"We are fairly sure they are in the Seattle area. Homeland Security is directing the FBI and Seattle police in the checking of all buildings large enough to house 95 people. There are not many so I expect we will have some word soon."

"How will they get to Anchorage," someone else asked.

Harrison again smiled. This was the second of three questions he wanted to answer. It was as if he had been salting his own news conference. "Homeland Security is making arrangements to have them flown to Anchorage. If we cannot find an empty plane they will be put aboard every available flight. As they are loaded aboard, we will announce the names so you will know exactly when each person has left Seattle."

"Are these guys going to get away with it?"

Harrison felt like yelling Bingo! Three out of three and the first three questions out of the gate. He leaned forward, tilted his head a bit. "Right now our first obligation is to the hostages. Once they are free then we can concentrate on running these miscreants to ground. *They can run but they cannot hide.* Once they have the final payment and the hostages are released, well, ladies and gentlemen, it becomes a brand new ball game." He looked at his watch. "This is all for the moment. I will try to be back here in an hour for an update. Thank you very much."

With a bureaucratic flurry, he was gone.

Chapter 61

Right on the dot of 5:30, Ayanna got the call.

"You want what?" snapped Ayanna into her cell phone. She was incredulous.

"You heard what I said, Love," came the voice again. "Start filling Unicorn 739 with fuel. When it's filled to capacity, I'll call back. I'll know when the plane is fully fueled when the trucks pull away. No tricks now. Just fuel the plane. While you are at it, have the ridiculous collection of guards pulled off the security detail. We don't want any trouble this late in the game."

"Are you planning on flying out?" She was incredulous. "Where do you think you can go?"

"Never you mind," said the voice. "Just fuel the plane to capacity. When it's full, have the fuel trucks leave the area. I also want security sweeps of the plane. Run your security people through it to make sure no one is on the plane. I mean no one. Not a human, not a dog, not a GPS. Nothing. Got it?"

"I got it but it's going to take some time. Getting a large plane ready to fly will take an hour of so."

"You've got time – but not much more than an hour. Don't play us for fools this late in the game. When the plane's full, clear all runways for takeoff."

"You don't think you'll get away with this do you?"

"So far we have," the voice was no sweet. "When I see the fuel trucks pull away, we'll talk again."

"What about the hostages? When will they be released?"

"As soon as we are over international waters. Relax, everyone is well. No one is going to be released until we are well on our way."

Before Ayanna could say anything else, the cell phone went dead.

Ayanna turned to Noonan. "You won't believe what they want."

"Sure I can. I heard what you said. They want to fly out."

"Where are they going to go? It's a long way to any place from here. Who's going to let them land?"

"No way of knowing but so far they've been one step ahead of us. They must have some sort of a plan."

"You don't sound as sure of yourself as you did a few hours ago."

"Until this all plays out we're not going to know what is what. Like you, I'm concerned about the hostages first."

She was exasperated. "We can track a plane. We've satellites and radar and AWACS. Even if they drop below the horizon they've got to land somewhere."

The detective shook his head. "Clever people, these thieves. I'm sure they have something elaborate planned. Do you have the final $10 million in diamonds?"

"Not yet. We should get them within an hour or so. Probably about the same time the plane gets refueled. Of course, we can slow down the re-fueling."

"I wouldn't do that."

"Why not?"

"I'll give you 95 reasons. Until the hostages are released we've got to play their game."

"This does *not* make me happy."

Chapter 62

"Gerry, dahling, it so good to talk to you."

"This is getting old and I haven't got much of anything. All I've gotten is a handful leads everyone else is getting a few minutes later."

"Gerry," the voice was soothing, "this is a very big game with lots of players. You've been treated well and it hasn't cost you a thing."

"May be true but you've got this whole city on edge. Everyone's a detective now. We've got people listening to the radio driving up and down the streets waiting for something to happen. It's crazy."

"All in the plan. All in the plan. The more people there are on the street, the better. Now, we're about ready for the last drop. $10 million in diamonds. You want to make sure you are in the right place at the right time. It may be a bit difficult but I am sure a woman of your ingenuity can swing it. Let me tell you where to set up your camera so you can see our greatest feat."

"I'm listening."

Chapter 63

"So this is what $10 million in diamonds look like," said Ayanna as she ran her fingers over the stones. She picked one up and held it to the light. "Beautiful."

"Now you know why they call them 'a girl's best friend.'" Noonan smiled.

"You've got to find a man to go with 'em," said Ayanna. "A rich one."

"Best of luck," Noonan said as he fingered the leather pouch. He played with it for a moment and then handed it to Ayanna. "In they go."

"Yeah," she sighed. Then she rolled the diamonds into her hand and poured them into the pouch. Noonan cinched the pouch shut and she held up her empty hands toward the AIC. "See, nothing in my hands."

The AIC did not smile. He did not think anything was funny.

"OK, listen up." The AIC gave a whistle bringing the room to instant silence. "This is the last drop, the end of the $25 million. The second we drop these off we are through with the negotiations. Then three things happen at once. We wait for the hostages to be released. We track the airplane these buggers are going to be flying and we bring the dirt bags in."

There was a round of here, here.

"Now," said the AIC, "we have to wait."

Chapter 64

Pandemonium was the only word to describe the runway around Unicorn 739.

Then it got worse.

The moment the fuel trucks arrived, the radios carried the news to every home in Anchorage. Ten minutes later everyone in America was glued to their television sets. Unicorn 739, Alaska's ghost airliner, was going to take off for parts unknown. Elmendorf Air Force Base had two AWACS aloft and there were rumors cameras of the spy satellites were being focused on the Anchorage International Airport. In Washington D. C., the President of the United States issued a statement condemning the hijacking and said there would be dire consequences to any nation giving haven to the extortionists.

In Anchorage, everyone with a camera and a tripod had staked out every square foot in the open field beside the runway ready to see history being made. Try as they could, even though Airport Security was fully manned, it had a hard time keeping order on the runway. So the Anchorage Police had to be called for assistance. When the men and women in blue did not prove to be enough manpower, the Alaska State Troopers were called. So, as Zero Hour approached, there was a massive plug of humanity surrounding the plane waiting to see what was going to happen.

Compared to the crowd outside, the people inside the terminal were civil. The end of concourse had been taped off and the tourist traffic had been moved back to the main hallway so the tourists would be away from Unicorn 739 when it took off. There were still plenty of people in the terminal – in addition to the press, Homeland Security honchos and every politico Alaska had to offer. With so much down time before the plane took off, there was plenty of on-air space for everyone and anyone in public office to get a minute or two of their 15 minutes of fame. Everyone wanted a piece of the journalistic coverage.

From the runway, the windows of the terminal looked to made of human flesh. They were people shoulder-to-shoulder all the way down the terminal. Those who could not make it to the tarmac were watching from the windows. History was going to be made here and everyone wanted be part of it.

No one seemed to notice two figures at the far end of the runway. They were barely visible from Unicorn 739. All someone could see if they looked hard enough was one of the figures was obviously a cameraman and he – it was probably a he – was aiming his lens right down the runway toward the plane.

Chapter 65

"Show time!" The Fisherman locked his car in the parking lot. He walked around the empty boat carriage and down to the floating dock. It was high tide and the dock was just a foot below the level of the parking lot. No one was there. Everyone was down at the airport. The Fisherman was alone. He stepped into the boat and then turned around to untie it from the dock. Then he pushed free of the timbers. He let the boat float a dozen feet and then turned the motor on. Slowly he putt-putted out into Cook Inlet headed for Knik Arm.

Chapter 66

It was still pouring when the Corporal came to the fence. It also had razor wire on top. Unlike the fence surrounding the barrack warehouse, this fence had a gate. Better yet, the gate was open.

This did not seem right. It smelled fishy. If these guys were so security conscious, why leave a gate open? So he spent some time looking into the woods on the far side of the fence. There was still a heavy rainfall so everything was moving under the cascading water. If anyone was over there, he couldn't see them. After ten minutes he cautiously moved forward until he was as close to the gate as he could but still have coverage. Then he sprinted through the gate and disappeared into the trees on the far side. Ten yards in, he fell flat on the ground and listened for sounds of pursuit.

He heard none.

He waited another ten minutes and then got up. Slowly he picked his way through the forest and ran head-on into the back of a building. Sliding along between the wall and the forest he rounded the corner of the structure and found himself at the edge of a rural mall. People were scurrying about in the downpour trying to get into their cars without getting their packages wet. Slipping more than walking, he made a beeline for the Security Guard at the Walmart at the far end of the shopping center.

Chapter 67

The instant the fuel trucks pulled away from Unicorn 739, Ayanna got a call on her cell phone.

"Very good. Very efficient."

"Thank you. Now let's get this charade over."

"It's almost done. Now, you do have the $10 million in gems?"

"Yes."

"They are in a pouch like before?"

"Just as you instructed."

"Fine, fine. Now, I want you to take the pouch and go into the Unicorn 739 down the corridor from the terminal. You are to place the pouch on the pull-down seat next to the pilot's cabin door. The pull-down seat on the left as you are facing the front of the plane. Do you understand what I am talking about?"

"Yes," Ayanna looked at Noonan with a helpless look. "You want me to put the diamonds in the pouch on the pull-down seat on the port side of the pilot's door."

"Correct," the voice said. "You are to enter the plane from the terminal, not the back of the plane. Do you understand?"

"Yes," again she repeated the instructions aloud so the Command Center could hear her.

"You are to leave the plane door to the Terminal open but you are to close the back staircase, the tail entrance, and remove the walkway from the side of the plane. Do you understand? You are to close the back staircase and then you are to exit the plane into the terminal. Are my instructions clear?"

Ayanna repeated what had been said.

"And I want Noonan there when you walk onboard to drop off the gems. I don't want him mucking up the works."

Ayanna looked at Noonan as she repeated what she had been told. Noonan just smiled and nodded.

"Now," the voice continued, "tell me what you are going to do in the order I told you."

"I," Ayanna started.

"No," the voice said. "You and Noonan."

"Yes, I and Captain Noonan are going to place the $10 million in diamonds in the pouch on the pull-down seat on the port side of the pilot's cabin entrance. We will enter the plane through the hatch opening into the terminal. We will close the back staircase, order the mobile sidewalk pulled away and then exit the plane."

"Good. The instant we get aboard I want to be cleared for takeoff. We will arrive, check to make sure the stones are there and then the plane will take off. No one will say anything. I expect there will be no trouble."

"When do the hostages get released?"

"As soon as we clear American air space."

"Your people. How will I know who you are?"

"There will be three people, me and two smaller persons. I am six feet six so you will have no problem recognizing me. All three of us will have helmets with dark visors so you cannot recognize us. We will all be dressed like Unicorn pilots. Does this description make you happy?"

"I'll be happy when I see you in jail."

There was a chuckle on the other end of the line. "Let's just stick to the matter at hand. The first thing for you to do is get those diamonds onto the plane."

Chapter 68

"What are we doing down here?"

Gerry looked at her camera man. "This is where we were told to be. My inside source says this is going to be best spot for a shot."

"This place ain't anywhere. We're at the end of the terminal concourse. The only shot we're going to get is the belly of the beast as it flies over. There's nothing down here except empty trucks."

"Patience. If this is where the action is going to be, this is where I want to be."

Chapter 69

Harrison took the call just as he was about to enter the Command Center. He made occasional appearances just to inform everyone he was in charge. Homeland Security never sleeps. When he looked at the incoming number he recognized it as the Seattle Headquarters and stopped just outside the door.

"Harrison."

As the voice talked, Harrison broke into a wide smile which he quickly turned to a granite expression.

"Are you sure?" He said. "All 95?"

There was some mumbling on the phone.

"What you are saying is everyone is accounted for. No one missing. No one hurt?"

There was a short affirmative on the line.

Harrison did not even bother to open the Command Center door. He headed straight for the warehouse room where the press was gathered. "Come on," he said loudly to the gathered journalists. "I've got some breaking news."

Chapter 70

Ayanna and Noonan entered Unicorn 739 from the terminal and walked to the pilot's cabin. Noonan pulled down the seat on the left side of the cockpit.

"Do you think they'll get away with this?" She was clearly angry.

"Don't know," he replied. "This is a long way from over. Until the hostages get released we play by their rules." He waved his hand helplessly.

Ayanna put the pouch with the gems down. "Never in my wildest dreams did I believe this would ever happen."

"The night is still young," smiled Noonan.

Ayanna followed the instructions she had been given by the control tower and flicked the switch to raise the rear staircase. The sidewalk had already been removed so she had done what she had been instructed to do. She didn't hear anything so she sent Noonan back to make sure to make the sure the staircase was up. Two minutes later he came back. The rear staircase was locked in place. Then the two of them exited the plane and the walkway.

The terminal walkway was empty save for a half dozen security personnel just standing around. No one knew what was going to happen next. Ayanna and Noonan then stood by the police tape and waited. For what they were not sure.

"How is their pilot going to get into this terminal? It's locked down."

"They've thought of everything else. I'm sure this is in their game plan."

"Well, I'm not sure."

And that was as far as she got.

In the distance – behind her *in the plane* – she heard a pop and whine and then a pronounced roar. She and Noonan turned around and looked back toward the entryway of Unicorn 739 just as a motorcycle exploded out of the walkway and careened into the Terminal. Its wheels hit the constellation carpet and shot down Concourse A. By the time the security personnel had recovered their collective wits, the motorcycle had snapped through the yellow police tape and was breaking the land speed record heading to the far end of the terminal.

"How is he going to get out of the building?" yelled Ayanna as she charged after the disappearing motorcyclist.

Noonan stood at the entrance to the walkway simply smiling.

Chapter 71

Hollywood could not have choreographed the next 10 seconds better than true life. Every person in the Terminal was pressed to the bank of windows watching the runway so there was not a soul walking around to slow the motorcycle's progress This gave the rider a straight shot at the east end of the combined concourses.

There may have been no one ahead of the rider but as soon as the motorcycle passed, everyone who had been pressed to the window was in pursuit. The human wave stalled Ayanna and the rest of the security personnel. The further the motorcycle ran, the more people joined in the chase.

Then something strange happened. One of the pursuers noticed some small, glittering objects were falling off the back of the motorcycle. Not a lot of them, just a few. It didn't take a genius to figure out what those objects were.

"Diamonds!" Someone yelled and there was an instantaneous crowd scrounging around on the floor looking for diamonds. That stopped the pursuit dead in its tracks.

Chapter 72

Gerry was watching as tail door to Unicorn 739 was being closed. "Oh no!!" snapped the cameraman. "We've missed it."

"Not yet." Gerry said. "We're where we're supposed to be. Get ready to shoot."

"Shoot what?"

Just then they heard the sound of a motorcycle.

"Is the sound coming from inside the Terminal?"

"Yeah," said Gerry. "Get the camera rolling. Focus on the terminal. We're here for a reason."

"But the plane's down there!"

"Yeah, but the action is here!"

Just as the cameraman focused on the terminal the plastic sheeting on the window being repaired exploded outward.

"Momma Mia!" said the camera man as the motorcycle went airborne.

"Did you get it? Did you get it?" Gerry was so excited she jumping up and down.

"I'm getting it!"

He was getting it. Right in the center of his lens. The motorcycle came out of the second floor window with streams of plastic sheeting from the window. The cycle fell about four feet and landed on top of a glass repair truck which had obviously been placed in exactly the right location to receive the motorcycle. The bike took a single bounce and landed on the angled staircase on the front of the truck. The ladder still had the wood board covering the steps so the new glass window, which was on the tarmac leaning against the truck, could be slid into place. The plastic sheeting ripped off and the motorcycle was now across the runway headed for the tree line of Kincaid Park half a mile away.

10 seconds later, everyone who could run, jump or hop was headed for the moose gates on the far side of the runway and Kincaid Park.

Chapter 73

The Fisherman was idling near the bank when he heard a crashing in the underbrush. Casually looking over his right shoulder he watched as a black motorcycle leapt off the ledge of Kincaid Park and dropped into Knik Inlet. There was a deep *kerplunk!* and the water swallowed the vehicle. It was high tide so the level of the water was almost flush with the forest floor. In six hours the water would be 30 feet lower. The motorcycle would still not be visible. It would be another 30 feet down, rolling back and forth on the bottom of the Inlet, being ground deeper and deeper into the mud with each tide.

The Fisherman nosed the boat toward a patch of rocks on the shore. As he did, a small figure reached into the brush and pulled a rope. The short ramp allowing the motorcycle to arch over the Inlet collapsed into the water. It did not make a splash, it just slid into the water. Then the figure was running toward him, stripping off the motorcycle helmet as she ran.

"Everything go according to plan?" The Fisherman looked at her expectantly.

She just gave him a quick thumbs up and reached for the nose of the boat. She jumped in and he slowly started to putt-putt out into the deeper waters. Beside him the woman stripped to her underwear and slid all of her clothing into the mesh laundry bag. As she was pulling on a sweatshirt, the Fisherman lifted the cement block and dropped it over the side of the boat. There was a slight splash and zinging sound as the rope ran across the gunnels and then the laundry mesh bag went overboard. The Fisherman and the woman each had a beer open and their lines in the water before the first Anchorage Police Patrol boat rounded the point and headed toward them.

Chapter 74

T here was not enough room to slide a playing card between the tips of the noses of Harrison and the AIC. Both were talking at the same time and each was index fingering the other's chest. It was the eruption of turf war at its finest. For those who had sweet tooth from this kind of confrontation – and from the looks on the faces of many of those in the Command Center this was indeed the case – it was pure Guerilla Theater. It did not get much better than this.

The AIC was accusing Harrison of grandstanding for the cameras and newspapers by announcing the hostages had been released unharmed. Because the AIC didn't know the hostage had been released he had been forced to pay the $10 million in ransom. Harrison said Homeland Security was in charge and he made the decision because the hostages were the first concern. Once the hostages were released it was his duty to inform the families.

This set the AIC off and he accused Harrison of getting a drop on the publicity. Harrison said if the roles had been reversed the most dangerous square foot in America would have been between the AIC and any news camera. The AIC said such was a lie. Harrison said it was true. The AIC threatened and Harrison stated he was in charge.

Then things got worse.

Ayanna had been able to get one of the diamonds off the floor in the terminal. That was only because she had actually retrieved it. Everyone else who was scrounging on the floor for the stones denied they had found so much as a sliver of a precious stone. One look at it and she realized it was not a diamond at all. Simply some costume jewelry. She could crumple it to shards in here hand.

The Anchorage Police had Kincaid Park completely cordoned off but there were so many people milling around looking for the motorcyclist it was impossible to tell who was a lookie-loo and who was the perp. Everyone coming out of the park was searched but this was not going to do any good because the perp had probably hidden the diamonds. The motorcycle was not found and there were so many scrambler tracks all over the Park so there was no way to follow the set left by the perpetrator's motorcycle. The police had stopped several boats in Cook Inlet near the park but none of the fishermen were suspicious. All boats were searched to no avail. It was as if the motorcyclist had simply disappeared into the ether.

The only person who seemed completely calm in the chaos surrounding him was Chief of Detectives Heinz Noonan. He sat back, sipping a cup of coffee watching the AIC and the Harrison accuse each other of all manner of malfeasance.

"Those creeps got away with it," said Ayanna as she down next to Noonan. "You'd think grown men could act better."

"Everybody's venting. It's to be expected."

"You don't seem to be too concerned. I mean, the bad guys won this one."

Noonan smiled. "Not yet. You've got a lot to learn about human nature."

Ayanna looked at him with questions in her eyes. "Is this going somewhere?"

"Sure. Do you want to catch the bad guys?"

"We all do."

"No," Noonan said. "What I said was do *you* want to catch the bad guys?" He emphasized the word *you.*

"Hey, I'm not very high up on the food chain around here."

Noonan shook his head. "These guys," he indicted the AIC and Harrison, "are political animals. They aren't detectives. They couldn't find chopsticks in a Chinese restaurant. Now, do *you* want to catch the bad guys?"

"Well, sure. How do we do that?"

"Logic," said Noonan. "Very quietly get four or five people. At least one has to be a cop. You'll need the cop to make the bust legal. Can you do that?"

Chapter 75

When the door to 457 Fleishacker Drive opened, Ayanna found herself looking at a man who was easily in his 90s. He moved slowly and smiled when he saw her.

"Hello there, young lady. What can I do for you?"

"Are you Jonathan Powers? Dr. Jonathan Powers?"

"That's right. I'm retired now but I'm still a doctor."

"I have delivery for you. I'm sorry it's so late but it came in on Unicorn 739 and the cargo could not be released until . . ."

"Oh, yes. I've been watching the television. Terrible what this world is coming to."

"This would have been delivered earlier but all of the cargo onboard was detained. Now the crisis is over we're delivering the cargo." She handed Powers a small box with one hand and a receipt pad with the other. "If you'll just sign here."

"No problem at all. I've been waiting for this."

Powers signed the receipt pad and handed it back to her. "Would you like to come in for some tea? I get so few visitors."

"Oh, no," replied Ayanna. "I'll be on my way."

As soon as the door closed Ayanna waved the receipt. Which was when the Anchorage Police officer hit the front door. He was too late. Dr. Powers was already out the back door and struggling to break free of the two Airport Security officers who had him pinned against the back fence.

"Going somewhere?" Ayanna asked as she pulled his wig off. Dr. Powers now had jet black hair. When she pulled off his bulbous nose of putty, he didn't look nearly 90 years old. Fifty was closer.

Chapter 76

"**I** would have loved to have been in the Command Center when the news of the arrest came over the television." Noonan was chuckling as Ayanna drove him across town. "I am sure everyone is fighting for time in front of the cameras."

"Better them than me," Ayanna said. "I hope you can salvage some of your vacation."

"Here, yes. But I don't see my Commissioner giving me comp time in Sandersonville. That's the way Homeland Security operates, Ayanna. If you did it on your own time it was for the good of the nation."

"Well, I'm happy this turned out so well. We didn't get them all. But there is a silver lining. Airport Security upstaged Homeland Security and the FBI. It doesn't happen very often but when it does it feels great!"

"Well, at least we got one guy and $10 million."

"How did you figure it out, by the way?"

"Logic, Ayanna, logic. Once I understood what was happening all the pieces fell into place."

"How so?"

"Well, take the airplane. Getting passengers to board early was no problem. Everyone wants to get on board so someone pretending to be the pilot – someone who had credentials and said they were new to Unicorn Airlines – said the passengers could load early. The gate attendants said fine. Loading early was no problem for them. The attendant had the authority to load passengers early. After all, they thought she was the Captain. So no one told her no."

"Wouldn't the crew have seen her face?"

"Sure. So what? The passengers and crew were going to be hostages. They would be held until the $25 million in diamonds were transferred. Then she'd leave the country. Live in some place where it's impossible to get anyone extradited back to the United States. She could have cared less who saw her face."

"Then they faked a bomb threat or something like that?"

"Yeah, something like that. After all the passengers were on the plane she directed them to a couple of buses. No one on board would have thought anything about it. They got into airport buses and left. No one at the airport would have been too concerned about airport buses at the airport. Once the buses started up no one could get off. The drivers were probably in security boxes so none of the passengers could get to them. I'll bet they drove right to where they were being held hostage. You'll probably find the buses there. All passenger cell phones and lap tops were confiscated and then Air Streaked to Juneau and Nome and wherever else they ended up. It was just more confusion."

"Just like the plane flying under the radar."

"Correct. Just confusion."

"So the hostages just sat in a warehouse for two days."

"They just sat. They were a bargaining chip. As long as the hostages were being held, the Police and Homeland Security was not going to be spending a lot of time looking for the perps. They were going to be spending their time getting the diamonds."

"How did you know where to look for the perp's address?"

"You mean their phony address? Another 30 seconds and your Dr. Powers would have been long gone."

"How did you find the address?"

"Simple. When I looked at the cargo manifest there were only a handful of specialty clients. There was nothing suspicious about any of them at first. Then we found the weight-losing igloo. It was clearly meant as a diversion. The perps wanted us to find the discrepancy. It was their way of distracting us from the real purpose of the cargo. Once I had eliminated the igloo I was left with the motorcycle and a lot of little boxes. I didn't know how the motorcycle was going to fit in so I took some preventative measures."

"Preventative measures?"

"I got some cocaine from the Crime Lab here in Anchorage. You see, I had a secret weapon."

"Do tell."

"The drug dog. I got to know the dog and his handler. When I first visited the plane the handler said he'd been through the plane twice and didn't find anything. No pilot and no cocaine. Then the plane was locked down. I knew there was no cocaine on the plane. Remember when I picked up the pouch when you were looking at the diamonds?"

"Yeah."

"Well, I dropped some cocaine into the pouch. I was pretty sure whoever was going to get the diamonds was not going to take them along."

"Why not?"

"Because there would be no way to get out of Anchorage with the stones. The perps have been very good at blending with crowds because they were part of the crowd. They dressed like airport people and had the run of the place. My bet was they *were* airport people. You've had a spy in your department the whole time. You have, what, maybe 200 employees. Look for the smallest woman. She will be your pilot."

"We didn't see anyone get off the plane! How did she do it?"

"You didn't see anyone get off the plane because you were looking for someone who didn't fit in. Everyone I talked with said they had looked over the tapes and had not seen anyone *who was not supposed to be there*. The pilot was a small woman who have crawled out of the plane and blended in with the security personnel. She was recognized as someone who should have been there so she was eliminated as a suspect."

"Hiding in plain sight, eh?"

"You got it. She probably had the previous day off. If you check your flights I'm sure you'll find her name on a flight to Seattle. I'll also bet she's got a military background. One person can fly one of the big planes but they've got to be very good. She was very good. If she had commendations and those can be traced."

"She's been working with the perps since the beginning."

"For months. She's been jiggling the paperwork for a long time. How do you think they got the window to the terminal out? They just faked some repair paperwork and took the window out. Then they moved the glass truck into the right spot for the motorcycle. I'll bet you'll find they had a fake work order for the window job. Oh, they had the airport security down perfectly."

"Was she the one on the motorcycle?"

"I'm betting yes. Somehow the person on the motorcycle had to get onto the plane without being suspected. On one of the security sweeps she probably just hid in the plane. Or just walked on as if she part of a security sweep. There were so many security people running around no one person was going to missed. Airport Security was expected to make sweeps of the plane and they did. She just walked onboard and hid."

"What about the diamonds?"

"Ah, the diamonds. Yes. The last shipment had to be delivered in town. There was no way the perps could leave the airport with the diamonds. Everyone everywhere was going to be searched. They could not take the diamonds and hide them in Kincaid Park because there would be too many people looking for them. You saw how many people there were at the airport as the plane was being refueled. So the diamonds had to be delivered in some other way. The motorcycle was a ruse."

"Well, it worked."

"Not really. You got those diamonds. The best way to get diamonds out of a secure area is to have them delivered to you. So that was the plan. The diamonds were put in a package which had just come up from Seattle. All it took was a pen knife and some tape. The box was split open, the pouch slipped inside and the box taped shut. It would have taken all of about five seconds."

"Right. And as soon as we cleared the walkway, she came blasting out of the plane," Ayanna shook her head sadly. "I should have seen that. We were waiting for a pilot to come walking in so he could take off. We weren't expecting someone to come riding out of the airplane on a motorcycle from the opposite direction."

"That could have been a flaw in their plan. I mean, how did they know the motorcycle could make it all the way down the concourse and not hit someone or slide onto its side?"

"Unlikely," said Noonan. "Everyone knew the plane was going to take off so everyone was looking out the window. They weren't walking around the terminal, they were glued to the bank of windows. As far as sliding, not a chance. The gosh-awful carpet on the floor runs all the way through the terminal. It gave plenty of traction. Or at least enough to get through the plastic sheet and onto the top of the glass truck."

"That must have been tricky."

"Maybe, but she did it." Noonan smiled.

"The fake diamonds were a good distraction."

"Absolutely. All she needed was a few seconds to make her leap perfect. If everyone who was chasing her was too close, she might not have been able to escape. The fake diamonds stopped everyone cold."

"You can say that again."

"What the thieves did not know was the one mistake they made – and all it takes is one. It wasn't a fatal one but it was telling. Remember when you were told to have the tail gate closed?"

"Yeah."

"It was their way of hinting they were going to be flying out. They could not fly with an open tail gate. So, to complete the deception, the tail gate had to be closed."

"So?"

"Well, if the tail gate had been left open, it would not have been difficult for someone to walk up the stairway, go through the bulkhead and pick up the diamonds from their hiding spot and walk out of the plane. No one was watching the plane; they were chasing the motorcycle rider."

"No one was watching the plane?"

"Well, I was. I didn't believe the motorcycle rider had the gems. So I didn't chase her."

"Which is where the drug dog comes in, right?"

"Right you are. The Dog Man and I just walked into the plane and dog found the drugs on the first pass. They were in a package to a Dr. Jonathan Powers at 457 Fleishacker Drive. I'm betting it's a lease. The perps needed a legitimate residence."

"Well, we got Powers. How many do you think there were?"

"Six or seven. As you pull the pieces together you'll get their names. That's when police work pays off. These guys – and at least one gal – gambled they could be in and out with the diamonds fairly quickly. They'd get the diamonds and be gone. After the clock stopped ticking they didn't care who knew who they were. They'd be in foreign country. No one got killed. No one got hurt. The diamonds are insured and they'd be set for life."

"Flubbed it."

"Sure did. I can't believe they blew the largest delivery. On the other hand they did get away with $15 million."

"Less one."

"Less one split, right."

"Did your office ever identify the perp, the one who said you had sent his brother up on a robbery charge?"

"Sort of. There were three possibles, none with Alaska connections we could find. The one I'm betting on had an older brother who was a Green Beret."

"Sounds like a fit."

"Except the brother was MIA in Vietnam."

"Good enough fit for me."

Ayanna pulled up to Noonan's in-laws. It was apparent to Heinz the twins, Otto and Fritz, were not there: his father-in-law's truck was not there.

But his mother-in-law was.

"Oh dear," he said turning to Ayanna, "do you know the difference between in-laws and outlaws?"

"No."

"In-laws aren't wanted."

Ayanna was still snickering when Noonan shut the door. Noonan reached in the open window and extended his hand to Ayanna. "You did a good job, girl. A very good job. Better than the law enforcement people."

"I had help."

"We all have help." He smiled and then suddenly reached into his pocket. "One last thing. Remember the business Harrison was looking for?"

"Anaktuvik? Yeah."

"I got a response from the Eskimo who works for the Seattle Police Department. He is an Eskimo, by the way, an Inupiaq. He said Anaktuvik Pass translates as the pass where caribou poop."

"Pass where the caribou poop?"

"Right. He said it's kind of an Inupiaq joke. Eskimos don't have horses. The closest thing they have are caribou so 'horse poop' to us is 'caribou poop' to them."

"So our perp was telling Harrison he was horse poop to his face?"

"Must have been. Kind of appropriate, if you know what I mean."

"Sure do."

Noonan pulled out of the open window and turned to face his approaching mother-in-law.

Ayanna started to pull out and then stopped. She took the car out of gear and opened the driver side door. Standing up she shouted at the Detective.

"Captain, er Heinz!"

Noonan turned around.

"Do you think we'll get the rest of them, the perps?"

"Ever gone fishing?"

"Well, yeah."

"Can't get them all."

And with that the Detective was reluctantly engaged in listening to his mother-in-law begin another long story of her latest medical emergency.

Chapter 77

"Gerry, dahling, I've missed you."

"Hey, everybody in the world is looking for you."

"I'm not an easy man to catch."

"No kidding. Where are you?"

"Far away. Where the Margaritas are cold and the *senioritas* are hot."

"Why are you calling me?"

"To congratulate you on your journalism prize. Very impressive. National award for a television reporter in America's **Gulag.**"

"We don't call it a Gulag. We call it home."

"It would have been impressive in New York."

"Well, I had inside help."

"Speaking of which. I just wanted to let know we'll be doing business again soon."

"Things are pretty hot for you right now."

"Ah, don't be so sure. I've still got my people. Lost one but he can be replaced. Just an out-of-work actor. Not one of my core people. We still walked away with $15 million. Not bad for two days work."

"So you will try again?"

"Of course. Ours is not a job; it's an adventure!"

"You will let me know when you plan on doing something illegal, right?"

"Of course. As long as you keep the same cell number so I know where to reach you."

"Will it happen soon?'

There was no answer because the line had gone dead.

Other Steve Levi Books

The Matter of the
VANISHING GREYHOUND
Steve Levi
Master Of The Impossible Crime

GOLDEN GATE BRIDGE DISAPPEARING GREYHOUND BUS CAPER

Cowboys
of the sky

The Story of Alaska's Bush Pilots

Steven C. Levi

WALRUS with a GOLD TOOTH
CRIME IN ANCHORAGE,
ALASKA—THE PIONEER WAY—UNORGANIZED!

STEVE LEVI